MOVIE SHOES

OTHER YEARLING BOOKS YOU WILL ENJOY:

YEARLING BOOKS are designed especially to entertain and enlighten young people. Charles F. Reasoner, Professor Emeritus of Children's Literature and Reading, New York University, is consultant to this series.

For a complete listing of all Yearling titles, write to Dell Publishing Co., Inc., Promotion Department, P.O. Box 3000, Pine Brook, N.J. 07058.

MOVIE SHOES

Noel Streatfeild

A Yearling Book

1

The Letter

It was the first week of the autumn term. The Winter children sat around the dining-room table. They were supposed to be working. Actually there was not very much homework being done. Even Rachel, the eldest, who was twelve and usually almost as conscientious about her homework as she was about her dancing practice—and that was saying a great deal—did not have her mind on her work. Tim, the youngest, who was eight, was not supposed to do any real homework but was supposed to "fill in the time usefully," really meaning anything except playing the piano, while the girls were doing their homework. On this evening he was drawing a picture of two cats meeting on the top of a brick wall, an inferior sort of drawing but one he sometimes did very well. Jane, the middle one, who was ten, never even on her best days worked at homework or, in fact, at anything else. The worst thing about Jane, as Rachel often said and so did those who taught her, was that she seemed to learn things without working. She did not know the things very well but she annoyed whoever was teaching her because when he or she said, "Jane, you're not listening. What have I just been saying?" she nearly always could reel off every word that had been said and looked smug after she had repeated them. The children's grandmothers, when they came to stay, said Jane had a difficult nature. And Jane was difficult to understand. Miss Bean, called by everybody Peaseblossom, a friend of the children's mother who had come to the house to give a hand when Rachel was born and had stayed on doing everything that nobody else wanted to do ever since, said that Jane was all right if you took her the right way. When she said that, it made Jane's mother sigh. Rachel and Tim did not exactly criticize Jane. Sometimes they groaned and made expressive faces, but mostly they just accepted her. There she was, with bad days, worse days, and worser days, but one thing she hardly ever had was a good day. The children's father, before the accident, had called her his little millstone, because he said she was a millstone around his neck which was bowing his back, but the way he used to say that made everybody, including Jane, laugh. You could see that though, like all the others, he often found her terribly annoying, he was very glad she was there, millstone or not.

Rachel was trying to finish her algebra. Mathematics was not her subject. Even when she was giving her whole attention to it, she was not often able to get the right answer. Today, with not even a quarter of her mind on what she was doing, the answers she was getting would have disgraced the jury in *Alice in Wonderland*. You cannot work out the sort of problem which begins "Let x equal the number . . ." when both ears are strained until they feel as long as a donkey's to hear little sounds that might tell you what is going on in the drawing room overhead.

Jane was not even pretending to read her chapter on the Magna Charta. She never had cared for history, and what she called "that old Barony bit" she hated worst of all. She was not pretty at the best of times, and now, with her braids untidy and a scowl on her face, she looked downright ugly. She felt a sort of emptiness inside which gave her a pressed feeling in front because she was frightened. Her ears were strained for sounds, just as Rachel's were strained, only

6

whereas Rachel tried to work to keep her mind off her worries, Jane let her feelings out by kicking at the leg of the table.

Tim looked up reproachfully.

"It's not a very important drawing I'm doing, but this was a nearly perfect cat. Now you've kicked the table, and the tail has run all down into the brick wall."

Rachel was in charge at homework. She knew, even if it was her duty to do so, it was no good telling Jane not to do something. Her voice showed she knew that what she was saying might just as well never have been said.

"Don't kick the table, Jane."

Rachel was pretty with the sort of prettiness that nobody argues about. She was small and fair; her hair, unlike Jane's, curled, and, even more unlike Jane's, her braids never got that hairs-standing-out-everywhere look. Even if Rachel got ink on her nose or had a cold, she remained more or less pretty. Jane thought it was one of the meaner things about life that Rachel should be pretty, and Tim noticeable, and she, in the middle, should be plain. There were so many things that Jane ranked as mean and hoped to put right one day that if she had written them out, they would have filled a whole exercise book.

"Doesn't make any odds if I kick the table; nobody wants to see Tim's drawing, and you'll get all the answers wrong whether I do or don't; you always do."

This gloomy fact was so true that Rachel could not argue it. "You couldn't be more right, but you know I've got to do them. I mayn't do any practice until they're finished."

Rachel's reasonableness was another thing that Jane found mean about life; she never felt reasonable herself. Now she said, "I couldn't think that any child wanted to practice dancing with its father ill upstairs and the doctor there deciding if he'll ever be well again."

7

The words had been said. They flowed into the schoolroom like a door opening, letting in a cold wind. Until that moment the children had been trying to pretend to one another that nothing unusual was happening, that this was an ordinary day. Nobody wished more than Jane that she could take the words back. She had been glad of the pretending by the grown-ups and themselves that there was nothing wrong, that one day things would come right and life would be as it had been before Dad's accident. Saying what she had said would not do any good; it just made them feel worse because they had to admit that there was something to fuss about. Angry with herself, she got up and marched over to the window. It was raining: long, straight, gray lines of rain, falling relentlessly on the London street.

Rachel finished her last problem; she looked at Jane's back. She guessed that Jane had said what she had said because it was her way of showing how worried she was.

"He'll get better," Rachel said. "It isn't as if he were really ill, in bed with a temperature and medicines and all that. It's just a matter of time."

Tim looked up from his drawing. "Everybody's been saying it's only a matter of time ever since it happened, and that was last January, which was months and months ago."

Rachel joined Jane at the window. "If only it didn't have to be winter soon. Dad's heaps better when the sun shines."

Jane thumped the curtain with her fist; she wanted to hurt somebody, and Rachel was the easiest person to get at.

"We ought to live in the country," Jane blurted out. "We *would* live in the country if it weren't for our dear little ballerina, Rachel Winter, the child wonder."

There was a pause. Rachel's insides felt queer when people talked about living in the country, and there had been talk of it since Dad's accident. Of course, if it would cure Dad to

8

go to the country, she would do her best to bear it, but it was something she did not want to think about, especially now when she had just had her twelfth birthday and Madame Fidolia was talking about auditions for Christmas pantomimes; besides, Rachel felt, she had sense on her side. In a pantomime she might earn some money. Money was needed now that Dad had been ill and unable to work for nearly nine months. She said at last, "There are Tim's piano lessons as well as my dancing, and actually the sun doesn't shine in the country any more than it does in London."

Tim sprawled across the table. "It isn't often that I agree with Jane, but I do think that's the most awful lie, if you don't mind my saying so. When I was evacuated to the country, the sun shone almost every day."

Rachel left the window and opened her attaché case, which was on the table, and took out her ballet shoes. "You don't really remember, Tim; you spent most of the time in a carriage."

This was true, but Tim did not like being reminded of the fact that he was the youngest. He said in his grandest voice, "As a matter of fact, you see the sun rather better from a carriage than you do standing up."

Jane gave a squeak and peered sideways through the windowpane up the street. "Here come Peaseblossom and Chewing-gum. I bet the poor darling is terribly wet. I told Peaseblossom it wasn't fit for him to be out."

Rachel tied on her shoes. "If it comes to that, it isn't fit for Peaseblossom either."

Jane was still peering up the road. "Oh, he is wet, the poor angel! His fur's sticking to him so tight he looks as though he hasn't got any. I'll have to rub him and rub him to get him dry." She turned angrily to Rachel. "That's like you to stand up for Peaseblossom, who's got a raincoat and galoshes while poor little Chewing-gum has to walk

9

along on his bare feet with nothing to cover him but his own fur.''

Rachel had tied on her shoes; now she raised herself onto her points. "Don't forget to see you use his own towel; it's not the sort of day to have a row about using the bathroom one.''

Jane had opened the door. She was about to make a rude answer when voices were heard. Dr. Smith and Mrs. Winter were talking at the bottom of the stairs. They were speaking quietly, but every word could be heard by the children.

"I know you're right," Mrs. Winter was saying. "He mustn't spend this winter in England. But you know how difficult things are.''

Dr. Smith was always in a hurry, and this made his voice have a permanent I-must-go note. All the same, the children could hear he was trying to be kind.

"If only you could persuade him to get this bee out of his bonnet that he can't go alone.''

"It's going to be difficult; he was away so long in the war he feels he must be with me and the children.''

"But it's only a few months, and it might be the answer. It might cure him completely. Would he get on with that sister of his?''

"I don't know, I've never seen her; she married an American who died two or three years ago. John hasn't seen her since she was eighteen. I don't somehow see him going off to her on his own.''

Jane suddenly realized that without meaning to, she and the others were eavesdropping. She softly closed the door but not before they heard Dr. Smith say, "All the same, you must persuade him. I assure you, another winter . . .''

The children looked at one another. Somehow, although they had been accustomed to being moved about during the war, that was years ago and they had almost forgotten it. They were used now to having a home and their father and mother with them. Tim spoke this thought out loud.

"Dad can't go away without us; all proper homes have a father and mother in them."

Rachel said to Jane, "That's Aunt Cora they were talking about, the one who offered to have you and me and Mom when London was bombed."

Tim felt he was being cut out of a relationship to Aunt Cora. "She would have asked me, too, if I'd been born."

Jane looked scornful. "If we had gone to Aunt Cora, you'd have been born after we'd got there, and that would have made you a citizen of the United States of America, and you wouldn't have been allowed to come back here after the war, which I often think would have been a good thing."

Rachel guessed that Jane was being nasty to Tim only because she was feeling frightened inside at the thought of Dad's having to go away. Rachel hurriedly tried to smooth things over.

"If Dad ought not to be in England this winter, we'll simply have to persuade him to go away, but I do wonder who's going to pay; it must cost heaps and heaps of money to go to the United States. I do hope I get a job in pantomime; then I could help."

Jane went out into the hall. She felt miserable, and not only because of all the talk about her father going away. She hated it when Rachel talked about getting into a pantomime. It was not that Jane wanted to be able to dance, but she wished she were good at something. Nobody knew yet just how good Tim would turn out to be, but he was admitted to be unusually musical, and Rachel, if she went on as she was doing now, was sure to be a professional dancer; but here

11

was she, good at nothing, unless you counted understanding dogs as something. She was sure that if only she had the chance, she could earn a lot of money as a dog trainer; but at present she had only Chewing-gum, and though he was willing, he was far from performing-dog standard. Even though he had learned to carry a newspaper, he had never quite understood that he must not bite the paper to pieces.

Peaseblossom was sitting on a chair in the hall, taking off her galoshes. She was the kind of woman who you could see had once been a splendid head of the school and captain of games. Even now expressions like "Play the game, old thing" came to her naturally. She and Mrs. Winter had been friends at school and remained friends after they grew up. When Peaseblossom saw the children's mother struggling, not very effectively, to look after newborn Rachel, she gave up being a games mistress and took charge. "You aren't fit to handle a baby and a house on your own, Bee, old thing," she had said. "Better let me lend a hand. If we all pull together, we'll manage splendidly." She was quite right; they had managed splendidly. The children's mother was the gentle, rather spoiling sort, and when their father had been away in the war, they might have grown up loathsome if Peaseblossom had not been there. Though she was nice about it, Peaseblossom believed in discipline. "Rules are made to be kept. . . . No good saying a thing and not sticking to it. . . . Play up and play the game." Now she looked up from her galosh at Jane's cross face.

"Quite true. Chewing-gum's sopping. Take him and give him a good rubdown, but for goodness' sake use his own towel."

Jane knelt by Chewing-gum and felt his coat. He was a red cocker spaniel and usually a lovely autumn-leaf color, but now his fur was dark with water. He had been given to Jane by an American soldier who had left him behind when he went back to his own country. The little dog had not had a name when he came to the children, for the soldier had just called him Pup, so Jane had christened him Chewing-gum because that was what the American soldier was always doing. She played with his wet ears. Then she said, "Did you see Dr. Smith, Peaseblossom?"

Peaseblossom gave Jane a quick look to see if she had heard anything. "Yes, he was just leaving as I came in."

"Where's Mom?"

"Up with your father in the drawing room. Run along, child, do, and dry that dog. Don't want a case of pneumonia in the house."

Jane got up, but she still loitered. She longed to think of a way to say to Peaseblossom, "We heard about Aunt Cora. Do go and find out if Dad's going away, and if you find out anything, please tell us," but she could not. It seemed difficult to say somehow, so after a second or two she called Chewing-gum.

"Come on, angel. Come on, poor drowned dog. I'll rub you until you haven't a wet hair left."

In the drawing room Mr. and Mrs. Winter were standing together looking down into the wet street.

"There's no harm in writing to her, John, dear," Bee Winter was saying. "It must be lovely in California in the winter. Fancy! Oranges grow there! I believe it's never really cold."

John scowled. "What a place to live—Hollywood!"

"It's not Hollywood itself. It's Santa Monica; she told you in one of her letters that her house was by the sea. If she had you to stay for two or three months, it would just get you over the winter, and then you might come back perfectly well."

Though Bee did not mean her voice to sound pleading, it

13

was pleading on the last line. She could not help remembering John a year ago, when he had been well. He was not always easy-tempered because he was a writer and got angry with himself and everybody else when he could not write well, but he had been gay and excited about things, rushing into the room after a good day's work to tell her about it. Since the accident, all that was gone. It was not his fault that a child had darted across the road to pick up a ball and had been killed. At the inquest John had been entirely exonerated; he had been driving slowly and carefully; it was the child, who had never been taught to cross a road properly, who was to blame. But that had made no difference to John; he had become ill from thinking about the dead child, so ill that he had what the doctor called a nervous breakdown, and when that got better, he had lost faith in himself and decided he could never write again. The only thing which did him good was sunlight. Sometimes when the sun shone, he would settle down at his typewriter and work away for an hour or two; then in would go the sun, and he would slide back to his gloomy mood, saying, "It's no good, Bee, I'm finished as a writer." Bee knew that was not true, but she also knew that if he did not get well soon, she would have to say, "Well, what are you going to do instead? There's this house to run; there are Rachel, Jane, and Tim needing breakfast, dinner, lunch, and tea, as well as new clothes, and we've been living on our savings since January, and they're nearly finished." Thinking of these things, she laid her face against John's shoulder.

"Just write to her, darling. Tell her what the doctor says. Write a nice long letter by airmail, and see what happens. After all, if she invites you and you don't want to go, you can always refuse the invitation; there's no harm done."

John shivered. He was so tired and ill that even sitting down to write a letter made him feel worse, but he hated to refuse Bee anything. He gave her a lopsided sort of smile.

14

"All right, I'll write to her if it'll please you, but I don't think she'll invite me, and if she does, I won't go. I'm not leaving you and the children."

Bee went to the writing table; she laid out a piece of airmail paper.

"You write it now. I'll ask Peaseblossom not to take off her coat. I'd like that letter to catch the six o'clock post."

2

The Important Wednesday

Wednesday started like an ordinary day. Rachel, as usual, flew out of the house five minutes before she need have started because she was so fond of her dancing school that she could not bear to waste time eating breakfast when she could be on her way to it. Jane and Tim went to the same school and every day had the same sort of argument before they started. This Wednesday was no exception. Bee said, "Hurry up, darlings, and finish eating. You've only five minutes before you start."

Jane immediately helped herself to another piece of bread and slowly spread jam on it. "Yes, hurry up, Tim. I always have to wait for you."

Tim had been just about to finish his milk, but at that insult he put down his cup. "That's the most monstrous lie. Yesterday Peaseblossom and Chewing-gum and I were standing at the gate waiting for you so long that we didn't get to school until prayers were over. That's why you and I got unpunctuality marks."

Jane stuck her chin in the air. "That was just once, and only because Mom made me change my socks for so small a hole that nobody but Mom would have seen it; but almost every day I'm made late by you looking for your music and—"

Dad had seemed to be reading the paper. Now he looked

up. His voice sounded as if it could very easily turn from a talking voice to an angry one.

"Shut up, kids. Scram."

Peaseblossom took Jane and Tim to school. It was not far, and they could have gone alone; but it was a habit which had never been dropped and had the advantage of giving Chewing-gum an early-morning run. Jane ran on ahead with Chewing-gum. Tim walked beside Peaseblossom, carrying his case of music. Usually they met the same people: the postman finishing his round, the sanitation men, and so on. This Wednesday, as they turned the school corner, coming toward them was the school music master, Mr. Brown, and walking with him was another man. Tim liked Mr. Brown better than anybody else he knew. Usually he ran to meet him, but this time he did not like to as Mr. Brown was not alone, so he just looked pleased. Mr. Brown said something to his friend, and when they were within speaking distance of Tim, they stopped.

"How are you?" Mr. Brown greeted Tim. "This is Mr. Jeremy Caulder. If you weren't a little ignoramus, you'd have heard of him."

Mr. Caulder shook hands with Tim. "How do you do? I stayed with my godson here last night, and he told me about you. You are fond of music, I hear."

Tim was surprised that somebody who was as old as Mr. Brown had a godfather. He had thought that stopped when you grew up, and Mr. Brown must have been grown-up for years because he had said he would be thirty next birthday. Tim was so amazed about this that he almost forgot to answer Mr. Caulder. At last he said, "Yes. Aren't you?"

Mr. Brown laughed. "Jeremy Caulder is one of the best piano players we have. He says I may bring you over to play for him this morning."

Tim looked hopefully at Mr. Caulder. "Could I come at eleven? We do French then, which I simply hate."

17

Mr. Caulder seemed a nice, reasonable sort of man. He said at once that eleven would suit splendidly. He and Mr. Brown moved on. Tim wanted to move on too, but seeing Mr. Caulder seemed to have done something to Peaseblossom. She stared after him as if he were a blue elephant or something equally unusual. Jane came racing back with Chewing-gum.

"Come on, Tim, we'll be awfully late. What's up, Pease-blossom? That's only Mr. Brown who teaches us piano and singing."

Peaseblossom's voice was hushed with awe. "That's Jeremy Caulder. I've heard him at the Albert Hall and often on the air. Tim's going to play for him at eleven."

Jane was not impressed. "More fool Mr. Caulder. Do come on, Tim."

Tim was not impressed either. "All right, I'm coming. It's not my fault if Mr. Brown stops and speaks. It would be awfully rude to walk on."

Peaseblossom laid a hand on Tim's shoulder. "This is your chance to show what you're made of. The family depends on you not to let down the side."

Rachel had arrived at the Children's Academy for Dancing and Stage Training as usual. She went down to the changing room, for she had an hour's dancing class before she began lessons. The moment she opened the changing-room door she knew something tremendous was in the air. The other girls tried to tell her what it was, but because they all spoke at once, she could not get the news straight at first; when she did, she understood the excitement. At twelve o'clock a theatrical manager was coming to the school, bringing the man who arranged the dancing for his shows. He wanted six children for a big musical production. The top classes were to dance for him.

Rachel changed into her practice things. Her heart was

thumping so hard she thought she could hear it. She must get chosen; she *must*. Imagine coming home and being able to say to Dad and Mom, "I've got an engagement." Mom wouldn't say much, but of course, she'd feel less worried; who wouldn't? Somebody earning money just now would make all the difference. Her best friend, Caroline, came over to her.

"I bet you get chosen. You and, of course, Miriam and Sylvia, Frances, Audrey, and Annette."

The six were all small and considered exceptionally promising. Quite honestly that was the list Rachel would have picked; only she did not dare put herself so firmly on it as Caroline did, and there was always the chance that the manager or the man who arranged the dances would choose Caroline, and that would take one of the rest of them out. Caroline was promising, all right, but nobody could call her pretty; in fact, she was plain. Rachel put an arm around her and said, "Counting you, with any luck we ought to be the ones he chooses: six of us to dance and one to understudy." Inwardly she added, "Oh, don't let me be the understudy, though that would be better than nothing."

Tim brought his news home first. He had a letter about it for his father. Mr. Jeremy Caulder would give him piano lessons. Not regularly, because he was away a great deal playing at concerts, but whenever he was in London. Mr. Brown, who wrote the letter, said Mr. Caulder agreed with him that Tim was an unusually musical boy and ought to have a chance, and for the time being the lessons would be free.

Dad had been sitting looking terribly tired and interested in nothing when the letter came, but after he had read it, he was quite different. He said he had often heard Mr. Caulder play and if he thought Tim was worth teaching, there might be more in Tim's strumming than met the ear. He was gay enough even to pretend to box with Tim, something he had not done for weeks.

On top of that excitement Rachel rushed in. She was in such a state she poured out her story so fast that her words tripped over each other.

"Mr. Glinken came to see us dance and brought the most marvelous man with him; he called him Benny. Benny showed us afterward some things we'd have to do. He's—Mr. Glinken, I mean, not Benny—putting on a simply enormous musical play, and I'm one of the six children. Real dancing we're doing. Madame Fidolia's no end bucked. He chose—Mr. Glinken, I mean, not Benny—me, Miriam, Frances, Audrey, Annette, and Sylvia, and Caroline's going to understudy. That's the only awful part. They took simply ages choosing between Sylvia and Caroline, and when they chose Sylvia, Caroline cried. But I was the only one who saw."

Though the drawing room was not very big and was full of furniture, Rachel felt that the family simply must have the thrill of seeing the sort of dances Benny was arranging. Without bothering to take off her coat and hat or change her shoes, she showed them Benny's steps as well as she could.

Peaseblossom glowed. "Well, this is a day! Up the Winters! Tim to be trained by Mr. Caulder himself and Rachel a real professional dancer. Our side's doing splendidly. I think this deserves a special tea. I'll see what I can find."

Peaseblossom did not get as far as the kitchen. A few moments after she had left the room she was back. She was holding two letters, a dull-looking long typewritten envelope for herself and a letter with American stamps marked "Airmail" for John.

The children knew that John had written to Aunt Cora and that Peaseblossom had posted the letter. They did not know Bee had put on enough stamps to send it by air. They had not expected Aunt Cora would answer for weeks. Because nothing more had been said about it, John's going to California had gone to the back of their minds. It was not a certain thing like Christmas or a birthday or the beginning of term; it was just a "perhaps." Now, looking at Dad's fingers opening the thin airmail envelope with Aunt Cora's name and address on the flap, they felt cold inside. Could Dad be going away? Going all the way to Aunt Cora?

John straightened the letter. Bee leaned on his shoulder and read it, too. All down one page, all over the next, all down the next sheet, and half down the back page, and while they read, the children's eyes were fixed on them. At the end John gave a half laugh, half snort and pushed the letter back into its envelope.

"Silly fool of a woman! What does she think I'm going to do for money?"

Bee said quickly, "That's not fair. You told her that it was what the doctor ordered and that it wasn't likely you'd really do it because of leaving me and the children, and she answers by not only asking the whole lot of us but Peaseblossom as well. I call it marvelous of her."

John looked at the children. "How would you like to go to California for the winter?" The children looked startled. "All right, don't worry, there isn't a chance of it. The fares would cost about a thousand pounds, and your father would be hard put to it just now to find a thousand pence. As for a grand piano for Tim and—"

Peaseblossom made a choking sound. They turned to look at her. Her face, which was always rather red, was the color of an overripe purple plum. She was holding out a crisp sheet of note paper as if, by looking at the back of the letter, they could read what it said. Bee ran to her.

"What is it, dear? Bad news?"

Peaseblossom struggled to get her breath, just as if she were getting it back after tea had gone down the wrong way.

"We can go. All of us. An old aunt whom I never met has died and left me a thousand pounds."

3

Will You? Won't You?

Talk went on all the evening. First of all, there was a terrific argument with Peaseblossom about spending her legacy on the family's fares to the United States. But it did not matter what John and Bee said; Peaseblossom had made up her mind. All her life she had wanted to travel. Up to that Wednesday in September it had been just dim wanting, but with the coming of the letter with the news of her legacy, she became like someone dying of thirst who sees water; nothing and nobody was going to stop her from having what she wanted. To every argument John and Bee put forward she had answers. Why should she save the money? What for? Why shouldn't she spend it on the family? What fun would it be traveling alone? Besides, if she went anywhere alone, she would have to live in hotels, which would cost as much and more than all their fares put together, whereas staying with Aunt Cora, she would be living free. Yes, of course, she would be expected to work for her board and lodging, but who supposed she wanted to be idle a whole winter? Had anybody ever heard of her ever wanting to be idle? All right, if they must be so businesslike, the money spent on the family could be called a loan.

Rachel sat on a stool, hugging her knees and trying to look cheerful. It seemed to her that nobody was aware her career was at stake. Here she was, one of six picked to dance in a big London theater, and her family, who ought to be bursting with pride, was discussing whisking her off to the other end of the world. The firmer Peaseblossom's arguments grew, the more miserable Rachel became and the more difficult she found it to look cheerful. Her lips kept dropping at the corners and had to be forced upward again. Toward the end of the argument, when it was clear Peaseblossom was winning, an enormous lump kept coming into her throat.

Just before suppertime Bee looked at John. She tried not to sound too pleased, eager and excited, but she did not succeed very well. She had not let John know how worried she had been since his accident, but she had been pretty desperate. Now it was as if a fairy had appeared and given her a wish and made it come true.

"Well, John, we seem to have produced every argument we can. If Peaseblossom really wants to spend her money like that, I think we ought to let her."

John was beginning to get a little excited. Not gaily excited, as he used to be so easily before the accident, but more as if the fog of depression which covered him most days had been blown on by a wind and was less dense.

"Let's accept for the moment that we're using Peaseblossom's money. What are we going to do about the children? There's this offer of Jeremy Caulder's; ought we to let Tim miss this chance?"

Rachel had to turn her head so that nobody should see her wipe her eyes. Tim indeed! The only thing that had happened to Tim was that somebody important had offered to give him lessons, while she had a professional engagement. Oh, it was too mean!

Tim had been playing an imaginary grand piano through most of the Peaseblossom argument. When the conversation turned to him, he took his hands off his imaginary keyboard and got up. He sat on the arm of John's chair.

"That'll be all right, Dad."

John put an arm around him. "That's what you say now, but what are going to say to me in ten years' time about the opportunity I'm letting you miss?"

Rachel had to turn her face away again and sweep some more tears out of her eyes. Opportunity Tim was missing! What about the opportunity she was missing?

Tim said, "I shan't miss any opportunity. Mr. Brown told me he didn't suppose Mr. Caulder would be in London much for a bit. Somebody in America can give me lessons while I'm there."

John gave him a friendly shake. "Don't you be smug, young man. Why should any American pianist want to be bothered with a little boy who's going to be his pupil for only a few months?"

"And who would pay for the lessons even if we could find someone to teach you?" Bee broke in. "Peaseblossom's money will mostly be used up, and we can't expect Aunt Cora to do more than keep us."

Tim refused to worry. "Mr. Brown won't mind as long as I practice every day."

Bee had suddenly seen Rachel's face. "Oh, my goodness, she thought, "how mean of us all, forgetting Rachel's great chance. But she mustn't let her father see how disappointed she is, or he may refuse to go because of her." She got up and went over to Rachel. She knelt by her and put her arms around her in such a way that Rachel's face was against her shoulder and so hidden from everybody. Before she spoke, she whispered, "Be brave, darling. Don't let Dad see how much you mind." Out loud she said, "We've forgotten our ballerina. Will you mind not dancing in this show and missing your lessons for six months?"

Answering was the most difficult thing Rachel had ever done. Bee's being so nice had broken her control, and she

25

was really crying; but somehow she managed a fairly nonwobblish voice and said the only thing she could think of: "Foreign travel broadens the mind."

Peaseblossom gave a quick look at what she could see of Rachel and broke in hurriedly. "Quite right, and a broadened mind helps all art. We'll bring back better pupils for Madame Fidolia and Mr. Caulder. Now that everything's settled, I'll get supper. Jane, it's your night to help."

Jane had been sitting in a corner. She had Chewing-gum on the piece of sheet he had to sit on when his toilet was done. She had combed him and brushed him until he shone like silk; then she had lain down beside him and listened with half an ear to the arguments. When first Tim and then Rachel came into the discussion, she sat up. She hugged Chewing-gum against her. There they went as usual, talking, talking, talking about Rachel and Tim; nobody seemed to care what happened to her. Peaseblossom's saying "everything's settled" was the last straw. Jane's voice was shrill with anger.

"I suppose it doesn't interest anybody if Chewing-gum and I don't want to go to America."

The three grown-ups laughed. Bee said, "I'm afraid not, darling. It'll be good for you."

Tim turned to his father. "Can Chewing-gum come? A boy at school's poodle couldn't go to Paris because he'd have been in quarantine when he came home."

Bee caught her breath. Of course, Chewing-gum couldn't go. She hadn't thought of that. Oh, dear, surely Jane would not be difficult! She could not leave Rachel, who was crying quite badly, so she held out a hand to Jane.

"We'll fix something very nice for Chewing-gum, but he can't come because it's the law that he must go into quarantine for six months when we get back, and he'd hate that, poor boy."

Jane was appalled. No Chewing-gum! How could she go

26

away and leave Chewing-gum? She got up and came into the middle of the room. She raged at them all.

"You can all go to America if you like, but I'm staying here. None of you seems to care what happens to Chewing-gum, but I do. Poor angel, you'd let him die in the snow and starve to death. All this talk about Rachel's dancing and Tim's piano, and nobody cares that they're taking from me the only friend I ever had, the only person who really and truly loves me. Well, you can't do it; I won't go to America. I'll chain myself and Chewing-gum to something so you can't get us away. You're beasts, all of you, to have thought of trying to do it. Beasts! Beasts! Beasts!"

Jane was wound up. She had lots more to say, but Peaseblossom felt they had heard more than enough. She went over to Jane and shook her. She raised her voice so it could be heard above Jane's.

"That's quite enough. California or no California, we mustn't get slack or let discipline slip. It's your night to help with supper."

4

Preparations

Once it was certain they were going to California, the days seemed to rush by. From the Wednesday when it was decided they would go to the day they were to sail was really a fortnight, but to the children it did not feel a bit like fourteen days. To Bee and Peaseblossom, though, it was the busiest fortnight of their lives. Every day was a scramble to get into it everything that was planned.

John was busy, too. It was he who managed to get them all passage on the *Mauretania*—a very difficult thing to do at short notice. The next thing was passports. All the passports were out of date, and the children had never been abroad, so they neither had passports of their own nor were down on their parents' passports. There were forms to fill in, and photographs to be taken, and hours to be spent in the passport office and, later, hours in the American Embassy waiting for visas, but John managed it all without bothering everybody else more than could be helped. He was like a very good sheepdog getting his sheep along at a nice speed in the right direction, with only an occasional little sharp bark. Oddly enough, though he looked terribly tired, hurrying about seemed to do him good; he was sleeping better than he had been since the accident. Best of all, when the tickets and the visaed passports were in the house, he labeled his portable typewriter and packed several packages of typing paper.

The children had their own affairs to put in order. The most difficult affair was, of course, Chrewing-gum. Jane stuck to what she had said. If Chewing-gum was not going, neither would she go. She made awful threats. They would have to carry her to the boat, and she would scream all across the Atlantic. It was Dr. Smith who found the way out. He stopped by on his round of visits on the Monday morning after the great Wednesday to ask if there was any news from Aunt Cora. He did not need to come far inside the house to see there was, for Bee and Peaseblossom were packing in the hall. The children were at school, and John was at the passport office; but Bee and Peaseblossom were glad to sit down for a minute and tell him all about it.

"The only trouble," Bee said, "is Jane. She says she won't go without Chewing-gum."

Peaseblossom broke in. "Don't think we are paying any attention to her. She will, of course, do exactly as she's told and be punished if she behaves badly."

Bee went on. "But we don't want anything to upset John, for he really does seem a little better. The other two are being splendidly helpful, and it's particularly good of Rachel, as she had just been engaged to dance in a musical show."

Dr. Smith thought for a minute; then he made a clicking noise with his tongue and held up a finger.

"Let me have a talk with Jane. You've all got to have certificates that you were recently vaccinated and that it took all right, before you can land in the United States. Lucky for you that I vaccinated you all this spring. You write a note asking me for certificates and get Jane to bring it around about four thirty and wait for an answer."

Jane and Chewing-gum turned up at teatime at Dr. Smith's house and were shown into his consulting room. He read the note just as if he had not known what was in it. Then he rang the bell.

"Your mother wants certificates to say I vaccinated you all. They will take time to write, so I suggest you and I and Chewing-gum have some tea before I get to work on them."

It was a good tea. Jane was surprised at the sort of tea Dr. Smith ate all by himself: sandwiches, buns, and even some ginger cookies. He talked about Chewing-gum's food, health, and coat until tea came, and it was only when Jane was eating a bun and Chewing-gum a sandwich that he mentioned America.

"Exciting business this, you all going off to California."

Jane laid down her bun.

"The rest of the family may be going, but I'm not. I'll chain myself to the furniture, and if they cut the chains, I won't walk; they'll have to drag me, and I'll scream all the way. I'm not leaving Chewing-gum."

Dr. Smith did not show any particular interest. He sipped his tea before he answered. "I see. Then it's no good my saying what I was going to."

"Not if it was to try and talk me around, it isn't."

"Not exactly," the doctor said. "It was to ask you to lend Chewing-gum to me. There are some shocking car thieves about. I was thinking of getting a dog, but if I could have an old friend like Chewing-gum whom I could trust to stay with me, it would be a great help."

Inside her, though she tried not to believe it, Jane knew she would not be allowed to stay behind, that she would be taken to America even if she did what she threatened and used chains and screamed. If she *had* to allow somebody else to look after Chewing-gum, Dr. Smith was the ideal person. At a doctor's Chewing-gum's health would be properly attended to, and he would have the right things to eat. However, she could not give way all at once. She had made such a scene for so long that it felt quite odd to think of stopping making a scene.

"Would you stand in a line for horsemeat?" Jane asked the doctor.

"Shouldn't have to. Patient of mine sells the stuff. He'll send around all I want."

"He's used to walking, not driving all day in a car."

"Always manage one good walk myself every day; shall enjoy Chewing-gum's company."

"He's never been a watchdog; he's not a biting sort of dog. I don't know how good he'd be at catching a thief."

Dr. Smith gave Chewing-gum some tea in a bowl. "Soon learn. I'll put a bone in the car with him. Any dog will bite anyone who comes near him when he's got a bone."

Jane thought that clever. "That's a very good idea. I'd be glad if he did learn to be a fierce watchdog. I'd be glad if he learned to do anything really well, because I hope to be a dog trainer when I grow up, and to judge by Chewing-gum, I've got a lot to learn." She lowered her voice. "As a matter of fact, he can carry a newspaper, but he's still inclined to eat it."

Dr. Smith nodded in the professional way he did when he visited anybody who was ill and someone explained to him what sort of being ill it was.

"Ah! Must see if I can help the old fellow about that. Very good of you, Jane, if you trust him to me."

Either because Dr. Smith was so nice or because talking about leaving Chewing-gum was the beginning of leaving him, Jane began to cry. She had been stubborn and angry since Wednesday, but she had not cried; now, when the tears started, they seemed to have been holding back an absolute river of tears. Dr. Smith was perfect. He sat her on his knee and let her cry and cry, and only when she had reached the hiccup and shudder stage did he talk. He told her about the dog he'd had when he was a boy and how terrible it had been when he first went to a boarding school. How he had thought

31

his dog would starve and die without him. How surprised he had been when he came home for the holidays and his father brought his dog to the station to meet him. The dog nearly had hysterics, he was so pleased to see him; but when that was over, he was surprised to find the dog looked splendid, and when he had remarked on this to his father, his father had said, " 'Course. Never make the mistake of thinking you're the only animal lover in the world, and never be such a fool as to get so tied up with an animal that you can't move without it. You'll be a nuisance to yourself and everybody else." Dr. Smith said he had found that was a very sensible thing to have said, and he thought Jane would, too. This going away for six months would be a useful way of getting used to leaving Chewing-gum if she had to and to trusting him to someone else.

Jane reached home as the family was finishing tea. She marched in and gave Bee the envelope of certificates. Then she stuck her chin in the air and said in a proud, don't-you-dare-look-surprised tone of voice, "It may interest you to know I've decided to lend Chewing-gum to Dr. Smith while I'm in America. He needs a watchdog for his car."

Bee had written on the evening of the great Wednesday to Madame Fidolia, to the head of Jane and Tim's school, and to Mr. Brown. The letter to Jane and Tim's school was just a notification that the children would be leaving England; the letters to Madame Fidolia and Mr. Brown said the same thing but were grateful and apologetic as well.

Rachel, knowing Madame Fidolia had been written to, did not tell her news to the other girls. She was quite sure Caroline would dance in the show in her place, but just in case somebody else was put in, it seemed better to say nothing. It would be too cruel to let poor Caroline hope again; she had not yet got over the first audition. It was so

32

awful, as Caroline told Rachel, to have been nearly chosen and then to end up as just an understudy. Rachel found it hard not to tell everybody her news. People kept coming up and congratulating her, and every time that happened she had a lump in her throat. She was glad when she got a message saying Madame wanted to see her before she went home.

Madame Fidolia was sitting in an armchair with Bee's letter in her hand. To anyone who did not know her she was an odd-looking old lady. Her hair was dragged into a bun at the nape of her neck; she was wearing a dress so old-fashioned in shape, it might have come out of a museum. Around her shoulders was a shawl kept in place by a large cameo brooch. Lying on the table beside her was a tall cane, which she always used when she walked. On her feet were pink ballet shoes. To Rachel there was nothing queer about her at all. Madame was not a person you could be fond of exactly—she was too grand for that—but Rachel respected and admired her and was a little afraid of her. Madame no longer danced, but she had been a very great dancer, and her arrival to watch a class sent a shiver down Rachel's spine. Madame could be patient, but she was very critical. Rachel dreaded hearing Madame's stick tap on the floor, and her voice with its faintly foreign accent say, "Precision, Rachel. Precision." That afternoon Madame waited for Rachel to curtsy and say, "Madame." Then she gave her a lovely smile.

"Come in, my child. This is disappointing news for you and for me."

That was so like Madame. She would understand at once. Lots of people would think it simply marvelous luck to be going to California for the winter, but not Madame. She would know just how awful it was to have your first stage engagement snatched away from you. Madame's understanding so well was a strain on Rachel's self-control. She felt tears smarting in her eyes and had to swallow before she could say, "Yes, Madame."

Madame did not seem to notice that Rachel was upset.

"But we must be sensible about it. A winter in the sunshine will be very good for your health. Nor are your chances much affected. I, of course, telephoned Mr. Glinken the moment I got your mother's letter and explained about you. He asked which you were, and when I described you, he said, 'Oh, it *would* be that one, but you tell her from me to work hard while she's away and not to let Hollywood discover her, and I may have something for her when she comes back.' "

Rachel could hardly believe she had really heard what Madame had said. Mr. Glinken remembered her! Mr. Glinken thought he might have something for her when she got back! She felt so gay, it was quite difficult to keep from giving a pleased skip. She clasped her hands and said on a gasping breath, "Oh, Madame!"

Madame nodded. "Nice, isn't it? We'll keep him up to that when you get home. In the meantime, your disappointment is great news for your friend, Caroline, and whoever I put to take Caroline's place as understudy, so you can look upon this California trip not as a misfortune but as the great adventure which it really is. Now, about your dancing lessons . . ."

Rachel dropped from happiness to despair.

"I shan't be able to have any. Aunt Cora, whom we're staying with, can't be expected to do more than keep us; she couldn't be expected to pay for classes."

Madame nodded again. "I quite understand that. Indeed, your mother says as much in this letter. She says that to save trouble and expense, Miss Bean, who is traveling with you, will be teaching you your schoolwork; she asks for a report on your work and a list of the books that will be needed. Fortunately I can arrange about dancing lessons. Let me have

34

your California address, and I will ask my old pupil Posy Fossil to look after you.''

Posy Fossil was a legend in school. There had never been a dancer to touch her. Everybody knew that Posy was dancing in the movies and that she had a sister who was a movie star. To Rachel, being told that she was to meet the fabulous Posy was like being told she was to meet Cinderella.

"Posy Fossil!"

"Yes, I don't know what she can arrange as she is out of pictures now and working hard. Manoff is forming his company again, and she is his star ballerina; but do not worry, my child, Posy will look after you. Now run along and send Caroline to me.''

Rachel curtsied, murmured "Madame," and left the room. Outside the door she stood still for a moment to get things straight. Thoughts poured in on her, making her so happy and excited she felt as if she might burst with being pleased. She rushed around the school, looking for Caroline. When she found her, she flung her arms around her.

"Oh, I'm so happy, and so are you going to be in a minute. Go to Madame; she wants to see you. But the second she's finished with you rush back here. I've got such marvelous things to tell you!"

Tim did not have a piano lesson with Mr. Brown until Friday. Because he was so excited about going to America, he had not practiced for two days. He knew Mr. Brown would understand, so he told him at once. Mr. Brown did understand; he said if anything like that had happened to him, he wouldn't have practiced either.

"Has this aunt you're staying with got a piano?"

Tim thought that a stupid question. "A piano! Every house has a piano.''

"On the contrary, very few houses have pianos. Doesn't matter a bit that you're missing your lessons for a couple of

35

terms, and Jeremy Caulder says it suits him better to start you at Easter, as he'll be in London quite a lot then; but you must practice. What are you going to do about that if your aunt hasn't a piano?''

Tim could not believe he had an aunt so dead to decency that she could live without a piano, but even if she was as peculiar as all that, *everybody* in America couldn't be queer. Somewhere there must be a piano. He sat down on the piano stool and, with one hand, made a brushing movement in the air, as if to brush Mr. Brown's foolish fears away.

"Don't worry. I'll find a piano."

Mr. Brown laughed. "All right, Tim, I'll leave it to you. I feel sure if there's a piano anywhere, you will find it, but mind you do. If you come back without having practiced, I shall take you to a pond and drown you.''

5

They Are Off

Light had just begun to sneak through the curtains when Rachel opened her eyes. For a moment she was suspended halfway between being asleep and being awake. Then, with a jump, she sat up. This was going-away day. She got out of bed, pulled back the curtains, and looked out. She let out a pleased "Oh!" for it was a glorious morning. The sun was shining, making the already autumn-turned leaves on the two trees that could be seen from the window a glittering gold; the sky was a clear pale blue, a flawless poem of a morning, just the day to start to cross the Atlantic.

"What's it like?" came from Jane.

Jane was sitting up in her bed looking pale, tousled, and cross. A hump under the eiderdown was Chewing-gum. As a rule he was not allowed on beds, but the night before, Jane had said, "Chewing-gum's sleeping with me tonight," and nobody, not even Peaseblossom, had argued. In a house bulging with excitement Jane was the one sad person. She was so miserable that she had not been bad or rude for days. This was so noticeable, it had made Tim say, "I do miss Jane's being cross. I've nobody to fight with." Rachel, turning as Jane spoke, felt a little of the gladness of the morning slipping out of the door. Poor Jane! Of course, nobody liked leaving Chewing-gum, but only Jane minded so

37

terribly that she could not be thrilled about going away. Rachel tried to cheer her up.

"It's a lovely day. No wind at all. I don't think any of us will be seasick."

Jane was not in the mood to like hearing good news. "Some people don't need waves; they're just seasick."

Peaseblossom came in just in time to hear this.

"Who's talking about seasickness? Your father's heard the seven o'clock weather forecast, and it's splendid. Not a mention of a gale. Up you get, travelers. Fold your sheets and pillowcases and put them in the laundry basket in the kitchen. No rush and scramble; everything in order, and everything in time; that's our way."

It was a funny morning, unlike any other. The boiler had been allowed to go out, so there was only cold water to wash in. It felt so queer packing each thing away as it was finished with: brushes, combs, washing things, pajamas. Nothing was left about to show anybody had slept in the house.

There was an unusually good breakfast, for there was no need to be careful of the rations; there would be no rationing on the *Mauretania* or in America. The tragedy was that when for once they were asked to finish their butter rations and to eat bacon and eggs, nobody was hungry, and although there was heaps of time, they felt they must hurry. Bee thought this quite natural and unimportant.

"Don't worry, darlings. When Mrs. Bones comes to tidy after us, she'll be very pleased to find we've left all this for her. I told her to take everything there was."

How queer that was to think of! Mrs. Bones, who came to help now and again and was a friend of theirs, coming into an empty house. Mrs. Bones, who would never touch a thing which did not belong to her, packing up their rations and carrying them home with her.

Their minds were taken off Mrs. Bones by the sound of a

car stopping outside. Everybody tried not to look at Jane, but they all knew whose car it was. The front doorbell rang.

It was all over in a couple of minutes. Dr. Smith said he was in a terrible hurry. He picked up Chewing-gum's basket, which Jane had packed with his biscuits and a bottle of his medicine, his brush and comb, his special soap, his spare collar and lead, his water bowl, his rubber bone, his half-eaten teddy bear, and his rug. Jane knelt by Chewing-gum and clipped on his lead. She gave the lead to Dr. Smith, who very tactfully did not speak to her but to Chewing-gum.

"Come on, old man. You wouldn't believe what a bone I've got waiting for you in the car."

The moment the front door shut behind Dr. Smith and Chewing-gum, everybody began to run. The night suitcases had to come down and join the rest of the luggage in the hall. Jane was handed a wet dishcloth and told to give all the stick-on luggage labels a final dab in the hope they would stick, for lots of the W's for Winter and the labels saying "Stateroom Baggage" were curling at the corners. Tim was given the job of counting the luggage and seeing that the tie-on labels were all securely knotted. Rachel had to search the bedrooms to be sure everything was packed and that nobody had packed the coats and hats he or she was traveling in. John went to the neighbors officially to say good-bye but really to remind them once more that this was the day they were going away, and would they please keep an eye on the house to see it was not burgled? Bee and Peaseblossom rushed around the house doing all those last things that they had forgotten to do or forgotten to ask Mrs. Bones to do for them. Then the clock struck, and John shouted, "Hurry up, everybody, or the cars will be here." They all rushed upstairs and put on their hats and coats, and only just in time, for as they came down again, the two cars Peaseblossom had hired stopped at the door.

They had a wonderful send-off. Every house in Saxon Crescent had somebody out to wave good-bye to them. There were extra people as well. The postman had loitered so that he could cheer. The newspaper boy had hurried through his round so that he could come back and see them off. Mrs. Bones, her hat on one side, came tearing up the street to have what she called a last peep at them. Even the policeman who was sometimes on the corner was there that morning, and he called out, "Good luck."

It hardly seemed possible that they really were safely on the boat train. They were in a long railway carriage with tables in it. Peaseblossom and the children were at one table, and John and Bee at another, which they shared with a Scots couple who were going out to America to see their married daughter. It was so funny to look around the railway carriage and think that they would be seeing all the people in it for the next six days. And to realize that they were not the only people starting on a great adventure. The journey passed wonderfully quickly. Just as it was beginning to be a bore, Peaseblossom ordered coffee for them all and, as a surprise, brought out of her case a most wonderful supply of chocolate cookies on which she had used what was left of the ration points. Now that they had really started and, with all their luggage, were safely on the train, they found the appetites they had lost at breakfast had come back. Even Jane, who had not spoken at all but glared out of the window, ate three chocolate cookies and seemed to enjoy them.

Southampton Docks was rather boring. There was a lot of standing in lines and answering questions, but just as it seemed as if the *Mauretania* must sail without them, John said, "We're through. Come on, everybody." They found themselves moving toward a sign marked Cabin Class Only, then up a gangway, and there they were on board the *Mauretania*.

6

The Mauretania

Days on land are like beads threaded on a string, big beads, little beads, gay beads for Christmas and birthdays, but days on a ship cannot go on the same string. They are different somehow and feel as if they need a special thread all to themselves. That is how the *Mauretania* felt to the Winters. As their feet touched the deck, it was as if a door slammed; behind it were Saxon Crescent, Mrs. Bones, Dr. Smith, everybody and everything that was life at home. Even Chewinggum was behind that door. Six days ahead was another door, which would open on America; but that was tight shut, and they did not even think about what was on the other side of it.

Peaseblossom and the children had a cabin on one deck, and John and Bee had one on another. The *Mauretania* seemed so big that Rachel felt a bit scared at seeing John and Bee leaving them. On a journey to the other side of the world it seemed safer not to be separated. A steward who had picked up most of their hand luggage saw her expression and understood at once.

"Don't you worry, you won't lose 'em, but by tomorrow they'll be lucky if they can find *you* when they want you. Never traveled with a child yet who didn't know the ship almost as well as I do before we were a day out."

It was quite a walk to get to the cabin. Down two decks,

along a passage, then down a tiny passage and there it was. It was the neatest place the children had ever seen. There were four bunks, two on each side, two cupboards and shelves, two chests of drawers, a porthole with little curtains, and a washbasin with hot and cold water. Of course, the first important thing to decide was who should sleep where. Naturally all the children wanted the top bunks. After all, you can sleep on the floor anytime, but it is something special to have a bed you have to climb to get into. Peaseblossom had to think quickly. She wanted to give Jane a top bunk because of Chewing-gum, but she did not want to say so, as, obviously for the present, the less said about him, the better. She decided to make a martyr of Rachel.

"I think we'll fix it by age. Rachel and I will have the lower bunks. We don't mind, Rachel, dear, do we? It's all going to be such splendid fun."

Rachel did mind and was just going to say so when there was a knock on the door and in came a steward in a white coat. He was carrying a long box and some telegrams. He was a cheerful man with a sunburned face and very blue eyes.

"I'm your bedroom steward. Name of Williams. Which of you is Miss Bean?" When Peaseblossom had taken the box, he looked at the telegrams. "Miss Rachel Winter. Miss Jane Winter. Tim Winter." He raised his eyebrows in a funny way. "Would that be you three?"

No one had thought that people would send parcels and telegrams. After all, they were the ones who were having the luck to go away, so if any parcels and telegrams were being sent, you would have thought they would have gone to people left behind. All the same, it was lovely to have them. Rachel's was from Madame Fidolia: GOOD LUCK DEAR FROM US ALL WE SHALL MISS YOU STOP POSY HAS CABLED SHE WILL TAKE CARE OF YOU MADAME. Tim's was from Mr.

42

Brown: HAVE A GOOD TIME BUT DON'T FORGET TO PRACTICE MICHAEL BROWN. Jane's was from Dr. Smith: CHEWING-GUM HAS BEEN WITH ME FOR AN HOUR AND HAS NOT YET LOOKED UP FROM HIS BONE ENJOY YOURSELF LOVE SMITH.

Rachel read her telegram out loud.

"Imagine Madame sending me a telegram! It's an awfully grand thing to have happened. Just fancy Posy Fossil having cabled about me, and her a star!"

Jane had climbed into the bunk over Rachel's to read her telegram. It was so nice to think of Chewing-gum happily eating a bone that she spoke in quite her old way.

"I'm glad I'm not a dancer and have to feel humble as a worm whenever that Madame noticed me. Now listen to my telegram. This is a sensible telegram."

They were so glad to hear Jane being herself again and to think that Chewing-gum had settled down that they said nothing about her rude way of talking but agreed it was a glorious telegram. In fact, Peaseblossom went on saying things about it so long that Tim, who had climbed up into his bunk, had to interrupt her.

"Everybody would think I hadn't had a telegram. Would you listen, please?"

They listened then, and Peaseblossom admired it very much.

"Splendid. Practice, that's the way. Mustn't let the side down." She was undoing her box while she spoke and took out some carnations. She read the card and looked pleased. "They're from a school friend, and listen to what she says. 'Hope you have learned to sing "California, Here I Come." ' "

They had never heard of a song called that, but somehow the line made them feel terribly gay and excited. Tim sang it to the tune of "Good King Wenceslas." "California, here I come, Cali-Cali-fornia. California, here I come. Cali-california." In a minute they all, even Peaseblossom, were

43

joining in. Tim knelt on his bunk and conducted. Among them they made such a noise that they did not hear a knock on the door and were surprised to find the stewardess in the middle of the cabin; she was laughing.

"I came in to tell you I was your stewardess. My name is Miss Mann."

They all said, "How do you do." Miss Mann was fat and cozy-looking, just the sort of person you would choose as your stewardess. Peaseblossom was particularly glad to find such a friendly-looking stewardess because she knew there would be lots of things she would want to know.

"I'm afraid we were making rather a noise," Peaseblossom said.

Miss Mann laughed again. "I gather you're going to California. My, I wish it were me." She came over to Peaseblossom. "Have you booked your sittings for meals? You'll want first sitting for the children, and if I were you, I'd get some unpacking done; it's a good thing to get things shipshape before you start."

Peaseblossom explained that John would be seeing to the table bookings, but she thought unpacking was a good idea. She looked around at the baggage. "I think I'll do better on my own in this small space. You children run along and have a look around, and on the way go to your mom and dad's cabin and show them your telegrams."

John and Bee's cabin was much smaller than the children's, and it had no porthole; but it was nice. Bee was alone in it, unpacking. She was thrilled by the telegrams and sat down on the lower bunk and showed the children all the telegrams that she and John had received. Almost everybody they knew seemed to have sent one, and there were five lots of flowers as well.

Rachel said, "Aren't we grand suddenly! It's almost as if we'd become royalty."

Tim, who had climbed up to the upper berth to see if it was as good as his own, shouted, "One, two, three, altogether," and started, "California, here I come. Cali-California." Rachel and Jane joined in at the top of their voices.

Bee put her hands over her ears. "Stop, darlings, we shall disturb everybody. Come down off there, Tim. Don't you want to see us sail? We shall be off in no time now. You'd better run up on the deck, where you'll get a good view."

The last person went ashore. The last gangway was pulled in, the last rope unhitched. There was a little gap between the *Mauretania* and the dock. People on the dockside waved and cheered. Hundreds of sea gulls wheeled and cried. The gap widened. It was too big to jump across. It was too big to swim across. They were off.

The wind got up a bit in the night. It made the *Mauretania* roll. The roll was quite gentle and made the family sleep as if somebody were rocking their bunks for them. In the children's cabin they did not know it was morning until Miss Mann came in with orange juice and tea. She drew back the little curtains which were across the porthole and started on Tim.

"Wakey, wakey. Rise and shine. Show a leg."

Tim blinked and sat up and, seeing who it was, felt pleased. "Good morning. What did you say?"

"What they say in the navy. Wakey, wakey. Rise and shine. Show a leg."

Jane leaned out of her bunk to take her orange juice. "Why do they say it?"

Peaseblossom had not moved, nor had Rachel, so Miss Mann put a cup of tea on the table beside Peaseblossom and orange juice beside Rachel. She shook a finger at Jane.

"I can see you're the 'why' sort. Never ask me 'why' anything in the morning. I've all my passengers to call and get to their baths. Now, when the steward knocks to say your baths

45

are ready, you're to run, or you'll have everybody late for breakfast.''

The word ''breakfast'' made Jane and Tim hungry. The food on the *Mauretania* was too gorgeous to be believed. There was so much to choose from, and you could eat as much as you liked, not just three courses as in a restaurant. Then, too, there was all the bread anybody could eat, and not just ordinary bread, but white bread. Most surprising of all, there was unlimited butter. They had not believed the table steward at first when he had told them this, but they found it to be true, because as soon as they had finished one dishful, they had started on another. Unfortunately, in spite of there being so much of everything, John, Peaseblossom, and even Bee were very strict about what could be eaten. With party food of every sort on the menu, for both lunch and supper, the children were allowed only cold meat or boiled fish and fruit afterward. John said, ''You've Dr. Smith to thank. He says if we let ourselves go at first, we'll all be ill for weeks afterward, and it's not worth it.''

Tim, sipping his orange juice, looked across at Jane. He sighed with ecstasy. ''Orange juice! A whole tumbler of orange juice coming in as if it were just ordinary.''

Jane nodded. ''And for breakfast, I wouldn't wonder, bacon and a real egg. That's the sort of food that's ordinary on this ship.''

''Even two slices of bacon and two whole eggs.'' Tim leaned out of his bunk and looked down at Peaseblossom. She had not moved. He lowered his voice. ''If only we could get to the dining room first and eat them before anybody could stop us.''

Peaseblossom half sat up. She stretched out a hand for her tea, then took it back again. She spoke in a much less brisk voice than usual. ''Good morning, dears. What are you talking about?''

46

Jane hung out of her berth so that she could see Peaseblossom. "Food. Bacon and eggs, actually."

The words "bacon and eggs" had an odd effect on Peaseblossom. She gave a queer moan and turned over on her back and shut her eyes.

Jane made a face at Tim. Tim, curious to see what was going on underneath him, hung almost upside down. "Are you ill, Peaseblossom?"

Peaseblossom spoke in a whisper. "Not ill. Just a little tired. Please leave me alone."

Rachel was awake and drinking her orange juice. She thought at first it was delicious. Then she was not sure. She put down the glass. Then she, too, rolled on her back and shut her eyes. Tim looked at Rachel in amazement. "You can't be tired, too. We've been asleep for hours and hours."

Jane climbed out of bed. She looked pityingly at Peaseblossom and Rachel. "They're not tired. They're seasick."

It was unfair, Rachel thought, that only she and Peaseblossom should feel the sea. Such heavenly things were happening on deck. There was a band. There were film shows. There was a game called bingo, and the lounge steward said there would be a horse-racing game, and when it happened, Jane and Tim would each have a turn at shaking the dice.

On the second day out the wind dropped, and just before eleven o'clock a very pale Rachel came up on deck. Bee walked on one side of her, and John on the other, but she did not need any help. Jane and Tim had a deck chair with a leg rest all ready for her. She got onto it and shut her eyes, while Tim and Jane solicitously tucked a rug around her. Presently Rachel opened her eyes. There were people all around sitting on chairs, laughing and talking. The sky was blue; the sun was shining. A solitary sea gull was flying above the ship. Rachel took a quick glance at the sea. It was dark green and navy blue, with gay white horses bobbing as far as the

47

horizon. She took a deep breath, and good, clear sea air filled her lungs, a lovely change after a stuffy cabin with a closed porthole.

A steward came down the line of chairs with a tray on which were cups. He stopped by Rachel. "Chicken soup? Crackers?"

"Chicken soup, please, and four crackers."

Poor Peaseblossom never really enjoyed the journey. She got up in the afternoon of that same day and each day afterward, but her getting up was a dreary creep to a chair, where she lay with her eyes shut.

Jane, who had got not only her spirits back but extra spirits to make up for having been miserable for so long, said, in a whisper loud enough for poor Peaseblossom to hear, "It's all going to be such splendid fun."

Peaseblossom was too depressed to say anything at hearing her words quoted against her, but she opened her eyes and gave Jane a look which said, "You wait until I'm on dry land."

Two nights before they landed there was a concert, and both Rachel and Tim performed at it. After she got over feeling seasick, Rachel had practiced. She tried to find a corner where nobody would notice her; but anything makes news on a ship, so the fact that Rachel was a ballet student quickly got around, and when the concert was discussed, it was taken for granted that Rachel would dance. Bee groaned when she heard the news.

"Oh, darling, and I don't know where Peaseblossom packed your audition dress, and she can't look for it; she'll fall over if she tries to unpack. I wonder if it's in a box in the hold or in the baggage room. You couldn't dance in an ordinary frock, could you?"

Bee and John were lying in chairs side by side. Rachel sat

48

down on the footrest of Bee's between the two of them. She lowered her voice so the people near would not hear.

"The only thing I can dance is m'audition."

Every pupil of Madame Fidolia's, when approaching her twelfth birthday, prepared material for auditions: something to recite, something to sing, and something to dance. These were called audition pieces, but the pupils always called them m'auditions, short for "My audition pieces." Once she was twelve, no pupil of Madame Fidolia's, even if she went to the other end of the world, as Rachel was doing, would be without the music for her m'audition song and dance any more that she would forget the words of her recitation. John was lying in the next chair, apparently asleep, but when Rachel used the word "m'audition," he opened one eye.

"You don't mean to tell me we've got to suffer 'Cherry Ripe' in mid-Atlantic."

John had been so gloomy and silent since the accident that Rachel had not known he knew how hard she had practiced "Cherry Ripe," for he had never before mentioned it.

"Did you hear me practicing it?"

John opened the other eye, and both were twinkling. "Could anyone miss it? As for Viola's speech from *Twelfth Night*, I can say it for you. I know just where to breathe. I heard Peaseblossom reminding you. 'Breathe there, dear.' " He got up. "I'm going to take a walk to get an appetite for lunch."

Rachel looked after John in amazement. "Dad sounds quite different."

Bee, too, was gazing at John's back. "Of course, it's too early yet to say he's better; still, it does seem as if there is a chance this holiday will work. When we see him thumping at that typewriter, that's when we'll know he's well." She lay back in her chair. "But talking about Dad isn't getting us anywhere. What about this frock?"

Rachel tried to think helpfully. The audition dress was red

49

crepe de chine. It had been made out of an old evening dress of Peaseblossom's. It was so old that the crepe de chine was cracking here and there, and there had been no thought of its being worn on the ship; it was much too precious. The clothes that had been left out for ship wear were sweaters, a pleated skirt, shorts, and two cotton frocks to change into in the evening.

"Nobody could feel like dancing in a cotton frock everybody had seen a person change into for the evening. Would it be rude to say I couldn't dance?"

"Disobliging, I think. I don't suppose there are many people on board who do things."

John had been once around the deck. He stopped for a moment. "Scrape her hair back and tie something on as an apron and turn her into Alice."

As soon as John spoke, Rachel and Bee saw he was right. With a ribbon around her hair and an apron tied over a cotton frock Rachel could easily look like Alice in *Wonderland*. Bee said, "I'll make an apron out of something this afternoon, and you go tell whoever's arranging the program that your dance is called 'Alice in Wonderland.' If they announce it like that, everybody will know who you are meant to be, even if you don't look much like it."

Tim had practiced every day. The day they sailed he found out there was a piano in the lounge, and the next day he sat down to play on it. The lounge steward came hurrying over to him.

"Now then, young man, none of that; no strumming here."

"I don't strum. I'm going to practice. I have to practice every day. I promised Mr. Brown, who teaches me, that I would."

Tim had nice manners as a rule, and the lounge steward had already noticed him with approval as a child who would not be as much of a nuisance as some; but Tim changed when he

50

was at a piano. He could be as difficult as Jane if anyone interrupted him when he wanted to play.

"Can't have every child in the boat practicing; got the rest of the passengers to think about."

Tim glanced around the lounge. Most of the passengers were on the deck. Those sitting about had not yet got their sea legs and had their eyes closed and anxious, suffering expressions on their faces.

"Them! I wouldn't miss my practice for them." Tim struck a fine scornful chord to express his feelings.

Grown-up people who have no particular talent themselves are apt to think that talent in a child is miraculous. The lounge steward was that sort of man. He looked at Tim's fingers and marveled that they could find the notes at all, let alone make a big noise like that.

"You professional?"

"Of course not. I'm going to be, but not for ages."

"Let's hear you play a piece."

The lounge steward had a face and a voice which were just the sort of face and voice Tim liked best. There was a look and a sound about them as if, at any minute, there would be an enormous loud laugh coming. Besides, playing pieces was what Tim liked doing.

"Actually I'm supposed to do some special things first, but I'll play my favorite tune for you."

Tim was an unusually musical boy, as Mr. Brown and Jeremy Caulder had found out. Of course, there were years of work ahead of him, but already, when he played, it was nice to listen. Even the passengers who had not got their sea legs opened their eyes and cheered up a little. The lounge steward leaned on the piano and found himself forgetting where he was and was carried in his mind to the village in Hampshire where he lived, especially to his garden. He found himself thinking, "Must pick the last of those toma-

51

toes before the frost gets them.'' It gave him quite a shock when Tim stopped playing and he found himself leaning on the piano in the cabin-class lounge.

"That was nice. What was it?"

"It's by Debussy. It's called 'Jardins sous la Pluie.' "

"And what might that mean?"

"Mr. Brown says that turned into the English we speak, it means 'Gardens in the Rain' "

The lounge steward blinked. "Crikey, and that's just what it sounded like; as soon as you started, I thought of my tomatoes."

After that Tim practiced as long as he liked, and of course, when the concert was suggested, it was taken for granted that Tim would play. To please his friend the lounge steward and himself, Tim said he would play "Jardins sous la Pluie."

The concert would quite honestly not have been much of a success without Tim and Rachel, for the talent was poor. Tim was on in the first half of the program, and everybody applauded so heartily that after he had bowed several times, which made the passengers laugh, he played Rachmaninoff's Prelude in G as an encore. Rachel danced at the end of the program. Her dance was quite short but arranged to show managers what she could do, so it was showy. The passengers were enraptured, and cheered as well as clapped. Rachel curtsied several times, but when the clapping and cheering went on, she hurried to Bee and John.

"What shall I do? I don't know another solo, and I've no more music."

John was pleased that his children had given enjoyment to everybody, but he thought it was time the concert finished and they went to bed.

"Tell them so, then, and thank them nicely."

Rachel went back and curtsied again. Then she cleared her throat. She had never made a speech before, so her voice squeaked a little. "I'm afraid I can't do another dance. I haven't any more music, and it's the only one I've practiced."

The audience clapped again, and a voice shouted, "Well, let's have the same dance."

Rachel danced the dance again. It was not very good that time as she was excited and wobbled on her pirouettes and her arabesque, but the audience, who knew nothing about dancing, thought her wonderful and clapped louder than ever.

After "God Save the King" had been played, the passengers crowded around Bee and John, and words like "wonderful" and "genius" buzzed about. Jane, who had been sitting between John and Bee for the concert, tried to get out of the crowd and off to bed, but it was difficult. Just as she reached the door, she heard a woman say to a man, "That child going out of the door is a sister, you know, but she doesn't do anything."

The man answered, "Queer having that plain kid with the other two so good-looking."

When Jane reached the cabin, Rachel and Tim were telling Peaseblossom all about the concert.

"But it's so odd," Rachel said. "They clapped just as much when I danced my worst."

Jane shut the door and began to undress.

"That's what is known as an undiscriminating audience, dear," Peaseblossom said, "but I feel sure our side did splendidly."

Rachel folded her apron. "Tim bowed beautifully."

Tim nodded. "I thought that was rather good. It was copied from Sir Malcolm Sargent last Christmas when we went to the carols at the Albert Hall."

Jane felt so miserable she would have liked to cry, but she cried only over desperate things like leaving Chewing-gum behind. What mattered was that what those silly fools said was true. She couldn't do anything, not anything at all,

53

and she was the only plain Winter. She looked so sour that at last the others noticed. Peaseblossom said, "What's the matter, dear?"

Jane was brushing her teeth. She took the brush out of her mouth. "Nothing. It's just that I've already listened to that awful concert, and I was not exactly enjoying hearing about it all over again."

Peaseblossom was shocked. She had known that Jane had been getting out of hand ever since she had quoted, "It's going to be such splendid fun." She spoke in her usual voice and not the fadeaway, gentle voice she had spoken in ever since her first morning on board.

"Jane! That's a disgraceful way to talk! You're jealous. Jealousy is a horrible fault. We may not all be equally talented, but we can all be equally nice people."

Jane said no more. She climbed into her bunk with indignation sticking out all over her. She lay down and turned her face to the wall and for the first time since the *Mauretania* had sailed missed Chewing-gum so much that it hurt. Chewing-gum, who thought her much the nicest of the family; who even thought her the best-looking; who did not care a bit if she could dance or play the piano; who liked her just as she was with no alteration at all. "I'll say exactly what I like," she told herself. "I don't mind being plain, and I don't mind not doing anything. I hate them all; I'll just be me whether they like it or not."

The whole family, even Peaseblossom, was on deck to catch a first glimpse of the Statue of Liberty. After so long at sea it was thrilling to see land and ships darting about. At first there was no sign of the statue. Then one of the crew held out a finger, pointing. "She lies there. You watch." The statue was on an island. She was even bigger and more like herself than she looked in photographs. The man grinned

54

at her affectionately. "Looks a bit of all right, don't she, bless 'er? Now you look over there. Watch close."

At first there was nothing to see, for where the man pointed was a bank of mist. What happened was like the end of the Sleeping Beauty's story, that part where the prince fights his way through overhanging branches and cobwebs and sees a magic castle. The mist broke away as if it were overhanging branches and cobwebs, and out of it came what seemed a magic castle: pinkish in color, an irregular outline stretching almost to the sky.

Awestruck, Rachel gasped: "What's that?"

The man laughed. "That! That's good old New York!"

7

New York City

John and Bee were met at the dockside by a friend of Aunt Cora's. They were very glad to see him because he had dollars for them. By the law of England they might not change pounds into dollars, so if they had not met the man, they would have had no money at all. The children, though they tried not to, stared at the man because he was so exactly like a rich American in the movies. He was very welcoming, so welcoming that at first the children supposed he must be an old friend of John and Bee's. When they found out he was a stranger, they decided that to be welcoming must be an American habit, and a very nice one, as it made the whole family stop feeling they were strangers in a strange land. After he had got over telling them all how fine it was to see them, he became suddenly brisk and bustling. He said he would take them over to the railroad, where they could check their baggage and turn the railway vouchers they had bought in England into railway tickets for California, and then he would show them around a bit and give them lunch. He said all this so obviously only to John and Bee, not including Peaseblossom or the children in his plans and invitations, that the only thing they could do was to separate. Bee said in a scared voice, "We've none of us been in New York before. I suppose my family won't get lost?"

The man laughed. "Why, no. What these kids will like will be to go to the top of the Empire State Building and then fill themselves up with ice-cream sodas. Come along, you folks, we've go a lot to do." With that, he put one arm through John's and the other through Bee's and hurried them away.

Peaseblossom and the children looked after them, feeling rather deserted. Rachel said, "He's a friend of Aunt Cora's. Do you suppose Aunt Cora's the sort of person who thinks children never want to do the same things as their parents do?"

Peaseblossom tried to sound confident.

"Don't talk nonsense, dear. Naturally that nice friend of your aunt's doesn't want the whole lot of us hanging around. Besides, we'll manage splendidly on our own, won't we? Up the Winters!"

They would have managed perfectly if the effect of New York on Peaseblossom had not been to turn her from her competent self into something rather like a sheep in a narrow lane trying to go the opposite way from the rest of the flock. Everybody was kind and helpful and told them how to get out of the docks and which way to go when they were out, but Peaseblossom could not take in what she was told. She kept saying in an agitated way, "I beg your pardon?" and even "What?" which shocked the children, who had been told since they were babies that to say "What?" was rude. Worst of all, she behaved as though the directions were being given to her in another language, commenting on them to the children in loud whispers, which the people politely trying to help must have overheard. "I can't make out a word he's saying. . . . Better ask somebody else. I don't think he knows where the Empire State Building is."

The children were so ashamed that at last they took control. Rachel gripped one of Peaseblossom's arms, and Jane the other, and they hurried her out of the docks and across the road; but once there, they forgot the directions they had been given and found it was difficult to get them again because nobody in New York walked slowly. Instead the people moved at the same pace as men use in England when they are practicing for a walking race. First one of the children and then another stepped forward to ask the way, saying politely, "Excuse me," but by the time they had got that out the person they had spoken to was almost out of sight and never even knew he had been addressed. At last a man who was held up by the traffic lights noticed them and leaned out of his car.

"You folks need help?"

They all explained at once. He was a terribly kind man. He told them to get into his car, and he would drive them to where they could get a bus. As they drove along, he told them that he knew they came from Britain because of their British accents. This surprised the children, who had supposed that it was America which had an accent and not England, unless, of course, you were Scottish or Welsh or something like that, but they kept this thought to themselves. The man was most considerate; he put them down where he said the bus would stop, and told them that in the bus they would have to travel only six blocks. He had been so kind that as he drove away, they felt they had lost a friend.

The thing they all had forgotten, and had not noticed when the man was driving them, was that traffic drove on the opposite side of the road from the way it did at home, so, in spite of the man's having told them that they were at the right stop, they thought they must cross the street. Even when they did grasp which bus to take, they made a very silly entrance, for they tried to get on the back end, as they did at home. Peaseblossom looked so flustered that Rachel said comfortingly, "We couldn't know."

Tim was indignant. "If you ask me, American buses are like tortoises; I mean, like you have to give a shut-up tortoise a buttercup at each end to know which end's going to eat."

Peaseblossom had always known the values of American money and had carefully restudied the subject before she left England, but by the time she was on the bus she was in that state of mind when people say, "I'll forget my own name next!" When the driver told her how many nickels he wanted she became deaf again and repeated in an ever-louder voice, "I beg your pardon?" Fortunately John had given her a lot of small change, and Jane had the good idea of taking her purse from her, tipping the money into her hand and letting the driver help himself. It worked all right, though the driver did not seem pleased, for he made international bus-driver noises.

Tim was surprised at this display of grumpiness in a country where everybody seemed so welcoming. As he sat down he whispered to Jane, "It was because you didn't put the money in that slot machine. Do you think I could go and tell him we aren't stupid really; it's only we've never seen one of those before?"

Jane was cross because though she would not admit it, the driver's being angry fussed her. So she said, "Don't be a silly idiot; interrupting him when he's driving will make him hate us worse."

To make up for the driver, the people in the bus could not have been kinder. Nearly all of them had expressions on their faces to show they thought seeing strangers get off buses at the right place was the most important thing in life. Tim was so charmed by this that before they left the bus, he thanked everybody. This seemed to cause quite a sensation, for the Winters got off to a hum of "Isn't he cute! . . . Isn't he darling!"

Tim looked after the departing bus with affection. "Did you hear what those people said about me?"

59

Rachel looked at Peaseblossom. Neither of them said anything, but they made faces which showed they hoped Tim was not going to be spoiled in America. Jane as usual spoke what she thought.

"You aren't cute, and goodness knows, nobody could call you darling."

There would have been a quarrel, but fighting their way through the half-running citizens of New York took up all their attention and breath.

The Empire State Building was a wonderful thrill to the children but not to Peaseblossom. Her insides could not comfortably have stood a ride up 2 stories; 102 were nearly fatal. She arrived at the top looking green as grass and holding a handkerchief ready. Actually they got the best view when they came down one story because there they could go outside and lean over a wall. The mist of the morning had gone, and it was a marvelous sight. On the top of the highest building in the world the skyscrapers of New York ceased to tower; instead they seemed to be straining to be as tall as the Empire State Building. On one side of the city wound the Hudson River, the ships on it looking from that height like toy ships made to float in a bath. The children saw how neatly arranged the New York streets were, almost as neat as a chessboard: long roads stretching across the city and across them other roads east and west. The children would have stayed up there twice as long as they did; only Peaseblossom said it made her feel queer even to watch them hanging over the wall, so out of pity they had to take her down.

When they came out of the Empire State Building, they remembered the other thing Aunt Cora's friend had said they would like: ice-cream sodas. Peaseblossom looked around at the hurrying, swirling crowd.

"I must find a policeman. He will be sure to know somewhere nice."

It took time, but at last Peaseblossom found a policeman. At once she felt more at home than she had done since she arrived, for policemen always knew everything, never minded how many questions you asked, and were never in a hurry. She went up to this one with a confident smile.

"Constable, could you tell me of a nice place to take these children to drink ice-cream sodas?"

Peaseblossom waited for the brotherly smile, for the pause while the virtues of various places were considered, for the final advice, "If I were you, I'd take them to . . ." Nothing like that happened. The policeman never smiled, scarcely looked at Peaseblossom. He paused all right, but it was the pause of somebody marveling why a stupid woman should bother him. Then he moved away; as he moved, he said, "Drugstore opposite."

Peaseblossom's faith in the United States of America quivered. What kind of land was it where policemen were not everybody's friend and adviser?

"What a strange man! A drugstore! Why should he think I want a chemist?"

Tim was thirsty and unwilling to wait longer for his drink. He knew now that in New York it was no good saying anything slowly because nobody heard you. He laid a hand on the arm of a passing lady.

"Where do we buy ice-cream sodas, please?"

She was the nicest lady. Not only did people in America, once they had stopped hurrying, seem to have not only lots of time to help strangers, but all put on that special helpful-looking expression. The lady called Tim honey and said "surely" twice and then showed them the same drugstore the policeman had shown them. She laughed when she saw Peaseblossom's surprised face and said it was clear they hadn't been long over, and she remembered being just as mixed up when she first visited Europe. She explained that a

61

drugstore in America was not the same thing as a chemist in England; it sold drugs, all right, but everything else as well, including ice-cream sodas.

The drugstore was beautiful. All down one side was a counter with men behind it in white coats. A most friendly man mixed their drinks. He tried to persuade Peaseblossom to have a soda, too, but when she explained about the sea and the Empire State Building, he quite understood and said he had just the drink for her and mixed her something which looked like fruit salts.

Whatever it was, it did her a lot of good. She made three loud hiccuping sounds, but once those were over, it seemed to be the end of her feeling peculiar, so much the end that for the first time in six days she was hungry.

"I don't know about you, but I would be glad of something to eat."

The rest of the time in New York seemed to fly away. They had a lovely lunch, and after that they went around to a big store and did a little shopping. Of course, they had no money to buy clothes, but they saw the loveliest things that people who had money could buy.

They went to the station in a taxi. The taxi driver had been in England during the war and was full of chat. He told them what he thought about England, which was not all very complimentary, and asked them what they thought of New York. Peaseblossom and Rachel said politely it was lovely, but Tim told the man he thought it was a noisy town, for he had taken a dislike to the sirens screaming on the ambulances, fire engines, and police cars, and Jane said that she didn't think much of the manners of policemen and bus drivers. The taxi man seemed surprised at there being anything to criticize and looked hurt and said no more.

As soon as they were out of the taxi, Peaseblossom turned on Jane and Tim. "How dreadfully rude you were!"

Jane thought this shockingly unjust. "He told us what he didn't like about England."

"Well, he's got a right to. He was over with us long enough to have an opinion, but you've been in New York only one day, and you start to criticize. I'm ashamed of you."

It took nothing to make Jane angry, but Tim was usually fairly even-tempered. Such apparent injustice, however, was more than he could stand.

"If you think all the time I'm in America I'm going to be polite to people and say everything's perfect while they say what they like about England, you're wrong. You couldn't make me."

"I've always said what I think," Jane said, "and I'm not going to change just because I'm in America."

Peaseblossom had a special tone of voice which she used only rarely, but when she did use it, even Jane seldom disobeyed her.

"Be quiet, both of you! I'll talk to you about this another time."

Bee and John were waiting with Aunt Cora's friend outside the gate that led to their departure platform. They could feel in a second that something was wrong, and if they had not felt it, a glance would have told them. Jane looked at her most black-doggish. Tim's lips were sucked together, and he was frowning. Rachel had a don't-get-me-to-take-sides expression. Peaseblossom had two bright pink patches on her cheekbones, always a bad sign.

There was no opportunity to find out what was wrong with Aunt Cora's friend there, and the great thing was to let him think the day had been enjoyed, whether it had or not, so John asked what they had done. Rachel answered, helped by Peaseblossom, and presently, as his temper wore off, Tim joined in. Jane said nothing at all. If Tim was weak enough to let Peaseblossom think she was forgiven, let him be, but not she; she would go on being angry until Peaseblossom apologized. Aunt Cora's friend was glad to hear what a good time they had enjoyed. Luckily Tim kept off the subject of policemen and bus drivers, so the man thought that they had admired everything and everybody.

The train was just like a train in the movies. All the cars were pullmans. Aunt Cora's friend came onto the train to see that they were what he called fixed all right. There were seats with room for two facing each other; each seat belonged to one person. Aunt Cora's friend showed them where presently the top bunks would come down and told them that the porter would make up their beds when they were ready for them and where he would fix curtains across so that each one of at night would have complete privacy. Then he led them down the train and showed them the places where they would go to wash and dress, and where the diner was, and the club car. After Chicago, he said, where their through pullman would be hooked onto a train called *The Chief,* they ought to sit in the observation car because the scenery would really be something.

When they had waved good-bye to Aunt Cora's friend, John led the way back to their seats and said with more enthusiasm than they had heard in his voice since the accident, "Isn't this fun!"

Jane was still very black-doggish, and was convinced she had a right to be. She had hoped John and Bee would ask her what was wrong so that she could tell the whole story. In her mind she could hear them say, "Well, Peaseblossom, I think Jane and Tim were right; if the taxi driver gave his opinion of England, there was no harm in their criticizing people and things in America," or something of that sort, which would squash Peaseblossom. Since neither Bee nor John appeared to have noticed she was angry, Jane had to open the subject herself.

"It would be more fun if people were allowed to say what they thought."

Bee saw Jane felt she must tell her grievance or explode. "What mayn't you say, darling?"

Jane explained. She was prompted by Tim, who, now that the whole story was repeated, was angry again.

While the story was pouring out, John seemed to be looking out of the window and not attending, but as Jane finished, he turned around. He held out a hand to Tim and pulled him onto one knee; he put an arm around Jane and nodded to Rachel to sit opposite him.

"Looks as though I ought to have had this talk on the boat. There's a thing we've got to remember every day and every minute of the day from now on. We are foreigners."

"Foreigners!" the children exclaimed.

Rachel added, "But the American soldiers weren't foreigners to us when they lived in England when there was a war."

"Yes, they were, and I expect they felt it."

Tim wriggled around on John's knee so that he could look at him. He did not feel he could expostulate well unless he could see his father's face. "We can't be foreigners; we all speak the same language."

"That's the snag. Just because we speak more or less the same language, we forget we're foreign and expect Americans to behave and think as we do; actually we are just as foreign as if we were Dutch, French, Belgian, or Swiss. Being foreigners means we are staying in somebody else's house. When you stay with Aunt Cora, you won't come down to breakfast and look at the food and say, 'We cook that better at home,' or, when some plan's made, 'I don't want to do that,' and you won't criticize the way her furniture is arranged or what she says. You'll be in her house, and you'll feel, as a guest does, that what she does in it is her business."

Jane was still looking very black-doggish.

"Do you mean that all the time we're staying here we've got to be visitors, and if somebody like that taxi driver says things about us, we can't say things back?"

"Well, he knew what he was talking about. He was in England for months probably and got to know us well, but what's the point in your flying out about manners of policemen and bus drivers when you've been in the country only five minutes? It's not only rude but ignorant. I don't want to preach to you, but it's common sense. Let's behave like visitors who hope to get asked again."

There was silence for a moment. The fact that they were now foreigners had surprised the children, for somehow they had not thought of themselves as that. It had been a shock to Tim and Jane to find that John sided with Peaseblossom in thinking they had been rude. Jane still wanted to argue. A holiday in which she was supposed to be on guest behavior with everybody was not at all her idea of a nice time. She had, of course, known that they would be Aunt Cora's guests, with all the being polite that meant, but being the guests of everybody in America was too much. She said as much. "I think it's idiotic that we can't say we don't like things if we don't."

John was losing the gay mood in which he had come on the train. He looked tired.

"I can't help what you think. I'm telling you how we're going to behave. When we've been here a month or two, it'll be different; we may be able to discuss ways of doing things, but not the moment we arrive. Anybody who yaps about somebody else's country without knowing a thing about it looks like a silly ass. You don't want to look like that."

66

Bee thought the lecture had gone on long enough. She was unwinding paper off a long, thin roll.

"Look what I bought for you all." She held out a piece of music. It was a copy of "California, Here I Come."

Tim had the music. The others leaned over his shoulder. He read it through; then, very softly, he hummed the chorus. In quiet voices, so as not to disturb the other passengers, Rachel and Jane joined in with him.

They laughed at the words, but singing them gave them a very happy feeling. After all, it was not just a song they were singing; they were really going to California. They were actually on their way.

A man across the aisle leaned over.

"Sing up, folks. Let's all enjoy it."

That was just what was needed; Americans seemed awfully nice on trains, not a bit standoffish. Soon lots of people were joining in, including Joe, the porter, and those who were not were laughing.

8

Aunt Cora

The morning they were due to arrive in Los Angeles, the most careful preparations were made for meeting Aunt Cora. Even Rachel's ears and nails were inspected. The children were not allowed to do their own hair and, once dressed, were scarcely permitted to move.

The only thing which helped make the waiting time pass was the view from the window. The sky was startlingly blue. There were mountains. Most amazing of all, there were oranges and lemons growing on trees.

"Fancy looking out of a train in October and seeing oranges growing," Rachel marveled. "At home now the last leaves are blowing off the trees."

Aunt Cora was on the platform. She was just a little like John but not a bit the children's idea of what a widowed aunt ought to look like; in fact, she was so unlike their idea of what any aunt, widowed or not, ought to look like that they wished Joe had not told them he would be watching the meeting. Of course, Aunt Cora had married an American when she was eighteen, but though they knew that fact, it had not prepared the children for an un-English-looking and -sounding aunt. Aunt Cora was thin with bright golden hair; she was wearing no hat and the oddest dress. To Tim and Jane it looked like any fancy dress, but Rachel felt it belonged to the first act of *Giselle*, for it had puffed sleeves and a peasanty look. Aunt Cora had a whiny voice with a queer accent that was neither English nor American but halfway between. She was wearing an American welcoming expression, and she said all the right American welcoming things; only somehow, perhaps because she was not an American, she did not sound or look sincere. The more welcoming her words and face tried to be, the more the whole family remembered how early she must have got up to meet their train. She did the proper things, kissing everybody, even Peaseblossom, and for each one had special words. "Bee! Why, isn't this too wonderful! . . . Miss Bean! I'm surely glad to know you. . . . This must be Rachel. We'll have to look after you, or we'll be losing you to the movies. . . . You must be Jane. Poor little thing, she needs feeding up. . . . Tim! Quite a little man, isn't he?" After a lot more of this she held John by the shoulders. "John! Big brother John."

John thought the welcome had gone on long enough. He said in a very brisk that's-enough-of-that voice, "Fine seeing you, old girl. Oughtn't we to be doing something about the luggage?"

Aunt Cora had borrowed a station wagon, which held them all and the luggage. She drove very fast, talking in her funny, whiny voice to John. Mostly she asked about people in England, and only John needed to pay attention, which was lucky because it gave the rest of them time to look around. Everything was unlike any place the children had been in before. Huge palm trees bordered the roads. There were no hedges or fences around the houses. Instead each garden came down to the edge of what the children called pavement but Aunt Cora, speaking to John, called the sidewalk. There were so many unusual plants and flowers about that Bee, who loved flowers, kept giving pleased squeaks.

"Oh, look, a plumbago hedge! . . . Oh, do look at that bougainvillaea!"

69

Aunt Cora looked over her shoulder.

"We're just leaving Beverly Hills; at the end of this boulevard we'll be in Santa Monica."

They were by the sea. There was a beach, restaurants with big signs outside saying Seafood, and houses built right up against the shore with steps leading down to the beach. A general gay seaside look everywhere. The children were thrilled.

"The sea! Look at the sea!"

Aunt Cora said, in a reproving way, as if the word "sea" were insulting, "You don't use the word 'sea' here. You say 'ocean'."

Peaseblossom hurried to cover the family's mistake. "Of course we do. We just forgot the Pacific was an ocean, didn't we, dears?"

Aunt Cora had built her own house, or rather Aunt Cora's husband, whom she called "My dear Ed," had built it for her. It was at the far end of Santa Monica. A lovely house, long, low, white, with what the family called a veranda and she called a porch overlooking the sea. From the porch, steps led down to the beach. The bedrooms were lovely. John and Bee had a big one with its own bathroom, and Tim had a dressing room opening off it. The two girls and Peaseblossom had a big room, and it had its own shower. Aunt Cora's room, which was too grand for words, had a bathroom, and there was another shower for Bella, Aunt Cora's black live-in maid. The number of bathrooms impressed the children very much, for in Saxon Crescent they had only one.

"I shouldn't think," Rachel said, "Buckingham Palace could have more."

The first thing they did on arrival was to have another breakfast. Just as if she had known what they would like, Bella had made popovers for them, and there was the most amazing fruit as well. Blueberries, the size of gooseberries,

70

served with thick cream. Purple figs. Little melons cut in half and iced. Queer soft orange-colored fruits called persimmons and, just to show they had come to the land of plenty, a whole bunch of bananas. There was a glass of chilled tomato juice; there was cereal; there were eggs, bacon, and coffee and cream. None of the Winters was sure if in America it was the right thing to talk about food, but they simply had to. Aunt Cora looked in a sad way at the table.

"I always provide good food, but I scarcely touch it myself. I have to be so careful to stick to my calories." She looked at herself and then disapprovingly at Peaseblossom, who had curves. "That's how I keep my figure."

Breakfast was served on the porch. While they all were admiring the food, Bella had come in from the back and was standing in the doorway. She was large and colorful in a bright flowered housedress, and her face had a wide, pleased smile; it could not have smiled more if she had been welcoming her own relations. At Aunt Cora's words she chuckled.

"Don't listen to Miss Cora. You eat all you've a mind to. Miss Cora eats no more than a bird."

Aunt Cora looked peevish. "And Bella eats enough to keep a family, and look at her!"

They looked at Bella. Just looking at her made them smile; she seemed so pleased about everything. Bella shook her head and gave another chuckle.

"I surely enjoy my food, but I'm not aiming to suffer from my nerves."

Aunt Cora waited until Bella had shut the door and was out of earshot. Then she lowered her voice.

"I expect you'll think Bella very familiar, but she has been with me ever since I married and thinks herself one of the family. Sometimes I think she thinks it's she who owns the house. You want to keep her in her place, or she'll be ordering you around."

71

The family went on eating and said nothing. Inside, they thought that they would not mind very much if Bella did order them around.

After breakfast the children were told to go on the beach while Bee, John, and Peaseblossom unpacked. Only Jane went straight to the beach. Rachel and Tim had first to see about their special things.

Ever since they had arrived in America, Rachel had been saying to herself, "I'm going to see Posy Fossil. . . . Perhaps there'll be a letter from Posy Fossil. . . . On the very day I get to Aunt Cora's I might meet Posy Fossil." The moment breakfast was over she had looked around the house. There had been no mention of letters, so apparently Posy Fossil had not written yet. Still, she might at any minute, and, thought Rachel, in the meantime, she must find a place to practice. It did not take long to find the place: the porch. It had a balustrade around it just the right height for a barre. She was just trying it out when she heard Aunt Cora call up the stairs.

"Oh, John! Here's some mail for you."

Rachel stopped practicing and listened. How perfect if Dad called out, "Where's Rachel? There's one for her." There was silence. Dad must be sorting the letters. Then she heard his voice. "Good. News from home. Three for you, Bee, two for Peaseblossom, and four for me."

Bella came to clear the breakfast. She smiled when she saw Rachel. "You enjoyed your breakfast."

This was clearly a statement and did not need answering. Rachel came over to the table and helped stack the plates. Bella did not look like the sort of person who would find it a nuisance answering questions.

"How often do posts come? I mean, posts from people who live in California?"

"Miss Cora opens the mailbox herself. Were you expecting a letter?"

72

"A letter or a message."

Bella stopped, a pile of plates in one hand. "I was remembering. I called Miss Cora to the telephone. There was a lady asking for you."

Aunt Cora was in the living room. Rachel peered around the door and looked at her. She was writing at a desk. She looked busy. Almost every day since they had known they were coming to California Peaseblossom had said something about their being as little trouble as possible to Aunt Cora. Interrupting a person who was writing was being a little trouble, but not a great deal of trouble, and if Posy Fossil had left a message, it would be too frightful not to answer at once. Rachel cleared her throat.

"Aunt Cora?"

Aunt Cora swung around. Though all the welcoming had not worn off her face, she looked as though she were hoping very much she was not going to be interrupted every time she sat down for five minutes.

"Yes, honey?"

"I asked Bella about letters, and she said she thought there had been a telephone message for me."

Aunt Cora looked vague. Then she nodded.

"That's quite right. A Miss Postle or Mossel called you up. She very kindly offered to see to your dancing lessons while you are here, but the studio was way over the far side of Sunset Boulevard, so I thanked her and said it couldn't be managed. I explained I was pleased to have you as my guests for the winter, but that did not include my acting as chauffeur all over Los Angeles." She gave a nod of dismissal and went back to her writing.

Rachel rushed up to her parents' room. John was arranging a table as a desk. He was putting out his typewriter paper and reference books, and as he arranged them, he whistled in a contented way through his teeth.

Bee was unpacking. She put an armload of John's clothes in Rachel's arms. "Hang these in that cupboard, darling. Only we mustn't call them cupboards anymore, must we? They are called closets here."

Rachel took the clothes, but she did not move. "Posy Fossil rang me up to ask me to take dancing lessons, and Aunt Cora told her I couldn't go; she said the studio was too far away."

Bee pointed at the closet. "Hang them up, and don't look so distraught."

"But I feel distraught; having a chance to learn dancing from Posy Fossil is just about the most important thing that ever happened to me."

As John stood back from his table to see how it looked, he said, "I don't think you need despair yet. I daresay there are streetcars, or we can borrow a bicycle. The great thing is not to rush your aunt for a day or two. After all, we've been in the place only about an hour."

Rachel hung the clothes in the closet. Nobody could have a nicer father and mother than she had, but sometimes they were disappointing. It didn't seem possible that anybody could think that seeing Posy Fossil in a day or two would do. It was the sort of thing that ought to be done the very first minute. She said no more, but she looked a lot.

Aunt Cora had no piano. Tim did not accept this strange fact without verifying it. He went into the kitchen and asked Bella; after all, the piano might just be away being repaired. Bella had a nice kitchen and seemed pleased to see him, and if the question of a piano had not been so urgent, he would have liked to stay and have a good look around. Bella was definite. She had looked after Miss Cora for years, and there hadn't ever been a piano.

Tim went in search of Aunt Cora. He arrived just after

74

Rachel had left. He did not make Rachel's polite entrance. He stalked in, looking severe.

"Why haven't you a piano, Aunt Cora?"

Aunt Cora looked up from her letter. Her face lost more of its welcoming look. Another child! Really!

"Why don't you go play on the beach? I do hope you children aren't going to run in and out the whole time. My nerves won't stand it."

Tim did not care what Aunt Cora's nerves would stand.

"I have to have a piano. I have to practice every day. I promised Mr. Brown I would. How do you get a piano in America if you haven't got one? Can you hire one for me?"

Aunt Cora saw that Tim was determined to go on talking about pianos until he had an answer. She laid down her pen.

"You can rent pianos in America, but they cost money. You haven't money, so you can't rent one."

"I'll have pocket money, I suppose. I do in London."

"I don't know from whom, unless you earn it," Aunt Cora said.

Tim was exasperated. "Children don't earn pocket money. It comes from their fathers on Saturday mornings."

Aunt Cora took up her pen in a very meaningful way. "In America it does not. You'll earn any you get here."

Tim was quite prepared to start earning if that was the way to get a piano. "How do I earn?"

"Will you stop asking questions? You make me so nervous. I don't know how children earn. I just know they earn. Now will you please run away? I'm busy."

Jane loitered up the beach. It was a nice beach, and the water looked perfect for bathing. She walked slowly along the sand, examining each house. She wondered if children lived in any of them; it would be nice if they did; with Rachel taking dancing lessons from that Posy Fossil and Tim practicing, she would need somebody for a playmate. She thought all the houses very nice and gave marks to each according to her view of its merits. She was just turning back to find out what was keeping Rachel and Tim when she saw something which stopped her in her tracks. She was in front of a nice white wooden house which would have got almost full marks had it not been that at the back of the lawn, fastened to his kennel by a chain, was a black spaniel. The spaniel seemed to be reasonably contented, but Jane was not contented for him. Without remembering any of the things she had been told about how to behave in a foreign country, Jane marched up to the gate.

The gate was locked. Jane shook it, but the lock was secure and would not come undone. She was just planning to climb over it when the gardener came around from the front of the house. He looked up, nodded, and said something Jane could not catch. She leaned on the gate.

"Do you know it's awfully cruel to keep your dog chained to his kennel like that?"

The gardener did not seem to have heard what she said, but he had caught the word "dog." He smiled. "Yeah, a fine doghouse."

Jane had never heard a kennel called a doghouse before, but she guessed what he meant. "However nice it is, he shouldn't be chained to it, poor boy."

The man scratched his head. Then he came over to the gate. He looked at Jane's angry face in wonderment. "He's gotta be chained.

"Why?"

"If he's loose, they'll take him."

"Who will?" Jane demanded

"Cops."

The gardener seemed to think the conversation was over. He took a look at the sprayer to see if it was working properly and walked away.

Jane gave the gate another angry shake. She leaned over to the dog.

"Poor boy! I don't believe a word he said. I think he made it all up. I shall ask Aunt Cora, and if it's a lie, I'll come and set you free myself."

When Aunt Cora saw the third interrupter come in, all signs of being a welcoming aunt left her. She looked like what she felt, an aunt who had got up very early to meet relatives, who felt she was being more noble than she could say in taking them in and, once they were in, wanted to see as little as possible of the adults and nothing at all of the children. She especially did not want to see this child, who she had already noticed was the plain one and unlikely, therefore, to be a credit to her.

"Well?" Aunt Cora said wearily.

Jane drew up a chair by Aunt Cora's desk. "Do dogs in America have to be chained up?"

Well, really! said Aunt Cora's face. What next? The first child looked as though you had hit her when you said very reasonably you could not drive her daily to Sunset Boulevard for dancing lessons. The boy had demanded a piano. Now here was the ugly one pulling up a chair as if she had come to visit, asking about dog laws. It was too much.

"Yes, they do, I'm glad to say. I've never liked dogs."

Jane eyed Aunt Cora with horror. Never liked dogs! What an aunt!

"Why do they have to be chained?"

"Hydrophobia, I guess. Now run along, and take the other two with you. Go play on the beach."

The children held a meeting on the beach. They walked until they were out of earshot of the house. They they sat down. The sun blazed down, warming them through and through. The sea made a lazy, lapping sound. Some seabirds of a new, interesting sort floated on the water, but for the three of them the day was a ruin.

"She said she thanked Posy Fossil and said my lessons couldn't be managed." Rachel moaned. "Oh, what will I do if Posy never rings up again!"

Tim threw a stone at an imaginary aunt. "No piano, and not even ashamed."

Jane rolled over on her face and kicked at the sand with her toes. "That Dad could have a sister who could say, 'I've never liked dogs'! To think we are going to live with such an aunt for six whole months!"

"And such a lovely place," said Rachel. "And Dad's put out his typewriter as if he really means to write again. If only Aunt Cora weren't like that."

Jane kicked at the sand again. "But she is like that, and she looked at me with a despising look."

Tim hugged his knees and rested his chin on them. "In America lots of children don't have pocket money given to them. They earn it. She said so."

"Earn it?" asked Rachel. "How?"

"I asked Bella. She said doing chores for the neighbors. I'm going to snoop at the neighbors this afternoon so I can see which would be the best to start on."

Rachel turned to look at him. "She wouldn't let you have a piano in her house if you did hire it."

"Then I'll hire a place with a piano in it."

"It will take a lot of money," Rachel warned Tim.

"I'll earn it."

Rachel felt a new respect for Tim. Here was she, feeling just hopeless, but Tim wasn't feeling hopeless; he meant to do something.

"If I can find out how you do it, I could earn, too," Rachel said. "I could earn money for carfare to go to my dancing lessons—that is, if Posy Fossil ever rings up again."

Jane brushed some sand off her nose. "Actually I'd be glad if Tim couldn't practice and you couldn't dance. It would make it much nicer in the house for everybody else. But if it's to help you to get things that an aunt who's so low she doesn't like dogs won't let you have, then I'll earn money to help you. I vote we all start trying. Let's see which of us can earn first."

9

Posy Fossil

It was not possible for the children to start earning the next day. On the trip over, Peaseblossom had planned that their days should be spent as nearly as possible in the same way as days in London—lessons, walks, meals, and bedtime. Aunt Cora, in a roundabout way, showed her that this could not be. In her funny whiny voice, she made it clear that Peaseblossom had been invited because house help was difficult and Bella was getting old and not able to do much more than the cooking.

Peaseblossom did not mind a bit about the housework; but she did mind that while she was doing the housework, there would be no lessons, and she had no intention of allowing Tim and Jane to sit up for evening dinner every night. However, she was tactful and did not say what she was thinking to Aunt Cora but smiled and said that she was sure everything would work out splendidly.

By the next day she had things arranged. Bee was delighted that Aunt Cora wanted help in the house; it was a way of repaying her kindness. She and Peaseblossom decided that they and the children would get the house cleaned immediately after breakfast. The children could then get in two and a half hours' lessons. After lunch they could have a good walk and education at the same time, studying flowers, birds, and places of interest. After tea there could be another hour of lessons or homework. Peaseblossom had got up very early and had a talk with Bella about meals. She found her most understanding. As long as she did not have to prepare it, Bella did not mind a bit Peaseblossom's giving the children an English tea. It was Bella herself who suggested they should eat it in the kitchen. Nor did she mind serving cereal and fruit for the children's suppers. She did not say so in words, but she managed, by the amused look in her eye, to suggest that she and Peaseblossom were conspirators planning strange goings-on behind Aunt Cora's back. Peaseblossom, as a good guest, thought this wrong but unavoidable under the circumstances

It was the children who resented Peaseblossom's planning. On Saturdays and Sundays and during the holidays they had helped clean the house at home, and they all had their days for helping to lay the table and wash the dishes; otherwise they did as little housework as they could and were glad of any excuse to get out of it. The very last thing they had expected in California was to find themselves doing more housework than they had ever done before. Even Rachel could not hide her thoughts. The first morning she was pushing an electric polisher up and down the hall with so sulky a face that Bee said, "Hurry up, darling, and don't look so cross. We want to surprise Aunt Cora when she comes down."

Rachel turned off the switch on the polisher. "I don't care if she's surprised or not. I think it's very mean of her to expect us to clean her house. She ought to do it herself, not let us do it while she stays in bed."

Bee was stern. "Sssh! Don't let Peaseblossom hear you. That's a horrid and ungrateful way to talk." She held up a finger. "Listen, can you hear the typewriter? Dad's very first morning. Isn't that worth paying for by a little housework?"

"Not to me. As far as I can see, we might just as well not

be in California. Every minute of the day we're going to be doing something. I shan't even be able to get in my proper practice, and what's the good of it anyway? I expect Aunt Cora's put Posy Fossil off for good, and if she has, she's ruined my career.''

Bee laughed. ''Goose! Get on with that polishing. Your career shan't be ruined, I promise you. Dad and I will find a way.''

Jane was making beds with Peaseblossom. She looked and felt shockingly black-doggish. Peaseblossom noticed, of course, but she did not ask what was wrong. Instead she kept up a cheerful conversation and did not mind getting no answers. After a bit Jane could not keep her grievances to herself any longer.

''One would think visitors wouldn't be the ones to work.'' She leaned across the bed and lowered her voice to a dramatic whisper. ''I'm beginning to hate Aunt Cora.''

Peaseblossom used her finishing-a-conversation voice. ''I'm ashamed of you. Not another word. Each one of you is as bad as the other. I shall speak to you all before lessons.''

Tim was in the kitchen cleaning shoes, a job he often did at home and did not dislike except when it interfered with his piano practice. He was appalled at the arrangements for the day. When was he to start earning money to rent a piano? He scowled at Bee's shoe, which he was cleaning, and slapped some polish onto it.

Bella shook her head. ''It doesn't do any good, honey, slapping the polish on that way.''

Tim put down the shoe.

''I'm angry, Bella. Very angry. Everybody knows I have to practice every day, but they don't care a bit. I've talked to them all, and they all say, 'Don't worry.' But I do worry.''

Bella's wrinkled face was kind but stern.

''You've no right to complain about your family. They're

82

right to see y'all educated. It's a fine thing. In Georgia, where I was raised, I didn't get so much education, but my family goes to college.''

"It's not that I don't want to be educated, and I don't mind cleaning shoes; but I must practice. I couldn't believe I had an aunt without a piano.''

"You've no call to go speaking that way of Miss Cora.'' Bella's voice softened. "Maybe I can help.''

Tim jumped up, scattering bottles, polishers, and shoes all over the kitchen. "How, Bella? How?''

"I'm not tellin'. You finish your work and do good at your lessons and maybe I'll tell you something.''

Lessons were on the porch. Before they started, Peaseblossom closed the doors.

"I don't want to say any of this again, and I won't hear one word of argument from any of you. You are selfish little beasts. You know how long it is since your father worked, and that he's started again this morning, and it's the first time since the accident that your mother has looked really happy. But what do you three do? Since we arrived yesterday in this lovely place, you've done nothing but grumble. Today I'm warning you. One more grumble, and you go to bed. Children who behave as you've behaved must be ill, so I shall keep you in bed and dose you until I see that you are your old selves again. Now then here are the lesson timetables I have worked out for you.''

It was no good arguing. Peaseblossom always meant what she said. As the three started working, they exchanged looks which said as clearly as though words had been spoken, "The meanness of her.''

The sun blazed down on the beach; the sea grew bluer and bluer and made an inviting, whispering noise. The children occasionally raised their eyes from their books and when they did, it was hard to go on being angry. California was a very lovely place.

After they had been working an hour, they heard Aunt Cora's voice. Again the children exchanged looks. So she had got up at last, had she, the lazy creature! She was calling to Bee.

"I'm going to market. You care to come?"

Market! That had a nice sound. That would be where all that gorgeous fruit was bought. If only Peaseblossom were not so strict about lessons, they could go to the market too. Evidently Bee thought it would be fun, because they heard her say something about a hat. Presently the front door shut.

Almost another hour went by. Then the front doorbell rang. There were voices in the hall. Then Bella's heavy, soft-shoed feet came shuffling toward the porch. She beamed at Rachel, though she spoke to Peaseblossom.

"There's a Miss Fossil asking for Miss Rachel."

Peaseblossom could be awfully nice. She said in a delighted voice, "Oh, Rachel, dear, I'm so glad! I think your aunt is out, so you could see her in the living room."

Rachel was suddenly shy. "I wonder if I'd better change."

She had on a shirt the color of her eyes and gray shorts. Peaseblossom thought she looked nicely and suitably dressed and said so. Rachel flung her arms around her neck. She only said, "Darling Peaseblossom," but they all knew that what she meant was she was sorry she had been cross. She dashed out.

Posy Fossil looked just as Rachel had imagined her. She was little and pretty in a way, but the most noticeable things about her were her hair, which was red-gold and curly, and a sort of eagerness, as if life were so exciting she couldn't stand still for a minute. She was wearing a green shirt and slacks, which surprised Rachel, who had supposed that somebody as important as Posy Fossil would be a crepe-de-chine

84

and-mink sort of person. Rachel wanted to be respectful, so though it was difficult to do in shorts, she curtsied as she did at the academy to Madame.

Posy Fossil seemed to think the curtsy terribly funny. She laughed and caught hold of Rachel's hand and asked where they could go to talk. Rachel, feeling shy and self-conscious, led the way into the living room, but once inside with the door shut, she could not feel shy long. Posy, still laughing, swept a curtsy to the ground and said, "Madame," in the most reverent voice.

"Fancy, I'd almost forgotten until I saw you do it." She curtsied again. "Madame. Mind you, everybody, even I, has to curtsy to Manoff. As we do it, we say 'Maître,' only most of them think it's very silly, so they do it like this." She curtsied and said "Maître"; only it was not a respectful, humble "Maître" but sort of I'll-do-it-if-I-must-but-I-think-it-ridiculous, which made Rachel laugh. Posy ran around the room, examining everything.

"I spoke to Mrs. Edward P. Beeson on the telephone."

"Aunt Cora," Rachel explained.

Posy picked up a plant in a copper bowl on the writing table. She came into the middle of the living room. She did a little dance. It was made up of quick steps, but she danced as if she were too tired to lift her feet, and as she danced, she kept opening her mouth in a hungry way at the plant and then jerking her head back.

Rachel laughed so much she had to sit down. Really, Posy was being very much like Aunt Cora. She even made her feet look whiny, like Aunt Cora's voice, and you could see she was dieting and wished she weren't by the way she looked at the plant.

"How did you know she was like that?" Rachel asked between laughs.

Posy put the plant back on the writing table.

"I felt her in my feet when she was telephoning. Go and get your shoes. I want to see where you've got to."

Aunt Cora's living room had a parquet floor and was perfect for dancing. Rachel was surprised that she did not feel scared dancing in front of the great Posy Fossil, but she did not. Posy rattled off strings of steps, and Rachel listened and then danced them. Sometimes Posy danced the routine first to show what she wanted. Rachel did not get much right the first time, but Posy kept saying, "Do it again. Do it again," and toward the end she was making a fair attempt at what Posy wanted. After about ten minutes Posy pulled Rachel down to sit beside her on the sofa.

"Yes. I could tell anywhere you were a pupil of Madame's. She's so thorough and so strict about precision and arms. You know about Manoff's ballet? You must come to a rehearsal; you can't believe how lovely some of his things are. Well, I can't teach you often because I rehearse every day for that—I'll get Manoff to let you come to his Saturday mornings sometimes. He teaches then himself, but for regular work you had better go to a woman called Donna. Madame Donna. She's good. I'll write it down for you."

Rachel saw Posy was the sort of person who saw no difficulty in doing things. She had evidently forgotten what Aunt Cora had said about not being a chauffeur. Posy was getting a piece of paper and a pencil out of her bag. Rachel gently laid a hand over Posy's to stop her. Then, red in the face because nobody likes explaining the sort of difficulties she had to explain, she told Posy everything. About Aunt Cora and how good it was of her to have them at all, and John's accident, and the British government's rules about money. Posy did not wait for Rachel to finish; she jumped to her feet.

"Where's the telephone?"

Rachel knew that using the telephone in somebody else's

86

house was a thing you asked permission to do, but Posy Fossil was not a permission-asking person, so she led her to it. Rachel only hoped Aunt Cora and Bee would not come back from their shopping in the middle of the telephoning. Posy looked up a number in the telephone book, talking all the time.

"You're like my sister Pauline. When we were at Madame Fidolia's, we never had any money, and she always thought we couldn't do things. When Manoff saw me dance and said he would take me as his pupil, Pauline tried to tell me I couldn't go to Czechoslovakia to learn from him. Imagine! Not learning from Manoff when he'd said he would take me! Of course I went." She got her number and asked for Madame Donna.

Rachel listened in a mixture of admiration and awe to the conversation that followed.

Posy explained to Madame Donna about Rachel and that she had no money. There was a pause after that, while Posy listened, looking bored and impatient, and then, unable to listen anymore, she appeared to interrupt. She said that she knew that was how Madame Donna would feel and that of course, she could not be expected to teach for nothing a child who would be in the country only six months and no lasting credit to her. That if the lessons were all, it would not matter, as Posy would see to it, but there was transportation as well. What about *Pirouette*? Wasn't it true that she was providing most of the dancers? At that, from the other end, there was a lot of talk which Posy interrupted with "You can easily arrange it. . . . No harm in letting them see her. . . . Very pretty indeed." Finally, still holding the telephone, she began to dance. Then she said, "She'll be there," and put the telephone down.

Posy turned to Rachel. "It's all fixed. Wait a minute." She danced again the steps she had done at the telephone. "I never can remember anything in my head. I have to remember it with my feet. The audition is at three, at the studio, but you are to be there at two so that Madame Donna can test you herself. You're to wear a tutu, which you probably don't have, so pack your shoes and tights and I'll take you with me and fit you into one of mine. Nana, our old nurse who lives with us, will alter it and take you to the audition. She's used to them."

"An audition for what?"

Posy looked surprised that Rachel didn't know.

"That film they're making. *Pirouette*. It's got scenes in a theater where a ballet's dancing. They'll want the girls they select on and off for three months. If they pick you, and I don't know why they shouldn't, you'll earn enough to pay for taxis to your lessons, and you'll be working at the studios under the man who's arranging the dances, as well as Madame Donna."

Rachel felt as if everything were going around. She in a film! It was too gorgeous to be true. She clasped her hands, her eyes shining.

"Oh, Miss Fossil!"

Posy laughed. "Don't call me Miss Fossil; nobody does. Now do go and get your tights, and take off the shoes. We haven't much time."

Rachel was just going to dash upstairs when she remembered Peaseblossom and lessons. She raced to the porch. She was so excited that she couldn't speak clearly. It took Peaseblossom a moment or two to grasp what the excitement was about. When she did, she got up.

"A film, dear? No wonder you're excited. Run up, and pack your tights and shoes. I put the tights on that hat shelf. I'll have a word with Miss Fossil."

Peaseblossom found Posy by the front door. She was dancing.

88

"This is very exciting news for Rachel," Peaseblossom said. "I don't suppose her parents will object to her being in a film if she gets the opportunity; but her mother's out, and I can't speak for her. I could ask her father; but he's been ill and has only just started working again, and it will be a mistake to interrupt him. I suppose attending the audition doesn't mean she has to take part in the film if her parents don't want her to."

Posy stopped dancing and said, "I wouldn't blame her mother for not wanting her to take part; I hate dancing in films myself; it hardly ever comes off, and the director usually wants the most ghastly things done which never could happen in a ballet. But I don't think she need worry about this one. I believe it's real stuff, barre practice and that sort of thing. I've only suggested it as a way around the money difficulty. She'd have enough for taxis and things."

Peaseblossom saw that Posy was not the sort of person to understand it was necessary to get permission to do things. It would be easier to trust to Rachel's sense. She took down Posy's address and telephone number, saying, "We knew we were going to hear from you, of course. Rachel's talked of little else since Madame Fidolia promised to write to you. But I should like just to know where she is so that her mother could telephone to you if she wanted to."

Posy was looking at Peaseblossom in a very interested way. Rachel would have guessed her feet were twitching to dance her.

"You'll have to meet my guardian and Nana," Posy said. "You three will agree about everything. It'll be especially lovely for Nana, as she doesn't often find people in America who think the same way as she does."

Rachel changed into her blue cotton frock and put on clean socks; she came flying down the stairs with her tights in one hand and her ballet shoes in the other. Peaseblossom felt disgraced.

"Rachel! No paper! No string! You're letting the side down."

Posy took the tights. "Nana will pack them properly with a tutu of mine. So don't worry. Good-bye."

Jane and Tim were listening to the excitement in the hall. This was a most extraordinary country they were in, a country where anything might happen. At one moment there was Rachel doing housework and lessons, with nothing but a rest and walk to follow, and the next somebody rushed up in a car and took her to an audition for a film. Tim's annoyance about the piano disappeared. In his mind Rachel was already a film star.

"She'll be able to rent me a music teacher as well as a piano," Tim told Jane.

Jane was stabbing angrily with her pencil at the sum she was supposed to be doing. She did not begrudge Rachel her luck, but she wished that just once luck would come to her. If only just once everybody—Mom, Dad, Rachel, Tim, and Peaseblossom—could look at her with proud faces and say, "It's Jane we have to think of. She's the one who's important." She frowned at Tim severely.

"If you're going to use American words, you should use them right. You rent pianos but not music teachers." Then, because she was not at all sure that her statement was true, she hurried on. "And if Rachel does get into a film, she'll have to spend all she earns on furs and diamonds, like the rest of them."

Tim could not be crushed. "It won't matter. I can do without her help. As a matter of fact, I'm already making arrangements."

Peaseblossom came back. Inside, she was feeling a little anxious. She did hope it was all right letting Rachel go off

90

with little Miss Fossil like that, but nothing of that sort showed in her face. She smiled at Jane and Tim.

"Our side's doing splendidly. Fancy, only here one day, and Rachel at an audition! It'll be your turn next, Tim, and then we must arrange something special for you, Jane. Now, how are the sums going?"

Jane bit her pencil and scowled worse than usual.

"Arrange something for Jane!" That was how they all thought. But wait. Someday she'd show them.

10

A Piano and a Dog

Lunch was over. The children were supposed to read for half an hour on their beds. Tim was reading *Treasure Island* for the third time. He had just got to the place where blind Pew's stick is heard tapping outside the inn when the door softly opened and Bella walked in; in view of where Tim's mind was, she made him jump. Bella put her finger to her lips and nodded at the other door, which led to John and Bee's bedroom, from behind which came the sound of John's typewriter. She creaked down on the bed, which made it sag over to one side. She spoke in a whisper.

"I have a friend who works in a drugstore. . . ."

It was a long story as Bella told it. Her friend from the drugstore had been around that morning, delivering bottles. He had told Bella·that she was right in thinking there was a piano in the drugstore. He also said his boss was a kind man, and he guessed if Tim asked him, he would let him practice on the piano at a time when customers weren't eating; then Bella held up a warning finger.

"Miss Cora mustn't ever know. She'll figure a drugstore is a trashy, no-account place."

Tim thanked Bella and watched her leave the room and close the door. He shut his book and sat up. He did not want a fuss, and there would be a fuss if he went out alone when he was supposed to be taken for a nature walk. Tim did not

92

want anybody with him; this was a matter between himself and the drugstore boss. There was only one person who could help, as Rachel was away at her audition. He slipped out of his room and moused along the passage to the girls' room. He listened outside the door. There was no talking, so it sounded as if Jane were alone. He opened the door a crack and peered in.

Jane was alone. She was lying facedownward on her bed, drawing. She was drawing an exceedingly fancy picture of herself in a circus ring, with Chewing-gum and six other dogs doing amazing feats around her. She hated to be interrupted, so she gave Tim one of her most disobliging frowns and said, "You're supposed to be resting, my boy."

Tim came in and closed the door and in a whisper told what Bella had said, adding, "Aunt Cora's not to know because she'll think drugstores trashy, no-account places."

Jane got off her bed; she thought better walking about. She had never heard the expressions "trashy" or "no-account" before, but she liked both.

"Which is just what I think of Aunt Cora. You go. I'll do delaying action. I'll probably have to tell Peaseblossom in the end, but with any luck not till you've finished arranging about the piano with the drugstore man."

Peaseblossom and Bee were lying on a blanket on the sand. It was so lovely and hot that at first Bee was too contented to speak. Then she murmured, "I feel too lucky to be real. In my wildest dreams I never thought of John starting to write the moment we got here."

Peaseblossom would have liked to go on lying in the sun and doing nothing, but she had gone to the beach not to enjoy herself but to talk about Rachel.

"I couldn't tell you before, as Cora was there, but Rachel not only has gone to lunch with Miss Fossil but is having an audition for a film."

93

Bee sat up. "Good gracious! For a film! But she can't act."

"It's a dancing film, I gather."

"Bless the child! Is she excited?"

"Of course. Who wouldn't be? But I wasn't sure what Cora would think."

Bee thought about Cora. "I think she'll approve. Oh, dear, I wish something like that would happen. The only thing that's wrong with this lovely, lovely place is our being poor relations. I don't believe even a saint could be a poor relation nicely."

Peaseblossom glanced at her watch. "I ought to go in and get Jane and Tim ready for their walk, but it's so lovely here I'll give myself another five minutes."

Bee lay down again and gazed through her half-closed eyes for a while at the blue, blue sky. Then it suddenly struck her that Peaseblossom was very quiet. She sat up. Peaseblossom was asleep. "Dear Peaseblossom! How good for her," she thought. "I'll go up and call the children; they can play on the sand instead of going for a walk."

It was so easy. Jane had nothing to do. Bee came to her first and told her she was going on to fetch Tim, so all Jane had to say was "Don't bother, I'll fetch him." Bee saw nothing queer in that and went back again to the beach and lay down on the blanket beside Peaseblossom. When Jane came down the steps to the beach, Bee was half asleep. She did mutter, "Where's Tim?" but all Jane had to do was to jerk her thumb at the house and Bee asked no more questions. "And not even a lie," thought Jane, "for my thumb might just as well have been pointing at the drugstore as anywhere."

Jane ran up the beach to see how the poor tied-up spaniel was doing. This time the people who belonged to the house, or at least what seemed to be the people belonging to the house, were at home. Two men were sitting smoking on the

94

porch. Even before she got to the gate, Jane heard the rumble of their voices. Evidently, when the people were home, their dog sat with them, for though his kennel was there, the dog was not. Jane was glad for the dog that he was having a nice time, but she was disappointed not to see him. Besides, she had plans about that spaniel. If Aunt Cora was right and it was usual for children in America to earn their pocket money, why couldn't she earn some taking that dog for a walk? She wondered what was the first step to becoming a professional dog walker. Did you go to the back door and ask to be hired, or did you write a letter to the dog's owner?

Jane was thinking so hard she was not noticing anything about her. From being engaged to take that spaniel for a daily walk it was no step to being engaged to take fifty dogs for walks. She had an imaginary conversation with Peaseblossom. "I'm sorry, but I've no time to help with the house or do lessons, I've my profession to think of. I've fifty dogs to take for walks. After all, I'm paying for Rachel's dancing and Tim's piano lessons." It was as she thought of these satisfying words that she saw a black shape down by the water, a black shape which, as she moved toward it, became a spaniel eating a fish. As she got closer, her nose told her it was a very dead fish.

Jane spoke to the spaniel severely.

"Bad, dirty boy! You'll be terribly sick, but it's not your fault, poor angel." In spite of the dog's furious growls, she kicked what was left of the rotten fish into the water. It was clear how the dog had got out. His collar must have slipped off, for he had none on. Jane took her handkerchief out of her pocket and tied it around the dog's neck. Then she took her belt off and put it through the handkerchief. She spoke to the dog persuadingly. "Come on, old boy. You'll soon be so sick it'll be nicer for you at home. Come on. Come along, old man." It was a slow start, but presently the spaniel began

95

to like Jane's voice and to trust her, and in the end he was trotting along as if he had known her since he was a puppy.

The two men were still on the porch talking and smoking. Jane looked up at them and sniffed to herself. Selfish beasts, lying up there, not caring a bit about their dog! She was going to shout to them when she saw the gate was ajar. So that was how the spaniel had got loose. Lazy brutes, they couldn't even shut their gate! She stalked in and, looking very cross indeed, climbed the steps to the porch.

The two men sat up, looking surprised. Jane did not care how they looked.

"Some people don't deserve to have dogs. They fasten them up to"—she hesitated for the right words—"doghouses. Then they leave their gates open so their dogs will eat bad fish and be sick, and"—she hesitated again—"cops will get them because of hydrophobia."

The dog made queer noises. One of the men got up. He was nice-looking, tall and thin with dark hair and amused gray eyes.

"I guess you're right about his being sick. Come on, Hyde Park." He picked the spaniel up and carried him down the stairs and out of sight.

Jane looked at the other man. He was older and fatter, with gray hair.

"Why's an American dog called Hyde Park?" Jane asked him.

The man had evidently not been told as a child it was rude to stare. He stared so hard at Jane that she almost reminded him about manners.

"I believe he came from London as a pup. Bryan served there during the war. You're British, aren't you?"

Jane nodded and said, "I should think he'll need medicine."

"Bryan'll see after him. He's crazy about that dog. How old are you?"

"Ten. He's got a funny way of showing he's crazy about him."

"Do you always frown? Can you smile?"

It was such a silly question that it made Jane laugh.

" 'Course. Everybody can. When my dog, Chewing-gum, got poisoned, the vet said a white of egg would have been good for him if we had a white of egg; only of course, we didn't have. But in America there are lots of eggs. Do you suppose a white of egg could be spared?"

"Sure. Did Chewing-gum die?"

Jane was appalled at the suggestion, and her face showed it.

"Of course not. If he had, I think I'd have died, too."

The man Bryan came up the steps and heard this. "Who's dying?"

Jane swung around. "How is he?"

"I've given him something to fix him." He handed her the handkerchief and belt. "Thank you for fetching him home. You fond of candy?"

The older man beckoned to Bryan. "Not so fast. Come and sit awhile." He looked at Jane. "What about a drink? I'm sure my friend here"—he looked at Mr. Bryan—"will get you a Coca-Cola."

Jane was delighted. If she stayed and drank a Coca-Cola, it should be easy to ask about walks for Hyde Park. Perhaps the old man had a dog, too, that needed a professional dog walker. She thanked him and sat down on the top step.

Mr. Bryan said, "Sure," and went to fetch the Coca-Cola, but he, too, had taken to staring. Jane wondered if perhaps staring at strangers was polite in America.

The Coca-Cola was lovely. Jane took a big drink and then, fortified, looked up at Mr. Bryan. "Who takes Hyde Park for walks?"

97

The old man said to Mr. Bryan, "You see what I'm thinking?"

Mr. Bryan nodded. "He doesn't get many, except maybe on a Sunday. How long have you been out here?"

"If you mean in California, one day; if you mean in America, five days. Dogs ought to walk every day."

"Sure. Where you living?"

Jane thought they were the most curious people she had ever met. Such a lot of questions. However, they were nice, and perhaps it was a good thing they should know about her, as Mr. Bryan mightn't trust Hyde Park with a stranger. She told them about John's accident and Aunt Cora's invitation, and that the invitation was for food and keep and did not include dancing lessons and piano lessons or being a chauffeur all over Los Angeles.

"So of course, we'll have to earn our pocket money, which Aunt Cora says children do in America."

Both men said, "Sure," to that. The older man, who was staring more and more, asked what the family consisted of.

Jane told him. She gave good descriptions of Rachel and Tim, though she bragged a bit, for she said Rachel was actually engaged to dance in the film.

Oddly enough, neither man seemed impressed by that. Mr. Bryan said, "And you? What do you sparkle at?"

Jane longed to be able to say something, but there was nothing to say. While she had been talking, she had looked cheerful, but at that question her face became its most black-doggish.

"If you want to know, absolutely nothing. And nobody need be despising because lots of people aren't good at anything special."

The two men exchanged more looks. Mr. Bryan said, apparently to nobody, "Extraordinary." Then he pulled one

98

of Jane's braids. "How would you like to have a chance to show what you can do?"

Jane beamed. "That's what I wanted you to say. I'm starting to be a professional dog walker. I'd like to start with Hyde Park." The two men burst out laughing. Jane thought that was rude. She got up. "There's nothing to laugh about. As a matter of fact, it's about time somebody thought of poor Hyde Park."

Mr. Bryan stopped laughing. "I'm sorry. Sure you can take Hyde Park walking. How much would you charge?"

Jane was hazy about American money. "Would one cent a day be too much?"

Mr. Bryan got up. He looked questioningly at the other man. "Too little, I think. Do you think I should visit her father to fix it?"

Jane thought that very grand. "That would be a good idea, though you'd better see Mom. Dad doesn't like being disturbed if he's writing; both Mom and Peaseblossom understand American money." She lowered her voice and spoke earnestly. "But do be careful to ask Bella for Mrs. Winter; otherwise you'll see Aunt Cora, and that wouldn't be a good idea at all."

Mr. Bryan was writing in a notebook. "Ask for Mrs. Winter; say I've called about Miss Jane Winter. And your aunt's Mrs. Edward Beeson. I know the house." He closed the book. "By the way, we haven't introduced ourselves and I think we should. May I introduce Mr. Benjamin Bettelheimer." The old man got up and bowed. "And my name is Bryan J. Browne."

Jane felt she ought to do or say something, but she was not sure what. She gave a bow like the one Mr. Bettelheimer had given her and behaved like somebody leaving a party.

"Good-bye. Thank you very much for asking me."

Mr. Bryan J. Browne came with her to the bottom of the steps. "Good-bye now, Jane Winter. I'll be seeing you."

Jane ran back along the sands and found Peaseblossom and Bee still asleep. She looked at them in amazement. "How queer to go to sleep in the daytime!" However, it was lucky for Tim. Given any luck, he would get back from his drugstore before they woke up. This was what happened, for as Jane came in from the porch, Tim came in at the front door. He spoke in a whisper.

"Is there a row?"

"No. Peaseblossom and Mom have been asleep on the sand all afternoon, and I expect Dad's still working."

"Where's Aunt Cora?"

Jane shrugged her shoulders. "Don't know. She said at lunch she was going to rest up. I expect that means bed again; she seems a very bed person. Did you find a piano?" Jane thought she heard someone moving. She caught Tim by the arm. "Let's go to your room. We shan't disturb Dad if we whisper."

They sat on Tim's bed, but Tim was so full of bounce because his afternoon had been successful that he found sitting still for long difficult.

"I found the drugstore quite easily. It's back the way we came when we drove from the station. It's not a bit like that drugstore in New York. It's got all sorts of slot machines, and it's a place where you eat. Tables and all that."

"Where was the piano?"

"In the middle on a sort of little platform thing. I came in, and a man asked me what I wanted, and I said I wanted to see the boss, because I didn't know his name. The man shouted, 'There's a gentleman to see you, Tony,' and Tony was the boss."

"Was he nice?"

Tim was not going to have his story interrupted. "He's

100

brown and curly with a funny voice which isn't American. His name's Antonio something, but he said everybody called him just Tony. I explained about the piano, and at first he said no.'' Tim got off the bed and gave an imitation of Tony saying no. '' 'I say no.' '' He ran his hands through his hair. '' 'I say no. I have the customers.' '' Then I said I'd come when the customers weren't there. Then Mr. Antonio's wife came from somewhere. She's fat, and her hair's black and very untidy, but she's nice; her name's Anna. She asked what I wanted, and when she heard, she laughed and said that the first thing was to hear me play. So I walked to the piano. It was very old, and it wanted tuning; otherwise it was all right. They were the sort of people I thought would like a noise on a piano, so I played Rachmaninoff's prelude.''

"Did they like it?''

Tim was so pleased with himself that he fell back on the bed and turned a somersault.

"It was marvelous. Mrs. Antonio cried, and even Mr. Antonio sort of sniffed, and they made sounds at each other in Italian and did this.'' Tim screwed up his face and threw up his eyes and hands. "So then I made an arrangement. I'll go and practice for one hour in the morning after breakfast, and then I'll go back and play for the customers after lunch.'' Jane made a startled sound. Tim stopped her. "That isn't all. Mr. Antonio will have the piano tuned, and he says the customers will give money, and half will be for me and half for him.'' Tim turned another ecstatic somersault.

Jane caught his legs as they came over and turned him the right way up.

"But, Tim, they won't let you. There's Peaseblossom's timetable, and I bet Aunt Cora won't like the idea of your playing in a drugstore.''

Tim flicked his fingers to show scorn. "They'll just have to like it. I'll call it all practice, which it is. I shan't say

101

anything about playing to the customers. Dad and Mom wouldn't mind, but they might give in if Aunt Cora thought it trashy, no-account.''

Jane was just starting to tell Tim about her afternoon when Rachel rushed in. ''Bella thought you were here. Where's everybody? Oh, I've had such a gorgeous, gorgeous day!''

The door leading into John and Bee's room opened. John came in laughing and looking exactly as he used to look before the accident. ''What's going on in here?''

They fell on him, each telling his and her own story. John sat on the bed. He pulled Jane between his knees, and Tim sat on one side of him and Rachel the other.

''Now, one at a time. And keep your voices down, because your aunt's resting. Let's hear Rachel first.''

Rachel was incoherent with excitement. She had lunched with Posy Fossil, who had a lovely house with a blue marble swimming pool in the garden. Her old nurse, Nana, had been heavenly and had altered a lovely pale pink tutu of Posy's for her and packed it and Rachel's shoes and tights in a box. There had been a gorgeous lunch, and then Posy had to go to a rehearsal, so Nana had taken her in a taxi to Madame Donna's studio.

''You can't imagine how I felt. Other girls were coming in, and they looked so grown-up and smart. Nana took me into a dressing room and dressed me and brushed and combed my hair. Then I went to Madame Donna.'' Rachel shivered at the memory. ''She asked me questions, and then I had to dance in front of all of them. Imagine!'' Rachel got up. ''She gave directions very fast, much faster than I'm used to, and then she showed me steps I had to follow. Like this.'' Rachel began to demonstrate.

John stopped her. ''Not here. You'll disturb your aunt.''

''Although I was always a bit behind, Madame Donna seemed fairly pleased, for she said that what I knew I'd been

102

taught thoroughly. Then she took me into her office, and told me about fifty girls were wanted for a film called *Pirouette* and that they were nearly all to be her pupils. That the man who was arranging the dances would see ordinary work going on and would choose the fifty himself. That it was all wrong my pretending to be a pupil when I wasn't, but she was permitting it to please Posy Fossil. And then she took down your name and address, Dad, because if I'm engaged, you'll have to see Madame Donna. And I warn you that'll be frightening for you.''

John did not seem to care. ''We can cross that bridge when we come to it. Did the man like you?''

''I don't know, but the other girls thought he did. He picked a lot of us out to do things alone. He asked me to do a few steps to show him how I moved, and I just did m'audition. The woman at the piano even knew the music. Oh, Dad, won't it be too gorgeous if I'm in a film! Imagine the glory!''

John looked at Tim. ''And what were you telling Jane you'd fixed? I heard the word 'piano' fairly often.''

Tim told his story about the concerts for the customers.

John was pleased. ''Good. I like you children to cope with things for yourselves.'' He put his arm around Jane. ''What are we going to do about you while all this is going on?''

Jane wriggled free from his arm. Her face was pink with triumph. It was so seldom she could say that anything was happening to her.

''As a matter of fact, a man is coming to call. I told him not to interrupt you, but to see Mom. His name's Mr. Bryan J. Browne, and he wants to engage me as a professional dog walker for his dog, Hyde Park. Oh, Dad, a lovely dog! A black spaniel. As a matter of fact, I've plans for being dog walker to lots of dogs, perhaps fifty.''

John rumpled her hair affectionately. ''What an enterprising family I've got. I shall tell Bella to fetch me at once

103

when Mr. Bryan J. Browne calls. If my daughter is going to become a professional dog walker to fifty dogs, I think I ought to see that the business begins on a proper financial basis.''

11

The Caller

Peaseblossom's plans for a good organized day were changed. It was obvious that if Rachel were perhaps to dance in a film, she must practice. So that was good-bye to her helping with the housework. Instead, as soon as breakfast was cleared, she changed her shoes and got in an hour's exercises on the porch.

And every day after breakfast and lunch Tim ran off to the drugstore.

The person who got no advantage from the new timetable was Jane. Six days went by, and Mr. Bryan J. Browne had not called, so she was still a houseworker. It had been bad enough doing housework when they all did it, but to be the only one was too much. The meanness of it ate into her, and she looked black-doggish even when she was eating a banana split.

Aunt Cora, though her voice whined as much as ever and she spent most of the day resting up, began to take a better view of the Winters. Her house looked like a new pin, for both Bee and Peaseblossom were good at housework. Bella was in wonderful spirits; she had not been what Aunt Cora called mean since the Winters had arrived. She smiled when she served meals, and she sang when she cooked. Then the children were turning out well, Aunt Cora felt, or at least, two of them were—Rachel and Tim. A niece in the movies would be a social asset. Aunt Cora watched the mail and listened for telephone rings almost as anxiously as Rachel herself did.

Posy Fossil was a person who expected everything to happen at once. Each day she telephoned to know if Rachel had been picked to dance in *Pirouette*. She sounded as if she were dancing with anxiety at the end of the telephone.

"Goodness, I do wish they'd hurry! This is such an awkward place to live in unless you have a car; there are no streetcars that go anywhere anybody wants to go. I can't make plans for your lessons until I know if you can afford transportation. I'm certain you've been chosen, and Madame Donna's certain, too. She says they had their eye on you."

Rachel tried not to be too hopeful, but it was difficult with Posy so sure.

Then one morning Bella was clearing breakfast when the telephone rang. Rachel was upstairs putting on her ballet shoes. Bella stood at the bottom of the stairs and shouted, "The telephone, Miss Rachel; it's that Miss Fossil."

Rachel ran down the stairs. She could imagine Posy at the other end dancing up and down, her red curls bouncing. She knew the quick way she would say, "Have you heard yet?" and the explosive "Oh!" when she said she had not. Oh, dear, if only, if only she could say, "Yes"! But this morning Posy's voice was different.

"I say, it's sickening, but I'm afraid that film's off; at least Madame Donna thinks so. The man did like you, but the fifty he's chosen are older, and they're nearly all dark." Rachel felt as if the sun had gone in. The hall was suddenly cold. It was awful to have hoped so much. Posy evidently could sense how Rachel felt. "Don't worry, I'll fix it up about your lessons somehow; it's just getting you there. I hate to go on raising your hopes, but there is still a chance that something else may work out; it's only a slim chance, but the man who engaged the fifty girls did take your name and address. It appears there are two or three days' work for a child dancer. Madame Donna thought he might be thinking of you for that.''

Rachel tried to be thrilled at that little straw of hope, but she could tell that Posy did not believe in it really. She had an awful lump in her throat, and though she swallowed most of it, there was enough left to get in the way, and her voice came out in miserable-sounding squeaks. ''Thank you so much for telephoning.''

Even over the telephone Rachel could hear Posy's feet dancing a sort of frustrated foot exercise.

''Don't sound like that. I tell you what, spend a Sunday with us soon. I'll have made plans by then and my sister Pauline, who's been making personal appearances, will be home. We'll swim in the swimming pool. I'll fetch you.''

It was a lovely invitation, but Rachel was too downcast to be pleased about it. Too downcast to be thrilled at meeting Posy's sister, who was a film star. Too downcast to be pleased about the swimming pool. So downcast that she could hardly say ''thank you.'' She put down the receiver and swallowed and blinked. It was silly to cry, but if only the film could have happened!

While Rachel had been on the telephone, the front doorbell had rung, and Bella had shown somebody into the living room. Breathing heavily, because she hated stairs, she had fetched John.

''There's a gentleman who's calling. I've put him in the living room.''

John had been in the middle of a sentence and would ordinarily have hated to be interrupted, but he remembered his promise to Jane.

''Quite right, Bella, thank you. I expect it's the gentleman

107

with the spaniel who's going to start Jane on that dog-walking career."

As Rachel turned from the telephone, fighting her tears, John was standing in the living-room door. His visitor's voice came down the passage.

"I've come to see if your daughter may come up to the studio for a film test."

Rachel's lump disappeared. Her tears dried. The man had not forgotten her. He had chosen her for that child dancer. She could not wait for John to call her. She flew down the passage.

"Dad, I heard! Here I am!"

John put his arm around her. "Here's the ballerina. This is Rachel."

The man looked at Rachel very kindly. His nice gray eyes were sorry.

"But it's not Rachel I've come about. Maybe the maid didn't tell you my name. I'm Bryan J. Browne. I've called about Jane."

12

Jane Chooses

Jane was helping Peaseblossom clean their bedroom. She was so gloomy she could not bother even to grumble. What a situation! Here she was, slaving while Rachel and Tim were busy with their careers, and no one seemed to see how awful her life was. Well, this very afternoon she would send a note to that Mr. Bryan J. Browne. He owed her the job of taking Hyde Park for walks; he had offered her a reward of candy for bringing him home, and she hadn't taken it. Not that she needed a reward for taking Hyde Park home, poor boy; all the same, Mr. Bryan J. Browne thought that she did, and he had to go on thinking it and engage her properly as a dog walker.

Peaseblossom was using the electric polisher, and the noise it made cut out sounds from downstairs. Jane did not hear the chime of the front doorbell, or hear Bella call John, or John call Bee. The first inkling she had that anything unusual was going on was when Rachel came in and told her she was wanted in the living room.

Jane, delighted, dropped the furniture polisher she was using on the floor. "Why?"

Rachel said in a funny voice, "It's your Mr. Bryan J. Browne."

Rachel was about to tell Jane to brush her hair as it was important that she look her best, but Jane did not wait. She shouted, "Galosh! Galoosh!" and ran down the stairs.

Peaseblossom did not seem to notice that Jane had gone out of the room; her attention was centered on Rachel, who looked so wretched Peaseblossom's sympathy went out to her.

"What is it?"

Rachel tried to answer, but she couldn't. She felt she must get away somewhere by herself and cry and cry. She gave a gulp and ran out of the room and downstairs. In the hall she hesitated, looking around in a scared way as if she were a rabbit chased by dogs. Mr. Bryan J. Browne's voice came from the living room; Bella's voice, singing, came from the kitchen. Peaseblossom was in their bedroom. Where could she go to be alone? Her one chance was the porch. The table was pushed back to leave room for her dancing practice; nobody would look underneath it. Thankful for even that little privacy, Rachel crawled out of sight, turned over on her face, and cried dreadfully.

Jane rushed into the living room. She was so pleased to see Mr. Bryan J. Browne that she forgot her manners and, without waiting to say, "How do you do?" exclaimed, "I'm glad you've come at last. Is Hyde Park better?"

John was walking about, his hands in his pockets, looking worried. He came over to Jane and held her by the shoulders. His voice was serious, almost as if she had done something especially bad.

"Mr. Browne hasn't come about Hyde Park. He wants to test you for a part in a film."

Jane was so surprised her eyes grew as round as oranges and her mouth opened and stayed open.

Mr. Browne was sitting in an armchair, smoking. He gave Jane a nod to show they were old friends. He said Hyde Park was fine and maybe Jane would take him walking in spite of the film. Then he said, "Mrs. Winter tells me you've read a

110

book called *The Secret Garden* by Frances Hodgson Burnett, who wrote *Little Lord Fauntleroy*."

Jane was still feeling surprised, but she knew she had read a lot of books for a girl her age and felt that when you had as little to brag about as she had, it was a pity to let a chance slip.

"Of course I have. I've read it lots of times. The first time was years and years ago."

Mr. Browne then explained. He was a director, and Mr. Benjamin Bettelheimer, whom she had met, was a producer. Mr. Benjamin Bettelheimer was the man who decided what movies people wanted to see, and bought the stories that were made into movies, and engaged the people to play in the movies. His company was called Bee Bee Films Incorporated, and Bee Bee Films, like every other movie corporation, had people who were under contract to act for them. This meant that they were paid money for so many years to act in the movies of that particular company. Bee Bee Films had three children under contract. David Doe—

At that point Jane interrupted. The Winter children did not often go to the movies, but they had been to see one in August on Rachel's birthday. It was about a circus, and David Doe had been the boy star.

"He was the one who saved the life of that pony and trained him and made him a circus horse."

Mr. Bryan J. Browne nodded. "That boy's something out of this world. He can imitate any accent, and he's wonderful with animals and birds."

Then he told Jane about the other children. There was a British boy called Maurice Tuesday who was Jane's age. He had been under contract for three years and was a big box-office draw. Mr. Bryan J. Browne did not say so, but there was something about the way his eyes looked when he was explaining about Maurice Tuesday's being a box-office draw

111

which made Jane think he was surprised that people liked seeing the boy so much. The last child was Ursula Gidden, a wonderful little film star who had been under contract to Bee Bee Films Incorporated since she was four. With these three children in the leading parts, Mr. Benjamin Bettelheimer had planned to make a movie of *The Secret Garden*. Shooting should have started this next week.

Jane frowned in a puzzled way. "Who's to be shot?"

Mr. Bryan J. Browne laughed and said that was the word for making the picture. You said "shooting it" instead of "photographing it." Everything was set. The garden had been built. Then, on the very morning of the day Jane brought Hyde Park home, Ursula had been rushed off to a hospital with appendicitis. Mr. Bryan J. Browne turned to John.

"I didn't see it right off. It was Benjamin Bettelheimer who saw Jane's possibilities. We had about decided to postpone production when in she walked. Chip on her shoulder, English accent, right age. Mistress Mary to the life."

Jane at last began to understand. "Do you mean I'm going to be Mary in *The Secret Garden*?"

"Maybe. We've got to test you first."

"Why didn't you say so when I was there?"

"Been waiting for a report on little Ursula. We've heard now she's not to work for six months."

The full meaning of what Mr. Bryan J. Browne was saying sank into Jane. He wanted her. The plain, ungifted one of the family. Not because he couldn't have Rachel or Tim, but because he wanted her. Mary was about the most important person in the story. If she played the part of Mary, she would be a film star. Then another side of the glory that had come to her filled her mind. The thing she most wanted in the world was coming true. She would be the one who was important, who earned money. She would pay for dancing

112

lessons for Rachel and piano lessons for Tim. She would buy clothes for them all so they wouldn't look like poor relations at parties. Her eyes shone more and more as these thoughts pushed one another about in her head. Jane's eyes could shine as if there were a candle in each of them, but they seldom did. In fact, neither Bee nor John had ever seen such a shine in them before. John said, "I can see you like the idea."

Jane looked at him in scorn. "Like it! Who wouldn't like to earn lots and lots of money and be a film star!"

Bryan J. Browne laughed. "Not so fast, little pal. Playing a part in one picture mighty seldom makes a star. As for money, you won't see much of that. Uncle Sam takes care of children in the movie business."

Bee, not knowing that money earning had been so discussed by the children, thought Jane sounded like a very mercenary child. If it had been Rachel, she would have wanted to know only about the work, and Tim would have asked questions about the piano; it was so like the general contrariness of Jane that she fixed on the two points that it would be hoped no child would mention.

"There are a lot of things to think about, and money is the least important," Bee now said.

Jane felt her parents were making a very poor showing before nice Mr. Bryan J. Browne.

"Mom! How can you say that!" She turned to Bryan J. Browne. "We aren't allowed to criticize anything in America until we've been here long enough to know what we're talking about, but if I could criticize, I would say that California seems to have fewer buses and streetcars than even a village in England has."

Bryan J. Browne looked surprised. "What would we use them for? Everybody has a car."

113

Jane knew John was on the verge of interrupting, so she hurried on.

"We haven't one. Aunt Cora has, but she won't act as chauffeur all over Los Angeles, so poor Rachel can't go to dancing lessons on the far side of Sunset Boulevard." Jane turned back to Bee. "And we do need clothes; you know we do. You were terribly pleased when Rachel told you she's probably going to dance in that film, and it was because she would earn money. Now, because I'm the one who's going to earn, you stop being pleased and say money's unimportant."

John looked apologetically at Bryan J. Browne. "I'm afraid Jane's inclined to speak her mind."

Mr. Bryan J. Browne smiled. "Go right on, Jane. Mistress Mary in *The Secret Garden* looked most times as you look right now."

John felt everything was going too fast. It was clear that Jane was only seeing the exciting rose-pink side of her chance. John had done some writing for English film studios and knew there was a gray, sometimes black side as well.

"Mr. Browne wants you along to his house this afternoon to go through the scenes you will have to learn for the test, which is to be tomorrow. Before we decide whether you'll go for the test . . ."

Jane gave an all-over bounce. "Of course I'm going."

John stopped her. "Not so fast. You've got to know what you're letting yourself in for. Mr. Browne told you Uncle Sam looks after children in the film industry. Mr. Browne told Mom and me what that means. If you make this test and do play the part of Mary, you become somebody who is looked after not by Peaseblossom, Mom, and me but by people who carry out the laws of the United States of America. You work eight hours a day, which includes three hours' lessons either in the Bee Bee studio school or with a teacher from that school in a room in the studio where *The Secret*

114

Garden is being filmed. To get to the studio in time for lessons or work will mean you'll have to leave here soon after eight o'clock each morning, and you won't be home until your bedtime. No fun except on Sundays. You won't see all the lovely things I hope Rachel and Tim will see, and I think you're going to find it very hard work and very boring. It would be different if acting were something you wanted to do, but you don't." He turned to Mr. Bryan J. Browne. "Jane hopes to be a dog trainer later on."

Mr. Bryan J. Browne stopped smoking. He held out a hand to Jane and asked her to come to him. He said that John was perfectly right, that it was hard work, and he could not pretend there was any future in it. Bee Bee Films would not want another girl under contract, as they had little Ursula. Nevertheless, he thought that Jane would enjoy working with David Doe. If she meant to be a dog trainer later on, David could teach her a lot; he could train any animal; he could probably train a gopher to jitterbug. Jane was just going to ask what a gopher was when Mr. Browne went on to say he could promise that if she played Mary, something would be done about transportation, for he could see that Santa Monica was an awkward place to live in if you had no car.

Jane listened first to John and then to Mr. Bryan J. Browne, and the more she listened, the more her eyes shone. As John was speaking, she imagined everybody talking at breakfast. "Jane, dear, have you everything you want? . . . No, Tim, you must wait until Jane has helped herself; she'll be leaving for the studio in half an hour." People would run about. "Has anybody cleaned Jane's sandals? . . . Don't bother Jane about anything; she must do just what she likes. She's so important." In the evening, when she came home, she could see in her mind's eye everybody, including Aunt Cora and Bella, standing outside the house, looking humble and admiring. They all would ask questions, but she would not answer. She would just sweep in and say, "Don't bother me now. Bring me my supper," and everybody would dash about trying to be the first to wait on her. When Mr. Bryan J. Browne was talking, she imagined David Doe looking mysterious and whispering secrets to her, such terrific secrets that when she got back to London, she had only to have a day or two with Chewing-gum and he would be so marvelous a performer she could get him into Bertram Mills's Circus the very next Christmas. As she heard the final words about transportation, she felt as Cinderella must have felt when she first saw her coach. The difference was that Jane saw not a coach but the largest car in the world, with a uniformed chauffeur and herself bowing out the window.

John said, "Well, Jane? Do you want to try for the part? This is a matter entirely for you to decide. Remember, if you are engaged to play Mary and don't like the work, there's no going back. You'll be slaving away at it practically all the time you're out here."

Bee added, "Dad says we've always let you children plan your own careers, and we must let you have a chance at this if you want it. But do think carefully, darling. It'll be terribly hard work, for you've never had an acting lesson in your life, and you'll be shut up all day, missing this glorious sunshine and all the nice times the others will have."

Jane was still standing by Bryan J. Browne. She thought the talk about not playing Mary silly. Of course, she would play her. Of course, she would be good. She'd show them! She'd surprise them all. She laid a hand on Mr. Bryan J. Browne's arm and said, "What time would you like me to come and see you this afternoon?"

13

The Other Mr. B.

Jane felt so proud it showed all over her. It showed so much that Tim, who came rushing home from his piano practice at the moment when she was waving good-bye to Mr. Bryan J. Browne, noticed.

"What's up? Who's that man?"

Jane spoke as if Tim had in his ignorance not recognized a world celebrity.

"That, my boy, is *the* Mr. Browne."

"*The* Mr. Brown! That's not *the* Mr. Brown. *The* Mr. Brown is my Mr. Brown. When anybody says Mr. Brown, they mean my Mr. Brown. That one is just Mr. Brown minor."

"You don't know whom you're talking about. Yours just teaches music, but mine is a director in the movie industry."

"Who cares! My Mr. Brown is a director in the piano industry."

Tim, feeling he had crushed the argument, marched past Jane into the house.

Jane could have stamped her foot. How tiresome of Tim to fuss about his old Mr. Brown instead of asking what her Mr. Browne had come about. She followed him into the house.

"Would you like to know why he came?"

Tim was going upstairs to put away his music and to wash before lessons, a thing Peaseblossom was fussy about.

"I'm not interested. Anyway, I know. You've talked and talked about Hyde Park and all the money you will earn taking him for walks."

Jane was so bursting to tell her news that she dropped her grand manner.

"He didn't come about Hyde Park. He came to see if I would be Mary in *The Secret Garden* in a film."

"The girl in that book Peaseblossom read me when I had mumps? The one who made that awful boy walk?"

"That's the one. Colin, he's the awful boy, is being acted by an English boy called Maurice Tuesday, but Dickon—do you remember the one who played a pipe and trained squirrels and things? Well, he's being acted by David Doe. We saw him in that film on Rachel's birthday."

"The one who trained that pony for the circus?"

"That's the one."

Tim thought Jane must be making up her story.

"And they want you to act with him? I bet they don't. Whatever for?"

"Because somebody called Ursula Gidden has appendicitis."

"But in all America they should be able to find somebody better than you."

Jane put out her tongue and made the rudest possible face.

"If you want to know, I'm exactly what he and Mr. Benjamin Bettelheimer wanted, so you needn't be hateful."

Peaseblossom spoke from the top of the stairs.

"And you needn't put out your tongue, Jane. I think it must mean that your tongue needs air. Go and sit at the table on the porch with your tongue out and keep it out for five minutes; perhaps by then it will have had all the air it requires and will never need to be put out at anybody again."

It was never any good fighting Peaseblossom. If you argued, things grew worse, but Jane was seething with rage. What a way to treat somebody who by tomorrow might be a film star! Wait until she was. She would crush Peaseblossom. Sit with her tongue out indeed! The insult!

Peaseblossom came down the stairs where she could keep an eye on Jane's tongue. She spoke in a quiet voice to Tim so that Jane should not hear. "You were rude, you know. I can hardly blame Jane for being rude, too, though of course, she shouldn't have put out her tongue."

"I didn't mean to be rude, but I just can't believe it. Why would anybody choose Jane?"

Peaseblossom had heard the news from Bee and was wondering just that herself. She had said "Jane!" when she heard. "Why Jane?" and she saw that Bee was bewildered, too. You can't change the way you see people all in a minute. Jane was the difficult one. Jane was the unartistic one. Jane was the plain one. Jane was by far the quickest at lessons, but that seemed hardly a quality to make someone pick her out for a film. If it had been just a tiny part, Peaseblossom would still have been amazed, but Mary in *The Secret Garden* could be only a leading part. She said in what she hoped was not a surprised tone, "And why shouldn't they choose Jane? She's having a test tomorrow, and if she's engaged, we shall be very proud, shan't we? Up the Winters!"

"I'd be much prouder if she was dog walker to fifty dogs, which is what she said she wanted to be. I should think she'd be simply awful in a film. So we won't be proud at all."

"That's enough, Tim. Go and wash and put away your music. We must start lessons. All this excitement has made us ten minutes late already."

John had not gone back to his typewriter. He wanted to, but instead he went to look for Rachel. He did not have to look far; the moment he reached the porch he heard a choking, hiccuping noise under the table. He leaned down.

"Come on, Rachel. Come for a walk. Jane's outside saying

119

good-bye to Mr. Browne, and Tim's not back; let's get out quickly before anyone catches us." John put his arm through Rachel's and tried to draw her down the steps. He thought she was trying not to go, for she was so incoherent with crying he could not hear what she said. Then she held out a foot. "Oh, the ballet shoes! Of course, Well, just come down the steps. We'll find a quiet spot."

They found a nice little place. John let Rachel mop her eyes and feel better; then he said, "Bit of a knockout, I know. You thought that they wanted you."

In a surge all the things she had been thinking while she cried poured out of Rachel. She explained about Posy's telephone call. How it seemed the end of all hope that she had not been chosen for *Pirouette,* especially as everybody had been so sure she would be.

"If you'd just heard you were not chosen, why did you think Mr. Browne had come about you?" Rachel explained about the faint hope of her being the child dancer. John was pleased. "Well, then there's still a chance of that."

Rachel's voice grew very small. "I don't want three days' work if Jane's to be Mary in *The Secret Garden.*"

"Yet Jane's playing that part, if it comes off, might be a help all around. There are a lot of rules about any money Jane earns, but Mr. Browne said there would be some sort of salary for whoever looks after her at the studio; she has to have someone there. That might mean we could arrange about your dancing lessons and getting you to them."

Rachel's voice was hardly a whisper. "I don't want things Jane earns for me."

"That's a clear statement. It's not nice to be jealous, but I can see that you might be just at first. Especially as, if we had stayed at home, you would have been our family star, appearing in your first show. But I think you'll get over jealousy pretty fast. If you'd danced in a film, it would have

120

been a money help, but it's nothing in your life. You are, we hope, going to be a real dancer; I'm reckoning by the time you're eighteen to be sitting in Covent Garden watching you dance *The Sleeping Princess* and whatever that leading part is in *Swan Lake*. I shan't care, and you won't care, that you were never one of fifty girls in a film called *Pirouette*. What we both shall care about is that in the six glorious months we spent in California you kept up your training, in fact, got some things you never could have got at home and turned the color of a peach as well because of the sun."

Rachel rubbed her cheek against John's shoulder.

"Oh, Dad, I do feel better, and I do see all that. Of course, that film doesn't matter. But Jane's younger than I am, and she's pretty awful now. Imagine what she'll be like if she acts Mary."

John laughed.

"Poor old Jane! I think if she gets this part, she's going to be sorry before she's through. But it may do Jane good. I believe it does everybody good to be the one to shine now and again. So far any shining in our family has been done by you and Tim."

"But she won't shine. She can't act. She's bound to be terrible."

"We shall see. I suppose these fellows in the film industry know what they're doing. I daresay we shall have to put up with a little grandeur from her at first if she gets the part, but she'll settle down. In the meantime, you be nice about it. Now go up to your bedroom and get on with your dancing practice. I'll ask Peaseblossom to excuse you from lessons this morning."

Peaseblossom took Jane to see Mr. Bryan J. Browne that afternoon. Jane strutted along ahead of Peaseblossom, feeling as though she had been rubbed the wrong way. Nobody had

121

done anything mean exactly, but nobody had done anything right. There had been no proper admiration. Nobody had said, "How splendid! Of course, I knew Jane was just the sort of person to be a film star"; instead everyone had looked startled and unbelieving.

Aunt Cora, who Jane had supposed would have been more pleased than anyone else, had been most annoyed. She was a great admirer of Ursula Gidden and knew somebody who was a friend of Ursula's parents, and she thought it almost insulting to Ursula that a child who had never acted in her life and was the plain, untalented one of the family should even have a test for her part. Of course, she had not said these things out loud, but she had half said them and looked them, and she had said in her whiny voice, "It won't happen. You've no idea, Jane, how these movie people go on. Every day you read stories of people who've been discovered. Often the movie company pays their expenses right across America just to make tests like this one you're to have tomorrow, but not once in a thousand times does anything come of it. I guess most of these so-called discoveries just get their railroad fare home, and nobody hears of them again. Now you take my advice, and don't expect anything, for you'll feel lower than a snake when they say you won't do. It's not to be hoped they'll use you, for that little Ursula Gidden is really something."

Even Bella, angelic Bella, whom Jane liked more than she had liked anybody for ages, did not have much faith in a movie career. She shook her head and looked more as if Jane were going to have a tooth out than a test. She had a grandchild who had had a test for the Our Gang films. The family had got so uppity about it that Bella could have slapped them. Then, when nothing came of it, they felt madder than hornets. Bella didn't want to see Miss Jane feeling that way.

John had teased Jane at lunch and called her "the little film star," but it was only teasing; he had not meant it. And he had backed Tim about the name Brown. He said Jane's Mr. Browne had an *e* on his name, but both Browns sounded alike, and Tim's Mr. Brown had been there first, and any other Mr. Browne would have to be called something else; he suggested Mr. Film Browne.

If there was anybody over whom a fuss was being made, it was Rachel. Peaseblossom, John, and Bee had treated her as if it were her birthday. On top of that Aunt Cora chose that afternoon to take everybody for a drive, and they all had sympathized with Peaseblossom because she could not go, but not with Jane. So what with one thing and another, it was a very black-doggish Jane who stumped up Mr. Bryan J. Browne's porch steps.

Mr. Bryan J. Browne had everything planned. A chair on his lawn and magazines waiting for Peaseblossom. He had even arranged to have afternoon tea served for her. Jane could see from Peaseblossom's expression that she approved of Mr. Bryan J. Browne.

Hyde Park gave Jane a fine welcome. He remembered her at once and bounced over, licking and barking. As soon as he settled down again, Jane knelt beside him and examined him all over. She could not find a thing wrong; his coat was in lovely condition. Evidently he had got over the effects of eating bad fish.

Mr. Bryan J. Browne had a big book with a paper cover. He sat down and opened it, and Jane saw that the pages inside were typed.

"I'm going to go over with you some short scenes I want you to learn by tomorrow. Are you a quick study?"

Jane wondered for a second what he meant; then she answered very fast because she wanted him to have a good opinion of her. "Actually very quick indeed."

123

"Can you cry?"

"Cry! Whatever for?"

"You'll have to as Mary."

"Why? Mary in *The Secret Garden* didn't cry, at least only in that bit at the beginning."

Mr. Bryan J. Browne laid the book on his knee and leaned forward and caught hold of one of Jane's braids. "Stop looking at Hyde Park and look at me. Do you want to be Mary?"

"Yes."

"Well, you won't if you argue about what Mary did and did not do. I'm the director of this picture, and nobody, certainly not unknown little girls, argues with directors. If I say Mary cries, Mary will cry."

"What's she going to cry about?"

"The first time she finds the garden. She looks around, and she cries because it's so good to be inside at last. But though she's crying, her eyes shine through her tears. Do you think you could do that?"

"Mary wasn't the sort of silly fool who'd . . ." Jane remembered about arguing. "I mean, getting into a garden you wanted to get into seems to me a funny thing to cry about."

"What makes you cry?"

Jane remembered the last time she had cried. That day at Dr. Smith's when she had given in about leaving Chewing-gum behind. She did not like remembering about Chewing-gum, so she said in a stuffy voice, "I did about leaving Chewing-gum."

Bryan J. Browne looked at Hyde Park.

"So would I, if I had to leave him any place." He got up and held out a hand to Jane. "Come over here, and see what you can do about this. Let's pretend that over here are the

124

steps down into the garden. You come down the steps as if you were stepping straight into fairyland. You say in a whisper, 'How still it is! How still.' Then you stand still and look around like this." He looked around as if he were in a strange garden. "Then you remember young Mrs. Craven's story. How she fell out of that tree. You don't see Mrs. Craven, but as she comes into your mind, she comes toward you—"

Jane was so shocked she had to interrupt. "She couldn't do that. She was dead."

"She *is* dead. It's her ghost who lives on in the garden. The ghost of the girl Archibald Craven loved."

Jane scowled. "Not in my book. There was only a robin in the garden."

"In my picture young Mrs. Craven's ghost is in the garden."

"Then, if you don't mind my saying so, it'll be a very silly picture. Nobody who has read *The Secret Garden* will know who she is."

"They will. Two very lovely people are playing Mr. and Mrs. Craven. The story opens with them long before Colin is born. We see her fall out of the tree, and we see him lock the garden and bury the key. It's young Mrs. Craven's love for her son, little Colin, that puts the idea into Mary's head to bring Colin to the garden."

Jane bit her lip to stop herself from arguing, but it was no good.

"Very well, Mr. Bryan J. Browne, if that's how it's going to be. But if you don't mind my saying so, it's not the story in the book called *The Secret Garden*."

Mr. Bryan J. Browne laughed.

"Perhaps not. But it's the picture I am going to make, and must you call me by my full name? Wouldn't just Mr. Browne do?"

"No. As a matter of fact, that's a thing I'm very angry

about." Jane explained about Tim's Mr. Brown. "Dad sided with Tim, although you're much the more important Mr. Browne. Dad says I could call you Mr. Film Browne, but I think My-Mr. Browne would be better, if you don't mind."

My-Mr. Browne said, "Fine," but his mind was back on his script.

"Now, let's get on without any more arguments. As you feel Mrs. Craven beside you, your eyes fill with tears. She kisses you. You look up, still crying but with your eyes shining, and you say, 'Robin, your wing brushed my cheek. It was as if you'd kissed me.' You look up at the robin, and you say, 'No wonder it's so still.' Then you clasp your hands and whisper, 'I'm the first person who has spoken in this garden for ten years.' Now, let's see how you do."

At first Jane did very badly indeed. She thought the line about the robin's wing silly and sounded as if she did, and though she made faces as if she were crying, her eyes were not even damp. It was a little better when she remembered the words without prompting, but there were still no tears and not a sign of a shine in her eyes. Then suddenly, just as she was pretending to step into the garden for the sixth time, My-Mr. Browne said, "Poor old Chewing-gum. I bet he's hungry and lonely. It's tough on a dog to be lonely. He doesn't know what it's all about. He thinks maybe you've run out on him." That did it. In a minute Jane was crying so hard that her nose was red and her eyes were swollen. My-Mr. Browne was nice; he said of course, Chewing-gum was fine, that everybody had something that made him or her cry and Chewing-gum was evidently a surefire way to set her off. Then he gave her a Pepsi-Cola, which was a thing she had never drunk before and which tasted very good. Then they started the little scene all over again. This time it went off almost perfectly. Having got upset about Chewing-gum, Jane found that the smallest whisk of a thought of his being lonely made the tears come. My-Mr. Browne was pleased. He said if she acted Mary like that at the test the next day and photographed all right, maybe she'd have a chance.

The other scenes were easy. The first was the one where she stood by Colin's bed and told him what she thought of him. She read the words from the script: "You stop! You stop! I hate you! Everybody hates you! I wish everybody would run out of the house and let you scream yourself to death. You will scream yourself to death in a minute, and I wish you would."

My-Mr. Browne took the script back and told Jane to learn the words and say them exactly as she had spoken them the first time.

The third scene was Mary's first meeting with Dickon. My-Mr. Browne said that Dickon would be sitting under a tree, playing on his pipes, and that all the wild creatures he was taming would be there. That Jane was to look very interested, as if seeing tamed squirrels, rabbits, and a robin were magic. This was so exactly what Jane felt that although she had to imagine the creatures, nothing could have been easier. There were a few lines to say, but most of the words were spoken by Dickon. They went over the lines two or three times for what My-Mr. Browne called inflections, but he seemed pleased and quite soon said that it would do. He would, he said, try to get David to bring along some of his animals or the robin for the test, and then Jane would be grand.

They went to find Peaseblossom. She was just finishing her tea. She looked with rather an anxious face at My-Mr. Browne. She did not say so, but she was sure his afternoon had been wasted. It was still impossible for her to believe anyone was thinking seriously of Jane in a film.

My-Mr. Browne gave Peaseblossom an envelope.

"These are the lines that Jane must know by tomorrow." He smiled at Jane. "A studio car will fetch you at nine."

14

The Painted Garden

The start for the Bee Bee studios was almost as grand as even Jane could have wished. Bee was taking her, and although neither Aunt Cora nor Peaseblossom said so, it was obvious that each wished she'd had the chance. There was almost the fuss Jane had wished for about getting her ready, enough to give her an idea of how it felt to be important.

The Bee Bee studios were in Culver City. Long before they got there, Jane and Bee could see the words "Bee Bee Films Incorporated" written on what seemed to be storage tanks which were built into the air. Close up, the studio looked rather like a prison. There were high walls all around the lot, guarded by a great many policemen and a great deal of barbed wire. The car stopped at gates with a policeman outside; evidently the policeman knew the driver by sight, for he said nothing and let them drive in.

Jane had hoped that Mr. Browne would be waiting for them; he was not, but he had told somebody else to look after them. She was a nice woman who said her name was Miss Delaney, though everybody seemed to call her Dot. As they walked along, they met all sorts of people, who smiled and said, "How's my darling Dot?" or, as if it were amazing to meet her, "Dot, honey!"

Inside, the lot was like a town. Wide streets ran up and down; only instead of houses on each side there were offices and studios. Cars and trucks drove up and down the streets, and there were even street cleaners with brooms. Miss Delaney showed Jane a long, low white building standing back in a little garden and said that was the Bee Bee school, where Jane would go for lessons if she got the part of Mary. Jane asked if that was where David Doe went to school, and Miss Delaney said it was, that all the children under contract went there. Jane would meet David as soon as he came out of school. The test scene with him would be shot after lunch so as not to interfere with his morning's lessons, because if he missed even a few minutes of his lessons between nine and twelve, those minutes had to be made up in the afternoon, for that was the law.

Miss Delaney took Bee and Jane to a big place she called the wardrobe. Evidently they were expected. A woman in a white linen coat came and was introduced as Mrs. Gates. She looked Jane over as if she could measure her just by looking at her; then she said to Miss Delaney, "Not far out. Of course, Ursula's a bit bigger." Jane was surprised to find Ursula was bigger than she was, for My-Mr. Browne had spoken of Ursula as "little." She had no time to say her thoughts out loud, for Mrs. Gates led them over to a place where clothes were hanging under cellophane coverings. She threw back the cellophane. "What would you like to wear, dear?"

Jane was thrilled. Of course, she liked dressing up, and this was dressing up in a big way. She had not thought of Mary in *The Secret Garden* as having a great many clothes, but evidently she had. There were whole rows of frocks and coats and some nightdresses and a dressing gown. Mrs. Gates said to Bee, "They look funny now, don't they? You wait till I show you the little petticoats and the frilled drawers that go with them. They're just darling."

With advice from Mrs. Gates and Miss Delaney, Jane

130

chose one of the plainer frocks. It was pink with a very full skirt. She was ashamed of the underclothes. Although the skirt of the dress was longer than her own, if she turned quickly the frilled pants showed. Miss Delaney said she thought they were cute, but Jane thought them awful. The dress needed a little altering, and while this was being done, Miss Delaney took Jane and Bee to another place where there was a hairdresser. He was a man with a lot of black hair and very sparkling eyes. He stood away from Jane, looking at her with his head on one side; then he made pleased noises, pulled out a chair, and gently pushed her into it. After untying her braids, he started brushing and combing her hair and trying out different parts in such a possessive way that Jane nearly asked him if he thought her head belonged to him.

Out again in one of the main streets of the lot, Jane felt dreadfully self-conscious. Her hair was brushed out and tied with a bow, and the ends had been curled. A warm wind was blowing, and though she kept holding her skirt down, she was sure those dreadful pants were showing. But she was the only person who seemed to think her clothes queer, for though there were masses of people hurrying along, nobody looked twice at her. After a while she saw why, for on a film lot it was more usual to be dressed up than not to be dressed up.

Mr. Browne was waiting for them in a huge room with lots of little rooms opening off it. Each of the little rooms had one wall missing, for they opened straight into the big room. The one nearest Mr. Browne seemed to be a bedroom, for there was a very grand bed in it.

They did not start on the test right away. Mr. Browne took Jane around and showed her things. The place they were in was studio twelve, where most of the interior scenes of *The Secret Garden* were scheduled to be shot. The garden was in another studio. Mr. Browne led Jane around and explained that what she had thought was a big room was a "floor"; she would hear people say a picture was on "the floor," and that meant it was being shot in a place like the one they were in. He explained that what she had thought were little rooms were really like scenes in a theater. Each one was built to fit the scenes in the script. Most of them were rooms in Misselthwaite Manor. He showed her the script where it was written that the scene was in Colin's bedroom, and then he showed her the piece of room with the grand bed in it and told her that she was going to act one of her test scenes there, and did she know which?

"Of course," Jane said promptly. "That's the scene where Colin's screaming and I tell him to stop."

Mr. Browne asked if Jane would like to go over her lines before the test and led the way to two chairs which were by themselves in a corner. Jane began to feel odd again the moment Mr. Browne mentioned lines.

Mr. Browne saw how she felt, for he laughed and said there was nothing to be scared of.

Jane knew all the words perfectly; she had almost known them when she had come home the day before, and Peaseblossom had been hearing them off and on until the car came, but in the fuss of saying them at that moment, Jane felt Mr. Browne could not be trusted to remember what he had said, so she gabbled very fast both her lines and his directions.

"There's steps I come down looking as if it were fairyland and I say how still it is how still and look at the tree Mrs. Craven fell out of and I remember—"

Mr. Browne stopped her. He said he thought she should take a deep breath and start again, and this time all she should do was to tell him what Mary said. This worked very well. Jane said every line in each scene perfectly, though with no expression at all, except a little in the scene by

132

Colin's bed, which was the scene she really liked. When she finished, Mr. Browne said they would go to the garden, as she was ready for her test.

The garden was the queerest garden Jane could imagine. It was partly real and partly painted. The trees seemed to be real, growing in real earth, but the roses were not real, nor were the little plants real—the pansies, delphiniums, larkspurs, lilies, pinks, poppies and all the other flowers that grew in the garden. Queerest of all was the grass, which looked just like grass until Jane got close to it and saw that it was artificial. It was easier to understand a made-in-the-studio garden when she and Mr. Browne came to the end of a path and found a different garden. That garden was not finished, for men were still working on it. It was going to be a winter garden; the trees had no leaves, and the ground was a tangle of plants all wound together. Jane said, ''That's going to be the place where Mary scraped about and found bulbs trying to come through.''

Many preparations had to be made for the test. The distance between the camera and where Jane was to stand was measured, and great big cameras were pushed around. A lot of people seemed to be gazing at Jane all at once; she hated that. Mr. Browne saw how she felt. He came and sat beside her on the top step leading into the garden. He said some people could be themselves one minute and then imagine themselves being somebody else the next, but he did not think Jane was that sort of person. That he did not want her to try too much; he thought that Jane and Mary could behave very much alike, and it was his job to try to use all the bits of Jane that were like Mary. Only in this scene Jane would have to think about Mary. If she did not, there would be a piece of film showing Jane Winter walking into a garden, looking at it scornfully as if she were saying, ''This isn't a real garden, just a painted one.'' Jane knew her words and knew what he

133

wanted her to do. Would she try very hard to do it? This was a picture he very much wanted to direct, but if she was not good in this scene, he was very much afraid Mr. Bettelheimer would decide not to make the picture now, and he would hate that. He was sure Jane would try hard, but he thought a prize might help. If she were so good that Mr. Bettelheimer and the other important men thought she should play Mary, he would give her a prize. Did she have a watch, or would she like one?

Jane gazed at him, her eyes shining. A watch! Would she like a watch!

"Oh! A wristwatch would be the grandest prize in the whole world." Then suddenly, as she said these words, she thought of Chewing-gum. It was awful to say no to a watch, but she had to do it. "There's something I want more than a watch. Something I made a secret vow I'd get somehow. A food parcel for Chewing-gum."

Mr. Browne looked at Jane in a funny way; then he pulled one of the curls the hairdresser had taken such trouble to make.

"That's a bargain. You get the part of Mary, and Chewing-gum shall get the best food parcel that's to be had in Los Angeles. We'll start shooting now; do what you can about those tears."

A film studio in Hollywood was a difficult place in which to feel miserable about a dog in London, and nobody left Jane alone. First a woman in a white coat combed out her hair, then somebody else dabbed at her face with a piece of paper, and then Mr. Browne brought up a fair girl in queer, old-fashioned clothes and introduced her. He said she was Betty, who was standing in for Mrs. Craven.

Jane thought Betty looked nice, but her mind was really on those awful tears.

"I do hope you won't think me rude if I don't talk much.

You see, I'm trying to cry. If I do, Mr. Browne will buy a food parcel for my dog, Chewing-gum.''

"Well, isn't that just darling! I suppose your dog is pretty hungry all the time."

"Not hungry, exactly. He has horse. You don't eat horse much in America, do you? It's nice, but you get tired of it. I think Chewing-gum does."

Betty was looking at Jane intently as if she were thinking of something. Then she said, in a dreadfully grave voice, "That's right. Must have variety. I don't think horsemeat is healthy food. I wouldn't let my dog touch it. I buy her food in specially packed cans. Sterilized, you know. I'm scared stiffer than a statue of germs. One germ and . . ." Betty did not finish but shook her head in a very frightening way.

Jane was horror-struck. She knew lots of things might happen to Chewing-gum, but that he might eat germs with his horsemeat was a new danger.

"You mean a germ could kill him?"

"Faster than an atom bomb."

A voice shouted, "Quiet, everybody." Lights blazed down on the garden.

Mr. Browne called, "Come along, Jane. Open the door, and come to the top of the steps."

Jane was not actually crying but rather near it because the idea of Chewing-gum dead of a germ was dreadful to think of. She opened the door and came to the top step and looked down at the secret garden.

Film lights are queer things. They are very bright and very hot, but they give special color to everything as well. When Jane walked around the garden with Mr. Browne, there had been no bright lights; now that the lights were on, the garden had changed. Jane found it was like opening a book to a painting of a lovely garden and suddenly finding she had the power to walk into it. She forgot about Chewing-gum, but the tears that had nearly fallen were still in her eyes as she looked around, entranced by the strangeness.

That was the only nice moment of making the test of that scene. Mr. Browne and everybody were so slow, and Jane could not see why. There were the steps. There was Betty ready. There was even a toy robin ready in a tree; all she had to do was to come down the steps and say her lines. But the moment she had finished looking around the garden and before she had time to come down the steps, Mr. Browne said, "Cut." All the bright lights were switched off, more measuring was done, and somebody came and looked at Jane and dabbed at her face again with another piece of paper. It was even worse when they got to the place where she spoke. For no reason that Jane could discover, Mr. Browne made her say "How still it is! How Still!" four times.

The bit with Betty was a little less tiresome, for Betty seemed to expect to have to kiss Jane several times even though she did it right the first time.

"It's so stupid doing everything so often," Jane grumbled, "and I hate having my face patted with that paper every time the lights go out."

Betty laughed and said they would look anything but pretty if it didn't happen. Under the hot lamps everybody perspired and needed wiping off.

Jane pulled down her pink skirts, for she was still conscious of her frilled pants. "Do lots of dogs die of germs?"

Betty's eyes twinkled. "Got to cry anymore?"

Jane shook her head.

"Cheer up. I never knew a dog to die that way. I was just trying to jerk a few tears out of you so your dog would get his package."

Suddenly the test in the garden was over. Jane wanted to find Betty to say good-bye because she liked her so much, but the woman in the white coat took her by the hand.

136

"Come along, dear. I want to change you."

Almost before she knew what was happening Jane was dressed in a nightdress and dressing gown, and she was standing with a candle in her hand talking to a strange boy who was in Colin's bed. The boy couldn't be Maurice Tuesday because everybody called him Ted. Jane never found out who he was because every time Mr. Browne said, "Cut," he got out of the bed and went and talked to one of the men who had something to do with the lights. When he was in bed, he half sat up, as he was told to do, and looked at Jane, but nobody could have looked at her in a more bored way. Jane told Bee afterward that he looked at her with a fish-queue face, and Bee said she knew exactly what she meant. Luckily it did not matter how Ted looked, for Jane was bored and tired and spit out her words at him to let off her feelings. Words spit out like that were just what Mr. Browne wanted. After Jane had recited them three times, he laughed and said, "Two o'clock, boys." The lights went out. Everybody, including Ted, went away. Mr. Browne turned to Bee.

"Get her changed quickly. She's meeting David Doe in the commissary."

15

David Doe

Miss Delaney had reserved a table for five in the commissary, and she took Jane and Bee straight to it. Jane was given a menu with so many lovely things on it to choose from that it would have been hard to make a choice even if she had her mind on it, but she had her mind on the door. What was he going to be like, this boy who tamed animals? Was he going to be friendly and sensible and explain exactly how training was done, so that she could make a skilled dog of Chewing-gum as soon as she got home?

Jane knew it was David the moment he and his father came in the door. He had a great mop of dark red hair, and queer wide-apart greenish eyes, and all over a sort of listening look birds and animals have, a look which makes you know that in one second, if they don't like the sound and smell of you, they will be out of sight quicker than you can feel a puff of wind.

David sat in the chair next to Jane, and Jane found that now that she was actually meeting David, whom she could feel she was going to like, she had nothing to say. David was obviously not a person who talked much; he gave Jane a shy smile and then stared at the menu. Bee said, "You must order your food, Jane, darling. You've only chosen clam chowder. What about fried chicken and ice cream to follow?"

Jane said, "Thank you, that would be lovely." Actually

she was so interested in David, she would have said "thank you" if Bee had said, "What about slugs on toast and grilled caterpillars to follow?"

Luckily Mr. Doe was a man who liked talking and was very nice to listen to, for he had an attractive soft accent and enchanted Bee by calling her ma'am, just in the way you say ma'am in England if you speak to the queen or one of the princesses. Prompted by Miss Delaney when he forgot the most interesting bits, he told Bee the whole story of how David came to be in pictures.

Mr. Doe had earned his living as a truck driver in the state of Missouri. He had two sons, Gardner and David. From the time he was a baby, David had gone off to the woods every minute that he could to play with the birds and wild creatures. The Bee Bee studios had a movie unit which was traveling through all the States looking for people who did unusual things. They chanced to come to David's village, and there someone told them about David. They went off to the woods and found him playing on a pipe he had made to an audience of a rabbit and a chipmunk. The movie unit took some pictures of him and his pets, and everybody thought that was the end of that, except that David's ma hoped maybe the "short" would be shown someplace near, where they could go and see it. Mr. Doe could never tell Bee how surprised they all had been when one day a letter came from the Bee Bee studios asking him to bring David to Hollywood for a movie test. Mr. Doe went to his truck company and showed them the letter, and they said he could have a leave of absence. The tests had been successful, and David had been put under contract. Just at first Mrs. Doe and Gardner stayed on in Missouri, for they still thought nothing much would come of David's career in the movies. Then suddenly a certain book became a best seller. It was the story of a boy who tamed a pony and got it a job in a circus; it was just the part for David. The company bought the book. David had a real wild pony and tamed it himself, and when the picture was first shown, David found himself famous overnight.

Bee asked if the Does liked living in Hollywood. Mr. Doe looked sort of homesick and said, "Why, yes, ma'am, we do. We've met some real friendly people, and we have a home in a nice neighborhood not too far from the Bee Bee studios. But we sure do miss Missouri, and I miss my truck driving. David is thirteen now, and maybe soon he'll be giving up movie work. When he does, we'll go right back to Missouri. Yes, ma'am!"

Bee asked what David was going to do if he gave up working in pictures, and Mr. Doe said he thought it would be nice to have a ranch. But at that, for the first time, David spoke. He had the same soft voice as his father; only his words came slowly and gently, as if they needed a little push to make them come out. It was not a ranch he wanted but land for a park. A place where wild creatures could live in peace, nobody hunting them, nobody stealing eggs, a place where they met human beings as friends.

Jane was puzzled by this ambition. If she had been David, she would not have wanted that at all. She would have liked a private circus where all the birds and animals she had tamed could perform: whole ballets of rabbits, squirrels as trapeze artists, and, of course, the star of stars, Chewing-gum.

Immediately after lunch David went to the garden. He told Jane he had a robin and a squirrel for her test, and he was going to get them to feel at home while she was changing. Jane's Mr. Browne took her to the garden. He told her to walk in very quietly and when she found David to do exactly what he told her. They would make the test as soon as David said he was ready.

David was sitting under a tree playing on queer homemade-looking pipes. On his shoulder was a robin, and lolling

140

against one of his feet a squirrel. He scarcely stopped playing when Jane arrived but whispered, "Stand still." Jane stood absolutely still. After a moment David stopped playing and said, "This robin is called Mickey, and the squirrel is Bob. Mickey and Bob, this is Jane." Then he played a few more notes and whispered, "I'm going to throw some food around you. While I play, come nearer, but move soft."

Jane was trembling. This was about the loveliest thing that had ever happened to her. This was magic. She crept inch by inch nearer to David, her eyes never leaving Bob and Mickey. Then something, perhaps a twig snapping or a stone slipping, made a disturbance. There was a flutter of wings, a hoppity-hop from Bob, and both Mickey and Bob were gone.

David was quite undisturbed. He still spoke in a whisper. "Come a step nearer. That's right. Now I'm going to throw the food. Then I'll play again, and we'll see."

David threw some nuts for Bob and crumbs for Mickey. Jane, scarcely daring to breathe, saw that one nut was almost touching her left foot, and a crumb was actually on the toe of her right shoe. She wished so hard it felt as if the wish must show coming out of her head. "Oh, let Mickey trust me and take the crumb off my foot. Let Bob fetch that nearest nut."

David was playing, and at first nothing happened. Then from behind one of the rose bushes a pair of gay little eyes and a nervous nose came peeping. Then, with a couple of hops, Bob was in the open, picking up the nut farthest from Jane, nibbling it, and looking at her while he ate. Then there was a flurry of wings and Mickey flew onto David's shoulder. David went on quietly playing, and Mickey, from the safety of David's shoulder, studied Jane. She could see him thinking, "Who is this girl? David seemes to think she's all right. Shall I trust her?" Suddenly he made up his mind. He fluttered off David's shoulder and, seeming wonderfully unfussed, began picking up his crumbs.

Jane held her breath. Although she could hear the dim hum of voices far away, there seemed nobody in the studio but herself, David, Bob, and Mickey. Bob's little teeth made a pleased chewing sound as he daintily picked up his nuts. There was only one left. The one near Jane's left foot. Would he trust her? Would he? Then suddenly he was there. For a second she felt his soft, warm body against her foot. She looked down. He had skipped away to eat his nut, but not far, and while he ate it, his eyes said, "You'll do." Suddenly Mickey was sitting on Jane's right toe. Jane was so proud she felt tight inside. "They trust me," she thought. "I almost believe they like me."

Jane's-Mr. Browne's voice came from behind David. "Grand. Can we get rolling?"

David did not stop playing; instead he nodded.

For Jane that part of the test was not a test at all; it was real. The garden was bathed not in artificial light but in real sunshine. It was not David sitting under a tree in a painted garden in Hollywood but Dickon under a real tree in Yorkshire. He spoke with Dickon's Yorkshire accent. "Don't tha' move. It'd flight 'em."

Jane was not Jane; she was Mary, standing still as a rock. Of course, she wouldn't move. It would be dreadful to "flight" Bob and Mickey.

David went on. "I'm Dickon. I know tha'rt Miss Mary."

Jane was looking just as Mary must have looked—her eyes shining because for the first time she was being trusted by wild creatures.

Jane would not have minded how long that test took, but suddenly it was over. The cameras stopped turning, the lights were out, and she was told to run along and get changed.

142

David stayed where he was. He said he would wait and take Mickey and Bob back to where they lived a little later on.

Jane's Mr. Browne seemed pleased; in fact, everybody seemed pleased. Mr. Browne said, "I wouldn't be surprised if old Chewing-gum got that package after all."

It felt queer to be outside the studio, riding home in the studio car. It felt queer to be just Jane Winter again.

Bee turned and looked at the storage tanks with "Bee Bee Films Incorporated" written across them.

"Well, it's been an exciting day, even if nothing comes of all those tests."

Jane stuck her chin in the air.

"I think something will come of them. I thought I was very good."

16

Something for Everybody

Tim was making money. Not a great deal, for the people who ate at the Antonios' drugstore took his playing as part of the service, like ice water. Mr. Antonio gave Tim a box in which to keep his money, and he made a ceremony of counting the daily total. As soon as the last lunch eaters had left, he would call out, "Tim, you come here." Tim would go into the office at the back. It had a red velvet tablecloth on the table, and there were artificial flowers on the table. The walls were covered with religious pictures framed in shells. Mr. Antonio would open a purse and tip what was in it onto the red velvet tablecloth. He did the counting because Tim was slow at American money.

Mrs. Antonio would waddle in and stand at the end of the table, making admiring sounds. When the count was good, her eyebrows, hands, eyes, and shoulders would go up, and she would say in a gasping voice, "Santa Maria! One dollar eighty-five!" or whatever the sum was.

On an afternoon soon after Jane's test the money-counting ceremony had a surprise ending. The count was extraordinarily good. Tim's share was nearly a dollar. He was just going when Mr. Antonio said, "Tim, see what is here." Like a conjurer bringing a rabbit out of nowhere, he laid a parcel on the table. Tim looked first at Mrs. Antonio and then at Mr. Antonio. Yes, the parcel was for him. They both were smiling in so pleased a way that Tim, without knowing what was in the parcel, smiled, too. He undid the string and pulled away the paper. It was music, but what music! There were about fifty sheets of it, and every one was the sort you could hear by putting a nickel in a machine called a jukebox. Tim did not know what to say. The Antonios were so pleased and proud he could not hurt their feelings, but what would Mr. Brown, and Mr. Brown's grand friend Mr. Jeremy Caulder, say if they knew he was playing that sort of music as part of his practice time? Tim had been able to feel he was not doing too badly because he was playing things Mr. Brown had let him play. But this music!

Luckily Mr. and Mrs. Antonio thought Tim was silent because he was too pleased to speak. Mr. Antonio winked at Mrs. Antonio.

"We make a surprise, Anna."

Mrs. Antonio, chuckling and shaking all over because any movement made her shake, said, "What did I say, Tony! It is no good to make the same music every day. Now Tim play the new music, and the patrons pay big money."

Tim took the music home. He could not, of course, play it; but he could read it through, and he could talk over the situation with Bella. He did not catch Bella alone until the evening. She was making what she called biscuits and the family called scones. She was nice to talk to because she knew the moment a person came into her kitchen whether it was just to visit or to discuss something serious. She could see that Tim's call was serious. She moved her cooking utensils and made room for him at the end of the table.

"What's on your mind, son?"

Tim undid the parcel and laid the sheets of music out so that Bella could read all their titles.

"This! Mr. and Mrs. Antonio want me to play this. They

bought it as a present. I just simply couldn't tell you how Mr. Brown hates this sort of music—at least, almost all of it.''

Bella looked calm and undisturbed.

"You earning money?''

"Yes. I don't know how much exactly, but I should think in English money it's almost a pound.''

Bella put her biscuits in the oven. She came back to the table. She shook her head at Tim. The trouble was, she said, he was not trusting enough. He was thinking he could decide the way things should be done, but the Lord had no time for that. He had seen Tim fixed right with a piano; but there had been no talk about music, and maybe the Lord was not aiming to fix the music. Or maybe He was aiming to fix it, and this was the music He would enjoy hearing Tim play.

Tim went to church every Sunday, but in England he had not thought of the things he heard about on Sundays as being mixed up with weekday matters like the Antonios' music. Bella, though, whom he considered about the most sensible person he knew, thought they did mix.

"Do you suppose, Bella, if I play all this music, the Lord's aiming to fix me another piano? Perhaps even one in Aunt Cora's sitting room?''

Bella looked solemn.

"You can't tell. You just relax, son. You'll see. The Lord may be fixing for Jane to go into movies just so you can have your piano.''

Bella was also a help to Rachel. Usually she was finishing clearing the breakfast dishes when Rachel came to the porch for her dancing practice. To Bella anything that you wanted enough came, though, as she had told Tim, not always in the way you planned to have it.

"But what I really need, Bella,'' Rachel explained, "is for Aunt Cora to think my dancing classes so important that she'll drive me to them every day, or let Dad drive me. The

146

classes are at five each day and all Saturday mornings. That's rather a lot to ask, isn't it?''

Bella's face cracked into one of her widest smiles.

"It's no good asking the Lord for that. The Lord'll just look down and say you should know Miss Cora better than that. No, what I figure the Lord's aiming to do is to fix up a car for Mr. Winter.''

After that, each time the front doorbell rang Bella would say to any of the family within earshot that maybe it was the car for Rachel or the piano for Tim. A few days after Jane's test the front doorbell chimed just after Tim had rushed off to his morning piano practice. Rachel was on the porch dancing. Jane was angrily helping Peaseblossom clean the upstairs passage. Bee was polishing the downstairs passage. The bell ringer was Jane's-Mr. Browne. He looked awful, Bella thought. Terribly tired, with rings half down his cheeks. He told Bella he would not come in; would she fetch Mr. Winter?

Because Jane's-Mr. Browne would not come in, they all heard what he said. Rachel came to the porch door. Bee leaned on the polisher. Peaseblossom and Jane hung over the stairs. Bella stood holding the front door. Mr. Browne sounded as if he were exhausted.

"She's got it. It's been a fight. We started on her tests twenty-four hours ago, and we went over them most of last night. Bettelheimer and I battled for her against the rest. We won somehow. Will you come up to the studio this afternoon at half past two to sign the contract? You'll have to take it to the judge of the Supreme Court to be ratified. Our lawyer will instruct you about that. Jane has to go with you. As soon as the judge has given his okay, Jane has to attend the studio school. You'll hear all about that this afternoon. So long. I'll be seeing you.'' He was just going when he remembered something. He felt in his pocket for a piece of paper. "That car you wanted. There's a friend of mine at this address who's going to Europe. He says you can use his old Ford. If you'll go to his place, he'll hand it over."

When the door shut behind Jane's-Mr. Browne, there was silence all through the house. Jane could not move or say anything. She could only think over and over again, "I'm going to be Mary. I'm going to be Mary. I shall see David, Bob, and Mickey every day!" Peaseblossom thought, "Good gracious! Jane! Bless the child, who could have guessed it! Quite a feather in the family cap. Up the Winters!" Rachel clasped her hands and thought, "I mustn't be jealous. I mustn't be hateful. I must just think how gorgeous it is about the car. But, oh, dear, I wish it were me." Bee, leaning on the polisher, thought, "I'm sorry. John may be right and it's good for Jane to shine, but I'm sure it's going to be terribly hard work, poor darling." John, standing by the shut door, thought, "Well, that's that. No going back now. I hope we're right to let her do it. We must wait and see."

The silence was broken by Bella. She clasped her hands and said, "A car! The Lord's sent a car! Next thing we know there'll be a piano standing right in front of this door."

Jane felt that the day should feel special, like a birthday. It did not. It went on in a dreadfully ordinary way. There was the excitement of John's fetching the car. He took them all for a run as far as the Antonios' drugstore to drop Tim off for his after-lunch playing; then he drove straight back to Aunt Cora's and turned them all out because he said he had to go to the Bee Bee studios. When Jane said she would go to the studios, too, he said nonsense, she would soon be seeing more than she wanted to of the Bee Bee studios. She was to go for a good walk with the others and finish up with a swim. Jane thought this was a very offhand way to treat a person who had just become most important, and she sulked for the rest of the afternoon. "Never mind," she told herself. "When I get to the studio, they'll almost bow, they'll honor me so."

Nobody noticed Jane's black-doggishness, for everyone had other things to think of. First there was Aunt Cora. They all supposed she would be pleased about the car. Almost every day she had said in her whiny voice that she knew they thought she was a meanie about the car, but her poor dear Ed had always said it ruined a car if you let anyone else drive it but yourself. So they supposed it would make her happy to hear she did not have to bother about them anymore because of the Ford. Not a bit of it. Aunt Cora, on hearing the news, had what she called one of her nervous spells. Her whiny voice rose to a squeak. She said John had been grumbling to the studio people about having no car. She would have gone on talking like that much longer; only Bella came in and took her away to lie down. The children exchanged looks which said, "What an aunt!" Bee and Peaseblossom were upset and worried and refused to believe Bella when she said it was just one of Miss Cora's turns and of no importance.

The other thing which was worrying Bee and Peaseblossom was Jane's engagement. It was the law of the United States of America that a child's parent, guardian, or teacher had to be with the child all the time it was on the studio lot. Who was that to be? Bee was the obvious person to go, but that would mean John would never have Bee with him in the afternoons when he was not writing. And for him to enjoy himself and get well was the whole point of their coming to California. Peaseblossom was rather keen to look after Jane at the studio, but if she did, what about Rachel's and Tim's lessons?

"I suppose," she suggested to Bee, "you couldn't teach them sometimes? Of course, not mathematics or Latin—those never were your subjects—but you can speak fair French, and you were quite a dab at English literature."

Bee groaned. She thought the future looked pretty bleak whichever way she looked at it.

"I hope it won't come to that. Anyway, I'll start off by taking Jane, and then we'll see." Then she added, "I'm sure John's right and it's good for darling Jane to have this chance to shine. But oh, how I wish Her-Mr. Browne had never seen her!"

Rachel, too, was wrapped up in worries. Tomorrow was Sunday. Posy Fossil had kept her word and invited her to spend the day. Since she had been in California, Rachel had been noticing American girls of her age. Not a great many came to this part of Santa Monica, but those who did come spent the day with neighbors, and sitting on the beach, Rachel had studied visiting girls carefully. They usually arrived in shirts and three-quarter-length slacks. A little later they changed into a sunsuit, and when they went into the water, the sunsuit came off, leaving a smart skintight bathing suit. In the afternoon they put on pretty frocks. Rachel hated to think of meeting a film star in an old cotton frock. Trudging along for the afternoon walk, she turned over various ideas. If only, oh, if only she had a pair of those three-quarter-length slacks, how gorgeously right she would feel! Rachel glanced back at Bee and Peaseblossom. Was it any good appealing to them? There might still be time to do something. One look at Peaseblossom's and Bee's faces, and she gave up that idea. Rachel set her mouth almost in the way Jane usually set hers. Very well then, she must manage something on her own.

Tim lagged far behind everybody else, singing at the top of his voice. He did not know the words of the Antonios' fifty songs, but that did not matter as they were mostly silly and very like each other, and he preferred words he made up himself. It was clear that the Antonios were right; even in one day the eaters had shown they liked that sort of music, for they had not only paid more but had bought him ice-cream sodas and Cokes as well. "Oh, lovely California,"

Tim sang, "where the sun shines every day . . . Oh, gorgeous California, where people pay money so the Lord can send me a piano."

John did not get back from the Bee Bee studios in time for a swim. It was getting late when he drove the Ford up to Aunt Cora's front door. He called to the family to come out and look at it once more before he put it beside Aunt Cora's in the garage. John had been looking better and better every day since they arrived in California, but the car seemed to be the final thing to make him absolutely well. Almost better and happier than he had been before the accident.

"You can arrange about your dancing lessons, Rachel. Here's your car and your chauffeur. Tim can be picked up at his drugstore in the afternoons, and we'll start our expeditions from there. We'll see everything. Do you know there's a place not so far off called Death Valley? What about that for an expedition!" He caught hold of Jane. "And we've you to thank, bless you."

John's gaiety was catching. Bee and Peaseblossom forgot Aunt Cora's nervous spell. Rachel, for the moment, stopped feeling like a worm or caring about her clothes. Tim was so enthralled by the sound of Death Valley that he hopped around the car, repeating the exciting words. Jane's black dog dropped off her shoulder. It was happening! It was coming true! She was the important one. "We've you to thank, bless you."

In California it did not get dark the way it did in England. In England there was a soft grayishness which very slowly grew thicker until it was black night. In California the sun shone; then it flamed into a sunset; then it popped out of sight all in a matter of minutes. It happened then. One minute they were looking at the car, and the next John had to turn on its lights to drive it into the garage.

151

"I do like nights in California," Rachel said. "There are such a lot of stars."

Tim was still hopping around, saying, "Death Valley." He stopped in the middle of a hop. "What I like is that singing from all the trees as soon as it's dark. Bella says it's tree frogs."

Jane took a deep breath. "I like it all, and it likes me."

That was a very Jane-ish remark, but nobody mentioned it. Instead Bee said, "I'm glad, darling. I can't tell you how much I hope you'll go on feeling like that."

17

Clothes, Inflections, and a Piano

Rachel's day with Posy Fossil made a great difference to her. On Sunday morning, as breakfast was finished, she decided what to do about her clothes. She would rush up and put on her m'audition dress, with her coat over it so that Peaseblossom and Bee would not notice what she had on. This worked perfectly. Posy turned up to fetch her punctually at ten, and Rachel rushed down to her. Peaseblossom smiled to see her so pleased and excited and shamed her by congratulating her on taking a coat. Bee kissed her and asked if she had her bathing suit and ballet shoes, and nobody noticed her frock.

The drive to Posy's home was lovely because they talked ballet all the way, and it was only when they were walking across Posy's garden to the swimming pool that Rachel remembered her frock, and then for the very opposite reason she had supposed she would think of it. Posy's sister Pauline, the film star, was lying on a chair in the sun. She got up when she heard Posy's voice and came across the lawn to meet them. One look, and Rachel saw that what Pauline was wearing was almost an exact copy of the cotton frock she had taken off as unsuitable. Pauline was not a bit what Rachel had supposed film stars were like. She was not as bouncy a person as Posy, but just as easy to talk to; in fact, the only thing about her which was what Rachel had expected was that she was beautiful. She kissed Rachel and told her the whole family was thrilled to have her with them, as they all wanted to know the latest news from England. Then she took her by the arm and introduced her to her guardian, whom she called Garnie, saying that most people called Garnie Aunt Sylvia, and Rachel could, too. The Fossils' old nurse, Nana, who had taken Rachel to the audition, was sitting by the swimming pool, darning a pair of Posy's tights. She gave Rachel a friendly, welcoming smile. Then came the moment Rachel dreaded. Nana said, "Take off that hot coat, dear, and give it to me."

Rachel took off the coat. Her cheeks were pink with shame when she had to let them see that she was wearing a red crepe de chine dress made from Peaseblossom's old evening dress. Aunt Sylvia gave Rachel a quick, surprised glance, and Rachel could feel she was thinking, "Funny, she does not look as if she would wear clothes like that on a Sunday morning." Posy was practicing dancing steps and not noticing what Rachel wore, but Pauline's face was half amused, half sympathetic. Nana, though, was a person who said what she thought.

"Good gracious, child, what did your mother send you in that dress for? There's no audition today. You've come to play in the garden. Take it off, and put on your bathing suit. Later I'll find you one of Posy's playsuits."

Rachel's cheeks grew redder. She wished a crack would appear in the ground so she could slide through it and disappear. She had never thought that the Fossil family would think Bee had let her wear that frock. She said in a whisper, "Mom doesn't know I'm wearing this. It's m'audition dress."

Pauline flung her arms around Rachel.

"I knew it! I knew it! Oh, Garnie, isn't she like us!"

After that the day became heavenly. Aunt Sylvia, Nana, Pauline, and Posy could not talk fast enough to tell Rachel about themselves when they had lived in London and gone to Madame Fidolia's academy. Rachel had never imagined that Pauline or Posy could ever have been poor. She had thought of them as always having been rich and successful, but they had been really poor once and had had a dreadful struggle to go to auditions in the right clothes. Pauline said the minute Rachel took off her coat she knew that she had on her m'audition dress and that she guessed she was trying to wear the right clothes for California, for that was just what she would have done when she was Rachel's age. The Fossils' conversation was all of the "Do you remember?" sort, and all the remembering was how frocks had been obtained for special occasions. When at last they stopped remembering, Rachel felt so at home that she found herself telling them not only about Jane acting the part of Mary but how she felt about it.

"Oh, don't I know!" Pauline said.

Posy, who was dancing, stopped dead at that.

"You don't. Petrova never could act at all, let alone have a part you wanted."

Pauline explained to Rachel that she, Posy, and a third sister, Petrova, were all adopted and only sisters because they had chosen to share the name of Fossil. That Petrova, the second eldest, had been at Madame Fidolia's and done a few things on the stage, but she had always hated it because she wanted to fly. During the war, she had been a ferry pilot, ferrying new airplanes from the factories to the air bases. Now she was working in the experimental part of an airplane factory.

Posy broke in there. "She's inventing something that's going to put the name of Fossil into the history books. You'll see."

Pauline nodded as if that were certain. "But I know how you feel about Jane. Because I've felt like that about Posy."

155

Posy stood on one leg, holding the other over her head. "Me! Why? You never wanted to dance."

"I shouldn't have thought," Rachel told Pauline, "you'd ever have felt left behind, because you've always been a success. You played Alice in *Wonderland* when you were twelve."

Pauline was pulling off her dress, under which she had a bathing suit. "Yes, but I've always wanted to be a great actress. I want to act Viola in *Twelfth Night,* and Portia, and Rosalind—oh, such hundreds of parts—and here I am making movies."

"You were sweetly pretty in that last one," Nana interrupted.

Pauline threw her frock onto a chair. " 'Sweetly pretty' just describes it." She undid Rachel's frock. "Put on your bathing suit, and thank your stars you haven't got the part of Mary or been picked for *Pirouette.* You be like Posy—know what you want, and scorn all the things that aren't part of what you want."

Nana took the red crepe de chine dress from Rachel. "You have a nice swim, dear, and later Posy can bring you up to her room. I'm going to look at a lot of things she'll never wear again that will come in nicely for you."

Aunt Sylvia looked worried. "What about your mother? Will she mind?"

Nana was moving toward the house with Rachel's things over her arm. "Nonsense, Miss Sylvia, putting ideas like that in the child's head! You can send a nice note to Mrs. Winter. Pretty things to wear will make you feel a lot better, won't they, dear?"

The clothes, the fact that Posy gave her a present of three dancing lessons a week with Madame Donna, and that John could drive her to them did make Rachel feel much better. It was a good thing, for she had a lot to put up with in the next few weeks. Jane and Jane's appointments seemed to be the only things anybody talked about.

Jane did not make life easy for Rachel. Rachel tried at first to be nice and talk about Jane's work, and in fact, she really was interested in everything that happened at the studio. But Jane was simply awful. She nearly always answered, "It's no good telling you about that; you wouldn't understand." Nobody could like that sort of thing from anybody, let alone from a younger sister. Many mornings and evenings, when Rachel and Jane were alone in their bedroom, it was all Rachel could do not to hit her.

Tim did not see nearly as much of Jane as Rachel, but the little he did see was enough.

"Jane was always terrible," he grumbled to Rachel, "but now she's nastier than I thought any person could be."

Aunt Cora was the only person who found Jane improved. Soon after Jane's contract had been signed, Aunt Cora gave her first party for the Winters, and she actually bought Jane a frock for it. It was of yellow muslin with little frills at the shoulders, and to go with it there were very short yellow socks and yellow shoes. To explain why she was outfitting Jane and nobody else, Aunt Cora said in her whiny way, "Your Mossel friends have given you plenty of clothes, Rachel, and Tim's all right, but Jane seems to have nothing to wear, and she should have now." She said "now" in such a way that it sounded as if acting the part of Mary had made Jane into somebody new.

Jane behaved beautifully to Aunt Cora. She flung her arms around her and told her she was the nicest aunt in the world. Rachel and Tim thought this the final awfulness of Jane, considering how she spoke about Aunt Cora as a rule. They gave very good imitations of people being sick to show how they felt; but that only made Jane worse, and she kissed Aunt Cora again.

157

On the night of the party Jane was a person none of the family had ever seen before. Not a sign of black-doggishness, not a sign of being bored at handing around plates; instead she was all smiles and politeness. Aunt Cora had explained that well-brought-up American girls curtsied when they met people, and Jane even agreed to that. Rachel and Tim, standing about unnoticed, heard over and over again, "This is my niece Jane, who has taken over little Ursula Gidden's part in *The Secret Garden*." Then they watched Jane curtsy and smile and saw Aunt Cora's friends look admiring and say she was cute and darling.

John, Bee, and Peaseblossom were enjoying the party so much, for they found Aunt Cora's friends amusing and gay, that they did not have much time to notice the children. Bee did say, "Oh, dear, do look at Jane playing up to Cora. She'll be dreadful tomorrow."

But John only laughed. "Won't do Jane any harm; it's the only time I've seen her give a display of good manners, don't stop her, for goodness' sake."

The real reason why Jane was being so especially awful was a reason nobody guessed. She was absolutely miserable at the studio. Being Jane, instead of admitting she was miserable, she stuck her chin in the air, pretended everything was marvelous, and behaved insufferably. Her hope that everybody at the Bee Bee studios would treat her like royalty had been dashed at the very outset. She was not used in the early scenes of the picture, and so, at the moment, she was just another child going to school. There was a little grandeur when the police at the gates recognized her and John drove the car onto the lot without being questioned, but that was the end of the grandeur.

Nobody could make a person feel more ordinary and unimportant than the people Jane met for the rest of the day. There was Miss Barnabas, head teacher of the school. She did not

158

think it was good for children, whether they were world-famous or not, to be treated differently from children in any ordinary school. She was in charge of a mixed collection of boys and girls between the ages of eight and eighteen. Many of them had faces as well known as Princess Margaret's, but that made no difference to Miss Barnabas: They were treated as ordinary pupils. Jane, whom nobody had ever heard of, really was an ordinary pupil, and to her great annoyance she was not even an especially bright one.

In the Bee Bee studio school there were more teachers than in an ordinary school because at any moment a boy or girl might be wanted on a set, and if that happened, a teacher would have to go along if the child had not completed three hours of lessons for the day. A corner of the floor where the film was being shot would be fixed up as a schoolroom, and to a minute the three hours of lessons would be made up.

Jane was handicapped in some subjects, like history, because it was taught differently and from a different angle in the United States, but even without that she knew that she was going to have to work very hard to keep up. Unfortunately for Jane, her way of trying to keep her end up when she felt it was down was to be truculent and unpleasant. Before she had been in the school a week, Miss Barnabas was saying to the other teachers, "Jane Winter seems badly raised." That remark would have scandalized Peaseblossom if she had heard it.

The other people Jane met each day were Mrs. Gates of the wardrobe department and Miss Steiman, the coach. The large wardrobe for Mary had to be made over for Jane, and this seemed to her to take hours and hours. She thought it all unnecessary, the dresses fitting well enough without being altered as far as she could see. She did not say what she thought about the fittings, for there was something about the cool competence of Mrs. Gates which kept her silent. But she

159

looked at her most black-doggish, and her expression did not escape Mrs. Gates. Several times she said to her seamstresses, "What a bad-tempered child that little Jane Winter is," and the seamstresses sighed and said how different from dear little Ursula. Ursula was loved by everybody, it seemed. She was a sweet-tempered, nice-mannered, clever child, and though Jane had never seen her, she grew to hate her. The more she thought about Ursula, the higher her chin stuck in the air and the sulkier she looked.

The worst trial of Jane's day was the time she spent with Miss Steiman. This happened every afternoon; Miss Steiman worked with Jane on her part. Every line that she had to say had to be said in a certain way, and that depended on what Miss Steiman called inflections. Every afternoon Jane heard, "Your inflections, Jane! . . . Your inflections!" The word "inflection" made Jane furious. She could not see, if she said a line in the right tone, that it mattered if she got the right inflection or not, and she fought Miss Steiman over every line. The truth was that Jane, who had never acted in her life, did not really understand what an inflection was, and she did not try to learn. Every day poor Miss Steiman, who was a patient woman, said, "I'd rather coach anybody else for twelve hours than spend half an hour with that little Jane Winter. That child just wears me out."

The one nice part of Jane's day was the time spent with David Doe. David had Bob, Mickey, two more squirrels, a baby fox, a crow, a pheasant, seven rabbits, and a pony in a kind of little zoo on the lot. Every afternoon Jane was taken by Bee to play with David and his creatures. Actually this was part of her work; but Jane did not know this, and the time spent with David was perfect. They never talked much because David was busy. None of the birds or animals was allowed to be fed by anybody but him. When they saw him, therefore, they connected him first with food and would fly or jump to him and nuzzle or peck in his pockets or at his hands. What Jane had to do was to be about every day so that they all would get used to her and treat David with the same confidence when Jane was there as they did when she was not. Actually better than that happened. Jane, so difficult with human beings, was a different person with birds and animals. If Miss Barnabas, Mrs. Gates, or Miss Steiman had seen her then, they would not have believed their eyes, for a gentle, shining-eyed Jane was not a person they had ever met.

One day Miss Steiman told Bee that the shooting of *The Secret Garden* had reached the place where Mary came into the story. Jane would start working the next day. In the funny way things seemed to happen in California, it was a day when there was news for everybody. Rachel had a phone message from Posy Fossil. Manoff had said she might attend a rehearsal. Everybody the Winters knew in England had written letters which arrived that day. A gentleman was taking an interest in Tim from the point of view of putting him on a radio show.

Peaseblossom had driven the Ford over to fetch Jane and Bee and knew none of the excitements. So when Jane strutted into the hall and announced, "They start filming me as Mary tomorrow," her words were drowned. Rachel danced up to Bee and flung her arms around her.

"Imagine! Tomorrow Monsieur Manoff will let me watch a rehearsal. Isn't it the most gorgeous thing that ever happened to anybody!"

Tim, who was playing his imaginary grand piano, stopped in the middle of a concerto. "I may be going to play a piano on the radio. A man's coming to see Dad about it."

The family gasped. On the radio! What a dream come true!

Aunt Cora clasped her head. "Radio! This is too much. You know, John, when I invited you all, I never thought

161

of such things happening. I'm worn out with all this excitement.''

John laughed. "Don't worry, old girl. You look upon us as you might upon a snowstorm—just a passing affair. When we've gone, you might miss us, you never know.''

18

The First Day's Shooting

Mr. Hiram P. Sneltzworther, who wanted Tim to play on a radio program, came to call the next afternoon, and in Aunt Cora's living room he did a lot of talking. Mr. Sneltzworther said he was a man who had made himself. He had started as a small boy selling newspapers, and today he was just about the most important dealer in secondhand cars. Surely John and Aunt Cora had heard of *Hiram's Hour*? Luckily Aunt Cora had. John took refuge behind Aunt Cora's saying, "Why, of course. Everybody knows *Hiram's Hour*," and just grunted in a way which could have meant yes and could have meant no. Mr. Sneltzworther said he never let himself rest. There was never a moment day or night when he was not looking for something new for *Hiram's Hour*. So when he ran out of cigarettes outside the Antonios' store and happened to hear Tim play, he had a brain wave.

"I can see him, Mr. Winter. The hall packed with people. And Junior sitting at a great big piano, playing something catchy and perhaps cracking a few jokes with the announcer. You needn't worry about the formalities. Approval has to come from the Society for the Prevention of Cruelty to Children; but it's not a complicated matter, and the radio people will give you all the help you need."

Aunt Cora was so pleased she was almost signing a contract for Tim when John stopped her. He said decisions of that sort he left to his children to decide, so he called Tim in.

John placed Tim between his knees so that he would not fidget and explained as clearly as he could what Mr. Sneltzworther wanted. When he finished, Tim thought for a minute and said nothing. Mr. Sneltzworther was afraid Tim might not be appreciating the wonderful opportunity he was being given.

"My announcer's the funniest man. I've heard folks say they laugh more at him than at Bob Hope. And just think of all you could buy with a few bucks. . . ."

Tim swung around to face Mr. Sneltzworther.

"Enough bucks to rent a piano?"

"If you go over big enough, to rent two or three pianos."

Tim's face was scarlet. How pleased Bella would be! Even she had not thought that the Lord would be sending more than one piano.

"I want only one piano, but if there are enough bucks, I should like some music."

John gave Tim an affectionate slap. "Excuse my offspring's sounding mercenary. They all understand that while they are over here, any money they need for lessons and so on they've got to earn."

Tim wanted to tell Bella about the piano. He said good-bye to Mr. Sneltzworther, who looked admiringly after him.

"Quite a kid!"

Rachel was having the day of her life. Manoff was working his company in a new ballet. It was very intricate and technical and full of lifts and difficult positions. When there was a pause in the rehearsal, the final touch was given to Rachel's happiness. Monsieur Manoff himself spoke to her. He asked her how she found his ballet. Rachel was too shy to say much, but she did stammer that it was lovely, and Posy quite perfect. Manoff smiled at that and kissed his fingers toward Posy's back.

"Such a one is born not once in a century. Each day I wake singing because I have the privilege to work with her."

Jane was having a horrible day. It started all right. She found she had a dear little dressing room with a yellow settee and yellow-painted furniture. It was the custom to send flowers to the leading artists on their first day in a new picture, and Mr. Bettelheimer had sent her a Victorian posy, and Mr. Browne a box of gardenias and a fat envelope. In the envelope was a typed list of dog foods. Every sort of delicacy a dog could fancy. Many of them were such grand things that Chewing-gum had never tasted them. On the bottom was written, "Please mark anything Chewing-gum would like and let me have his address."

That was the end of the niceness of the day. Shooting had been going on for some time on *The Secret Garden*. It was turning out to be a difficult picture to make, but everybody who had seen the beginning part of it run through was excited about it and said very nice things about it to Jane's-Mr. Browne. People had said, "If it goes on this way . . ."

Mr. Browne had smiled and looked confident and answered, "Why not? We've David Doe and young Maurice Tuesday."

All the important people had said, "That's so," and they had not said, what clearly they were thinking, "But you haven't got Ursula Gidden."

Jane's-Mr. Browne had sighed and thought, "How right they are, I have not," and he held his thumbs and said over and over again, "Jane will be all right. I know she'll be all right."

Jane, because she had felt unimportant and had made herself disliked ever since she had been at school on the studio lot, had counted more than anyone could have guessed on how wonderful life would be once she had started playing the part of Mary. It was an important part; everybody would be bound to treat her with respect.

As Mr. Phelps led Jane by the hand onto the set, all the people who were making the picture—Jane's-Mr. Browne, Mr. Phelps, who was the assistant director, Mr. Browne's secretary, the camera crew, the lighting men, the ground electricians, the sound control man, the greens men, who were in charge of special effects in the garden, the script girl, the men and women from the wardrobe department, the hairdresser, and the still-camera man—looked at her. They had kind, friendly expressions but, of course, showed none of the respect Jane had hoped for because she had done nothing so far for them to respect. They were a hardworking team of men and women whose business was making films, and they were looking at an unknown little English girl and hoping for everybody's sake that the big risk Mr. Bryan J. Browne had taken in letting her play the part of Mary was going to prove worthwhile.

Jane found that when he was in the middle of making a picture, Her-Mr. Browne was quite a different person from the Mr. Browne she had seen sitting on his porch. People were important to him only when they were part of making a scene, and he forgot they were even alive when they were not part of a scene. When Mr. Phelps brought Jane onto the set, Mr. Browne wanted her, but he wanted her to be like a piece of Plasticine that he could make into any shape he liked. He put his arm around her and showed her the set. He explained it was a railway carriage, and he was just going to tell her exactly how he wanted her to feel when Jane interrupted him. She honestly thought she was saving him trouble by letting him know he was wasting his time telling her things she knew already.

"I know all this. I sit there, and Mrs. Medlock sits there,

166

and we eat our lunch out of a basket and she tells me about my uncle and I tell her about India.''

Mr. Browne would have liked to take Jane by the shoulders and give her a good shake. However, Jane was not his to shake, so instead he kept his temper and beckoned Mr. Phelps over and told him to introduce her to Annie and see if she knew her lines. He would take the run-through in a minute.

Mr. Phelps was young and energetic. His mother had come from Ireland, and Irish people never mind saying what they think. Mr. Phelps was very much like his mother. He had a lot of black hair, and he ran a hand through it and looked sternly at Jane. "Will you hold your tongue and do what I tell you?''

Jane was angry and hurt. This was not the way she had expected things to be. "Why's My-Mr. Browne gone away? Why's he looking cross? I know what I've got to do, and I only told him so.''

"*Your* Mr. Browne, is it? Well, if you want to please your Mr. Browne, you'll not tell him anything. He'll tell *you*.''

"But why shouldn't I? I'm being Mary; it's an important part.''

Mr. Phelps threw his head back and roared with laughter.

"And you are the living, breathing image of Mary.'' Then he stopped laughing and looked stern again. "Now, look, I'm your friend. I want to help you. You get any nonsense out of your head about the importance of your part. Young Ursula Gidden, who's made more money for this company than you or I will ever see, is as mild a child as you would find in a walk across the world. Remember that, and maybe in a week or two, if you come to me and ask me nicely, I'll tell you something which you'll be glad to know.''

A stout elderly woman with black hair came onto the set. She wore a long, full dress of purple, with a black cape trimmed with sequins and a black bonnet with strings under her chin. She came straight up to Jane.

"Hello, my dear. I'm Annie Street. I'm English, too. Yorkshire, what's more."

Jane liked the look of Annie Street. "Are you playing Mrs. Medlock?"

"Yes, and you've got to hate me, so don't smile like that." Annie Street turned to Mr. Phelps. "Can we have a run-through?"

Considering that she had never acted, Jane did not find the first day's shooting very hard. Mary was a child who had been brought up in India, where, in the days when *The Secret Garden* was written, Indian servants spoiled English children abominably and allowed them to treat them in the rudest way. Jane's-Mr. Browne, having got over wanting to shake Jane, came back and worked hard on her. He was sure, from what he had seen of her, that Jane could be made to play the scenes with Mrs. Medlock just right. What he did not know was what a help Mr. Phelps was. During a moment when Mr. Browne was talking to Annie Street, Mr. Phelps whispered, "Get it out of your head that that's Annie Street. There must be somebody you'd like to snub."

Jane thought of cool, competent Mrs. Gates. Mrs. Gates in her white coat, looking at her as if she were less than a caterpillar.

"There is."

"A he or a she?"

"A she."

"Well, speak to her then, and you'll do fine."

Bee was, to her surprise, finding that she liked her first day in the studio. She had been scared that she would feel awkward and in the way with the actors and actresses. Actually there were not many actresses and actors about, for they were not needed in the railway sequences. There was, however, somebody who made Bee feel at home at once.

Jane had a stand-in, a girl called Shirley Norstrum. Shirley was doing lessons when Jane came on the set. Shirley's work was to sit or stand in the places where Jane would have to sit or stand when the shooting took place. Focusing on Shirley, the camera and lighting men got their correct positions. While Shirley stood in for Jane, Jane could have her clothes changed or finish her lessons. When she came onto the set, everything was ready for shooting. Stand-ins like Shirley saved time in picture making.

Like every other child who worked in pictures, Shirley had to have someone to look after her in the studio, and that person was her mother. Mrs. Norstrum was the perfect person for Bee to meet. There was nothing at all about studio life that Mrs. Norstrum did not know. Moreover, her life was much more like life as Bee knew it in England. Mrs. Norstrum had her housework and her shopping to do, and from what she said, shopping was hard work because many things to eat cost more than people like the Norstrums could afford to pay.

Listening to Mrs. Norstrum, Bee felt cozier and more at home than she had felt since she arrived.

"Oh, dear, I'm glad I met you! I was so scared of coming here. But you'll tell me all the things I want to know and give me a hint if Jane isn't doing the right things."

Mrs. Norstrum liked Bee and smiled, but inside, she felt worried for her. Shirley, of course, went to the studio school. She had not spoken much to Jane, but she knew her, and she knew what everybody thought about her. What Shirley had said was "That Jane Winter is certainly a horrid girl." So Mrs. Norstrum, wanting to help and liking Bee, dared give a hint. "If Jane does her best, and runs to her lessons when she's called and plays quietly between shots with Shirley or Maurice or David and their stand-ins, she'll do fine."

At that moment there was a call for silence, as a scene was being shot. Then Jane's voice could be heard answering Mrs. Medlock, "I shall not want to go poking about."

Actually it was said exactly right, in a mixture of Jane's worst black-doggish and being-grand moods. Although it was right, it made Bee sigh. Somehow she could not see Jane running to her lessons and playing quietly with the other children, and she wondered more than ever if she and John had been right to let her act in *The Secret Garden*.

19

Maurice Tuesday

Shooting had been going on for several days when Jane first met Maurice Tuesday. It was Miss Barnabas who introduced him.

"Maurice is British, too. You should get on wonderfully."

Though she had made no friends in the school, Jane had managed to pick up what the boys and girls thought of Maurice, and it was not complimentary. Actually Miss Barnabas was trying to be kind and helpful in bringing Jane and Maurice together. She thought that since they were of the same nationality and both difficult, they might get on well together. Jane, hating the school, hating Miss Barnabas, bitterly disappointed about the way a person playing the important part of Mary was treated, too proud to tell her family she was miserable, jumped to the conclusion that what Miss Barnabas meant was "You are just as bad as Maurice, whom nobody likes," which quite honestly Miss Barnabas might have meant, only she did not. So straightaway, without bothering to find out what Maurice was like, Jane pressed her lips together and thought, "We won't get on wonderfully. I'm going to hate him. I know I am."

Maurice was a startlingly good-looking boy. He had fair hair and huge blue-gray eyes, which he could, with no trouble at all, fill with tears. He had been brought to America by his mother as a refugee from London during the Second

171

World War. Even before he acted in pictures, Mrs. Tuesday thought Maurice the most wonderful boy in the world. She thought he was so precious he ought not to mix with ordinary children. She hated his going to the studio school and gave in only because the studio threatened to cancel his contract if she insisted on his having a private tutor. The truth was the Bee Bee studio company knew that if Maurice had a tutor, he would never do any lessons, for his mother spoiled him so, he had only to say he didn't want to do something and he didn't have to do it.

After two hours of lessons a call came for Maurice and Jane to go to the studio. Since they had still an hour of lessons to do, a teacher took them over. She walked behind, talking to Maurice's mother, and Jane and Maurice were sent on ahead. They just eyed each other at first, like two dogs who have a fight in mind. Then Maurice said, in the grandest, most irritating voice, "Wonderful chance for you, playing Mary."

Jane quickly turned over rude answers in her mind. "Thank goodness I'm not you, having to act that sissy Colin."

Maurice truly thought Jane incredibly ignorant. "That's in the book. Of course, he's quite different in the film script. My public wouldn't let me play an unattractive part."

Jane felt like a kettle when it's boiling and the lid's about to blow out. Maurice was the very top of annoyingness, and the most annoying thing about him was that he was being grand in the way she herself had always wanted to be. When she was able to speak, her voice was rude, even for Jane.

"Your public! Who are they? We never heard of you before, but we have heard of David Doe." Out of the corner of her eye Jane saw that Maurice didn't like that, so she added, "My-Mr. Browne said about David, 'That boy's something out of this world.' He didn't say anything like that about you."

172

Maurice gave a sniggering laugh. "*Your*-Mr. Browne! That's funny! I must tell everybody that. *Your*-Mr. Browne!"

Jane stopped, her eyes shining with temper. "He is My-Mr. Browne. He told me to call him that. Do you know, I think you're exactly like Colin in the beginning of *The Secret Garden,* and goodness knows I couldn't say worse of anybody."

They had reached studio twelve. Maurice marched in, but over his shoulder he whispered so the teacher and his mother would not hear, "And I know why they let you play Mary. You're exactly like she was when the children in India christened her Mistress Mary Quite Contrary."

That was the beginning of the bad patch for everybody working on *The Secret Garden.* Because Jane was acting Mary, Her-Mr. Browne was letting her be the real Mary, the sour, crabbed, bad-tempered little girl whom nobody liked in the beginning of the story. That was all right for a day or two, but of course, quite soon there were sequences where Colin and Mary should have begun to make friends with each other. That was hopeless. Maurice, who really could act, was delightful in the scenes, but Jane, who could not, went on speaking to Colin exactly as she went on feeling about Maurice. Her-Mr. Browne cajoled, beseeched, almost prayed. Mr. Phelps tried to help. Miss Steiman worked with Jane on inflections for hours. Nobody could understand why she could not look pleasant, and smile, and say simple lines like "The moor is the most beautiful place. Thousands of little creatures live on it. All busy making nests and holes and burrows, and chippering or singing or squeaking to each other." Miss Steiman swore Jane could say the lines charmingly, with shining eyes, as if she could see the moor and the little creatures that lived on it, but she did not when Mr. Browne wanted her to.

What nobody knew except Jane was what Maurice did to her. While he was acting, he looked like an angel, but the moment the cameras stopped turning and the lights were out he whispered things like "Now you're for it. . . . Look how depressed everybody is. . . . I should think you're the worst girl Mr. Browne—*Your*-Mr. Browne—ever had to direct." Or, just as they were starting a scene: "Even the camera crew have given up hope. They say you stink, which is the worst thing a camera crew can say." Then, on the words "Silence, everybody," there he would be, looking angelic.

Poor Bee suffered terribly. Mrs. Norstrum was as kind as she could be, but even she couldn't pretend that anybody was pleased with Jane. She knew that the studio gossip was that Mr. Browne was losing heart, and it was possible even now that he would postpone production. Jane's-Mr. Browne was as nice to Bee as he could be, but that was not very nice because he was feeling desperate. The cast was kind, and the crew working on the picture was kind; but Bee could see it was just the kindness of people who were sorry for her. The worst thing was that Bee did not know what to say to Jane. She knew that days were being wasted because Jane could not get her scenes right, but she could not blame Jane. After all, Jane had never said she could act; it was Her-Mr. Browne who had given her the part. It was quite natural, really, that Jane should not be able to act; it would have been surprising if she could. Bee thought it would be a mistake to talk about Jane's studio troubles at home; it couldn't help poor Jane, and it would perhaps spoil everybody else's good time.

Everybody else's good time was one reason why Bee did not even tell John she was worried. He was so happy and was writing well. Rachel appeared to be enjoying her dancing lessons. Tim, though he had not yet appeared on *Hiram's Hour,* was practicing for it and seemed in radiant spirits. Even Aunt Cora was cheerful. She was enjoying having her housework done for her and gave herself over to what she really enjoyed—parties. It was almost Thanksgiving, and she was planning a big party for that as well as for Christmas. Peaseblossom was living in a dream-come-true world. She had always wanted to travel, and now that John had the car, she was seeing California. They were leaving long expeditions until after Christmas, but already they had been up the mountains, to old Spanish missions along the coast, and to orange and lemon estates. Peaseblossom was a person who was determined not to waste her traveling opportunities. Wherever she went she took her camera, a notebook, and three reference books: one on the birds of California; one on the flowers, trees, and shrubs; and one on animals. And whenever the children were near, she tried to educate them.

Because John and Bee were always going to parties in the evenings with Aunt Cora, and because the California sun had given Bee's cheeks color and California food was making her fatter, John did not at first notice how worried she was. Then one Saturday he did notice and from that minute would not let any time pass before he knew everything.

"You can't think how dreadful I feel," Bee explained. "You said it would do Jane good to shine, but you ought to see what's happening, poor scrap."

"Does she say anything about the part to you?"

"Not a word. Only that she hates Maurice Tuesday."

"What's the boy really like? I've only heard Jane's view."

"I don't know. I must say he seems a conceited little horror, but he certainly can act. I don't think it's his fault he's the way he is. I simply can't stand Mrs. Tuesday. I never speak to her more than I can help. She's a really silly woman. The boy's father's dead, and the moment the war started she rushed across the Atlantic to stay with some unfortunate Americans, who must have been driven mad by her. She thinks Maurice is perfect and never stops talking about him, and I'm so ashamed because she's English."

John thought for a bit.

"Stop worrying. I'm sorry for the Bee Bee Film Company, and Jane's-Mr. Browne, but it was their idea and not ours that they should sign Jane on; if she's no good, that's their funeral. What we've got to worry about is Jane. I hoped this film was going to give her a chance to shine, but if it's going to mean that after all the excitement she's to be thrown out, she's got to see the situation straight. She must understand that to us she's our Jane and we don't care a bit if she never acts the wretched Mary. Thank goodness tomorrow's Sunday. I shall take her out and have a good talk with her."

Jane was surprised and pleased but a little suspicious when John said he was taking her for a drive. Everybody liked going for Sunday drives, and it was a bit queer that only she was going. It was particularly queer that the others did not make a fuss. Jane did not know that John had seen first Rachel and then Tim and asked them not to argue. Tim was quite willing. Some time ago Mr. Antonio had said, "There will come that Sunday when you don't go with your papa; then you'll come to us and eat ravioli," and Mrs. Antonio had nodded and smiled. "You play the hymns while I cook the food." Tim had no idea what ravioli was, but he was sure he would like it. And this was the Sunday for it.

Rachel was not so easy to handle. Aside from her three dancing lessons a week, which she enjoyed, she was leading a routine schoolroom life, while Jane went lioning off every day to the studio. If on top of that Jane was to have special treats on Sunday, it really was too much.

"But, Dad, why only Jane?"

John did not like tale-telling, but he thought he could trust Rachel. "I think she's bitten off more than she can chew up at the studio, and I want to find out all about it."

"You mean, she mightn't play Mary after all?"

"Your mother thinks that could happen."

Rachel had an awful wrestle with her voice not to let it

176

sound pleased. Inside, she could not help being pleased. Jane had been cocky and difficult, and in Rachel's opinion, a snub like that was just what she needed.

"Goodness!"

John held her by the shoulders. "And if that happens, you've got to be nice. You and Tim were the lucky ones when talents were handed out. If Jane loses this part, she's going to take it hard."

"I'll be as nice as I can, but she's not been a bit nice to me since she had that contract."

John gave her a kiss. "I daresay you've put up with a lot, but we may find old Jane has been up against it ever since she went to the studio. Anyway, you say nothing about my taking her for this drive, and next week you and I will have a jaunt."

"Just us?"

"Just us. We'll go out to lunch."

Sunday was a lovely day, with the sunshine at its most golden. John and Jane drove to Santa Barbara. It was lovely, built like a town in Spain, with white houses in beautiful gardens and bougainvillaea tumbling over white walls. They ate gorgeous Mexican food called tortillas. When they were pleasantly full and contented, John drove the car out of Santa Barbara and parked it by the ocean. Then he suggested that they lie on the sand and that Jane tell him all about *The Secret Garden*.

So at last Jane found herself able to pour out her misery.

On the whole, she was quite fair, and she did tell the whole story: what she had hoped and how things had turned out and how, in spite of everything, she still wanted to be Mary and would mind most dreadfully if the part were taken away from her.

177

John lay on his back and smoked his pipe all the time she was talking. When she had quite finished, he sat up.

"Then you haven't seen David Doe since the shooting began?"

"No. I don't meet him while we're doing interiors."

"Do you know where he lives?"

"Sort of. Why?"

"Because we're going off right now to call on him. I expect he's acted lots of times with people he didn't like, and he's probably got a way of dealing with the situation. Anyway, let's ask; I feel I shall like David."

Jane got up, her face happy for the first time for weeks.

"Could we! Could we really go and see him? Oh, Dad, what a marvelous idea! He knows how to tame anything. I believe he'd even know how to tame that awful Maurice."

It was not difficult to find David's home. The neighborhood children were playing around, and of course, they could point out where David lived. Mrs. Doe answered the door. She was more than thin; she was gaunt. Looking at her, you could tell that life had not been easy for the Does. She looked as if she had tried so hard, and worked such long hours, that she was like a spring wound so tight it could not unwind. Mrs. Doe was evidently used to visitors. She took the arrival of John and Jane as a matter of course and asked them out to the porch.

On the porch Mr. Doe was reading the paper, and Gardner, the older boy, a book. David was repairing a rabbit hutch. Mrs. Doe had evidently been mending, because her mending basket, piled high with Mr. Doe's and the boys' clothes, was beside a rocking chair. John apologized to Mr. Doe for disturbing him on a Sunday afternoon, but Mr. Doe said he was not disturbing him at all. He threw down his paper. At once a little breeze caught it and blew the sheets across the backyard. Jane and the two boys rushed after the sheets to

178

pick them up. While Jane was picking the paper up, John got a chance to tell the Does why he and Jane had come. It was easier when Jane was not listening because he could say bluntly that he believed she was no earthly good but that she still wanted to play the part and thought she could do it if only she could get over not liking Maurice Tuesday. Because Jane was not there, Mr. Doe, in his gentle, drawling voice, told John that he knew things were going badly, that they had been warned the picture might not be made after all.

Jane came back to the porch, her arms full of papers, and said, "We're not allowed to criticize things in America because we're visitors, but I must say I do wonder why Americans need so much Sunday paper. In our house Aunt Cora takes two, and Bella, her cook, takes another, and by Sunday evening everything's simply covered with paper."

Mrs. Doe looked at Jane with a soft expression on her queer, hard face. She knew from Jane's voice that what she wanted to say was "It's an idiotic waste printing all that." Mrs. Doe had all her life been a person who had wanted to say that certain ways of doing things were idiotic. She had been too busy since she married Mr. Doe to say anything much, but she still felt that way. She liked the look of Jane and even the rather truculent Jane-ish way in which she spoke. She took the papers from her, folded them, and laid them down. She said to Mr. Doe, "Pa, Jane'll come in the kitchen and help me fix something to eat. You and the boys stay right where you are."

Mrs. Doe had a lovely kitchen, full of little canisters painted bright scarlet. While she was frosting a cake, fixing milk shakes, and making coffee, she talked. At first Jane thought she was making just ordinary conversation. She told Jane about herself. How she had always planned to do things. Always wanted to start something and go places, but she never had. Then her elder boy, Gardner, turned out the spitting image of her. He wanted to do things and go places, and that was hard, for he needed expensive books and instruments. Then David got into the movies, which meant they had a little more money, and someone nearby had just the instruments and books Gardner needed, and now he was all set to go to college when the time came. She turned to Jane to be sure she was listening, and that was when Jane felt that there was a purpose behind this story. "Has David ever told you about his chipmunk?" Mrs. Doe asked.

"The one he was playing his pipe to when the men from the Bee Bee film unit first found him?"

Mrs. Doe nodded. Nippie, David called him. And Nippie—though Jane mustn't tell David she had said so—was just about the meanest chipmunk in the world. He was always good with David, but when David wasn't there, he stole things, upset things, and, worst of all, did all kinds of things just to be annoying. Mrs. Doe could see he hated her and wanted to anger her. Of course, because he was David's pet, she never touched him, never complained about him. And at last she found out how to fix him.

Jane sprawled across the kitchen table. David's chipmunk and Maurice were by then the same person.

"How did you?"

The coffee was boiling. Mrs. Doe poured it into a coffeepot. She smiled as she remembered Nippie. She said there was nothing that kind of no-good, stuck-up chipmunk hated more than not being noticed. It had occurred to her one day that if she acted as if he weren't there, maybe he would find it wasn't such fun trying to upset her. It worked wonderfully, she said. Nippie couldn't understand at first. There he was, like a child trying to attract attention, but no notice was taken of him. When he was bigger and David took him out to the woods, he was a different chipmunk. "Why, right to the day he died," Mrs. Doe went on, "which was just before David came to Hollywood, he never came near the house without looking in at me. Real neighborly, he was."

Jane sprawled even farther across the table. Mrs. Doe moved about so fast that she wanted, if necessary, to be able to catch hold of her and hold her attention.

"Do you know Maurice Tuesday?"

Mrs. Doe was at the refrigerator, pouring cream into a jug. "David never says much, but he's spoken of him."

Jane knew from Mrs. Doe's voice that whatever David had said was not very complimentary, and she was glad. She was certain nobody as nice as David could like Maurice; still, it was satisfying to be sure.

"But David's chipmunk couldn't speak," Jane pointed out. "You had only to watch him. I have to listen to that awful Maurice, saying things just so that I'll do Mary all wrong."

"What's words? Sounds as though he's acting mighty like David's chipmunk."

Jane began to have an idea. Her eyes shone.

"What's a chipmunk like?"

"Like a little squirrel."

Jane's eyes shone more than ever.

"Maurice is a chipmunk. Just a mean, no-good, stuck-up chipmunk. I'll watch him just the way you watched Nippie, but chipmunks can't talk, so if he says things, I just shan't hear him. I'll make a face as though I were thinking of other things. He'll be so cross."

"Madder than a hornet." Mrs. Doe picked up the tray. "Come on."

Jane was just following her when she thought of something. "How did you look at the chipmunk? Like this?" She put on a scornful, proud expression.

"No. I smiled. Just kept on smiling. Acting as if nobody could feel happier."

181

"I can't do that when I'm with Maurice. Nobody could."

Mrs. Doe led the way back to the porch. "I was glad I had. If you stop and think, it was that chipmunk that took us out here, and that same chipmunk will see Gardner through college."

Driving home, so full of strawberry shortcake and strawberry milk shakes that she could hardly bend, Jane told John all about David's chipmunk and how Maurice was a chipmunk.

"I'm beginning to see him. I've never seen a chipmunk, but this chipmunk has fair fur and blue eyes. He skips about, and I don't pay any attention. I just smile and look pleased, and when he speaks, it's just as if he never had, for chipmunks can't."

John had been talking to David and Mr. Doe while Jane was in the kitchen, and he'd heard that Jane's refusal to do anything but scowl at Maurice was part of the trouble.

"I'm glad you'll smile. It's nothing to do with me; I don't care if you are Mary or not. But if *you* want to be, you've got to look as though you were getting to like Maurice."

Jane considered that. "So I will. Chipmunks are sort of squirrels. Nobody could help liking a squirrel. I believe Mrs. Doe almost couldn't help liking Nippie. Anyway, she's glad now about him because David's brother, Gardner, is going through college, and in a way Nippie helped, being there when the Bee Bee film unit came."

"And you're going to be glad of Maurice, because you'll be Mary because of him?"

Jane stuck her chin in the air. "I'm never going to be glad of Maurice, but I'm going to be glad I tamed him. Because I shall; you'll see."

182

20

The Crisis

John did not tell Bee exactly what Mrs. Doe had told Jane, partly because Maurice was Jane's problem, and if she wanted Bee to know how she was handling it, she herself would tell her. Mostly, though, John kept quiet about it because if Jane's plan for taming Maurice was a failure—and John was very much afraid it would be—it was going to be difficult for Bee if people complained that Jane was behaving queerly and Bee knew the reason for the queerness. She could hardly say, "It's because Jane thinks Maurice is a fair-furred, blue-eyed, mean, no-good, stuck-up chipmunk," but her face might show that she knew the reason, and that would be awkward. So John just said that Jane had a new way of tackling the problem, and Bee, who felt more embarrassed every day because of the whisperings at the studio, said she was thankful to hear it, and she did hope it would settle things quickly one way or the other.

Jane's-Mr. Browne had spent an awful Sunday. Till late on Saturday night he had sat hunched up in a velvet armchair in the studio movie theater, watching the film that had been made so far run through. During the first part he kept muttering, "It's good. It's right." From then onward he ran his fingers through his hair till it stood on end, and as sequence followed sequence, he groaned, first to himself but finally out loud.

On Sunday he spoke to nobody. He went for a long drive

up into the mountains with just Hyde Park for company and thought and thought and could not make up his mind. He came home just as the sun was setting. He sat on his porch and looked at the telephone. Should he call up Benjamin Bettelheimer? Should he say, "Let's call the picture off?" Should he? He looked questioningly at Hyde Park.

"What'll I do? Give it a few more days? Give your tail a wag if the answer's yes." Hyde Park got up. He went to his bowl and had a long drink of water. Jane's-Mr. Browne smiled for the first time that day. Then he, too, got up. "Have a drink? Maybe you're right at that." He got himself a Coca-Cola, brought it back to his chair, and sat down. As he sat down, Hyde Park thumped his tail on the floor three times.

At first nobody at the Bee Bee studios believed in what seemed a miracle. There was no one to give a hint of improved times. Jane was no better in school. Miss Barnabas was patient and long-suffering, but there was beginning to be a weary note in her voice when she said the name Jane Winter. Miss Steiman was conscientious and did her duty by Jane's inflections, but she told everybody it would be a weight off her mind the moment she heard that shooting had been stopped on *The Secret Garden*.

The only people who did notice that Jane seemed different were the woman from Mrs. Gates's wardrobe department and the hairdresser. On the Monday following her visit at the Does' Jane was full of her thoughts. Her eyes shone as she let her mind wrap Maurice in fair fur and give him a tail. She was so busy doing this that she never noticed she was being dressed in her frilled pants and petticoat, nor was she conscious of the frock being put over her head. She didn't mind the hairdresser and her curling irons. When Mr. Phelps came for her, the hairdresser looked at the dresser as much as to say, "What's cooking?"

The scene was the one where Mrs. Medlock brings the bad doctor cousin in to Colin and they find him and Mary laughing together, having just found out that they must be cousins. This was the moment when Jane had to be gay and show that she really liked Maurice.

Jane's-Mr. Browne told Jane exactly what he wanted. He had not the faintest hope of getting what he wanted in spite of Hyde Park's faith in her, but there was nothing about the way he spoke to show what his inner feelings were.

The scene started with Colin in bed and Mary sitting by his bed looking at him in a very interested way. Maurice had to say, "Why do you look at me like that? What are you thinking about?"

In the picture Mary was supposed to be thinking how odd he was. Just like a boy raja she had once met in India. What Jane was thinking was "How queer. I'm not pretending anymore. He *is* a fair-furred, stuck-up chipmunk."

Movies are made with a long shot, a two-shot, and a close-up of each person, each taken separately with rearranging of lights, cameras, sound, and so on. After the first shot Maurice said, "Take that silly look off your silly face. They've stopped shooting, and anyway, nobody cares how you look. They're going to give up this picture. You're no good."

"Nibble, nibble at his nut . . . if it's nuts chipmunks eat," thought Jane. "I don't hear anything . . . nothing at all. Aren't chipmunks interesting!"

When the photographers took the next shot, a sort of stunned breathlessness came over everybody. Mr. Browne looked at Mr. Phelps. Mr. Phelps looked at Mr. Browne's secretary. The camera crew made faces at one another. The lighting men nearly dropped off the catwalks. The ground electricians made silent, whistling sounds, and all the people standing about nudged each other. Two shots had been taken and neither needed taking again. In both Jane's expression had been exactly right.

Jane's-Mr. Browne shook his head. His guess was that it was a bit of luck and that trouble would start again when Jane had to speak. But it didn't. Maurice could not think what had happened. He whispered every annoying thing he could think of, but it had no effect on Jane. Whether they were shooting or not, she went on staring at him with an amused, interested face and said nothing at all.

Jane's lines, carefully rehearsed by Miss Steiman, were "I am thinking two things. The first one is that you're like a raja . . . they speak the way you do. The other is how different you are from Dickon."

Jane enjoyed herself. She had never seen a raja, so it was easy to say it and mean a chipmunk, which she had never seen either. As for his being different from Dickon, that certainly was true! Dickon, who was David. Jane's eyes shone, and her lines came out not just as Miss Steiman had coached her to say them, but exactly right.

When the day's work was over and Jane and Bee had left the studio, someone called out, "A miracle. A doggone miracle!"

Jane's-Mr. Browne, who looked as though he had just got over having bad influenza, said to his secretary, "Make a note for me. Order a can of liver for Hyde Park. That dog's sure got sense."

21

Thanksgiving

Thanksgiving was a lovely day. You would have thought that in Aunt Cora's house there was no need for anybody extra to come for Thanksgiving because she had her brother and his family with her already, but Aunt Cora was a great person for parties. In her funny, whiny voice, which sounded as if she could never enjoy anything, she would say, "I could just do with a wonderful time." So for Thanksgiving afternoon she planned an especially gorgeous party, which kept her busy for days beforehand, decorating the house with horns of plenty with flowers and fruit pouring out of them, all of which she made herself.

In the morning John drove everybody to church.

On the way, Rachel said, "I don't think everybody goes to church to say thank you. Aunt Cora is much more interested in her party than in church or Thanksgiving dinner, and I think there are lots of people like her."

Jane stuck her chin in the air.

"As Dad's here, I won't say what I think about Aunt Cora, but I'll tell you who does observe Thanksgiving properly, and that's Bella; not only is she going to her church, but she's sung hymns all the morning."

Aunt Cora's party was a great success, and this time it wasn't only Jane over whom a fuss was made. Over and over again Aunt Cora's whine rose above all the other voices.

"This is my nephew, Tim. You must listen to him next week. He's playing the piano on *Hiram's Hour*."

Jane, in the yellow muslin frock that Aunt Cora had bought her for the first party, was fussed over by Aunt Cora and Aunt Cora's friends, but this time she behaved differently. She was polite, but she did not look half as smug and pleased with herself as she had at the previous party. "How queer," Rachel thought. "Now that Jane really is acting Mary and they're pleased with her, she's nicer instead of worse." What she did not know about was a conversation Jane had had with Mr. Phelps the day before.

It was between shots. Mr. Phelps came up to Jane.

"Come on, Jane. We're ready for you." He took her by the hand and led her to the set. On the way he said, "Seeing you sitting there playing with Shirley, I wouldn't have known you for the same girl I've been fetching all these weeks."

Jane knew just what he meant, but of course, Mr. Phelps did not know why she was doing so much better.

"I like it now. I like it especially now that we're using the garden."

Mr. Phelps stopped and looked at her. "That's not the reason, and you know it. I'm wondering what's made you decide to behave yourself."

Maurice's being a chipmunk was Jane's secret; nobody in the studio was ever going to know that. She wanted to change the subject, and she remembered a way of doing so.

"You said if I asked you someday, you would tell me something I'd like to hear."

"I did too, and now I'll tell you. You're the spitting image of that girl Mary, and though Ursula is the best child actress I ever saw, if you go on as you're doing you'll be better as Mary than she could ever have been."

"Why?"

Mr. Phelps shrugged his shoulders.

"You're contrary and Mary was contrary, but that's not the half of it. Maurice is contrary, and he could make the Statue of Liberty cry. I was saying last week it must be something in the blood, that there wasn't a pin to put between you when it came to conceit and contrariness; now I'm not so sure. There are times when you can be as nice as Ursula or Shirley Norstrum, maybe even as nice as David."

Jane turned scarlet. "I'm not a bit like Maurice."

"Everybody thinks you are. Too good to know anybody. Puffed up like a toad over nothing."

Jane for once was silenced. Was that what everybody was thinking? She was not like Maurice. She would not be like Maurice.

"It's not true; I'm not the smallest, tiniest bit like Maurice."

"We'll see. Personally, I don't believe you are, but everybody else does." Mr. Phelps lowered his voice. "You won't be with us very long. Why not show people they've made a mistake, that you are a darling girl?"

They were on the edge of the set.

"Like David?" Jane asked.

Mr. Phelps nodded. "Like David."

It was very difficult for Jane to change much, but she did notice what was worst in Maurice and tried to be the opposite. So when Aunt Cora's friends said, "My! So you're playing little Ursula Gidden's part! I'll say that's something!" Jane was careful how she replied and said sensible things, such as "It's because I'm like Mary in the book that they've let me act her," with the result that Aunt Cora's friends said to one another, "That little Jane is just the nicest child."

When the party was over, Aunt Cora stretched herself on a sofa while everybody else cleared up. She said giving a party was fun, but what it did to her nerves was nobody's business. Because it was Thanksgiving, the children were being allowed to stay up and eat turkey sandwiches. As they tidied the living room, they looked at Aunt Cora and wondered more than ever how she could be John's sister.

While Bella was fixing the sandwiches, the family went for a short walk up the street. The air was full of the queer, spicy smell which trees and plants seemed to give out in California. The sky was blazing with stars. The ocean rolled in with a gentle swish-swash. The tree frogs raised their nightly hymn. John stood still.

"Listen and smell. It's all so different from home and so exciting. We'll never forget our Thanksgiving here, will we?"

As he spoke, it was as if wild joy grabbed them all. California was exciting. It was different. It was queer. In a minute they were playing follow-the-leader up the street. John was leading. Then came Tim. Then Rachel. Then Peaseblossom. Then Jane and last Bee. John did the silliest, maddest things, which they all copied as well as they could. And as they skipped, hopped, and jumped, they sang a new version of "California, Here I Come," John making up the words as they went along.

22

Christmas

Tim's piano came the week after his first radio show, which was like putting whipped cream on top of an already iced cake, for Tim enjoyed every second of *Hiram's Hour*. Mr. Hiram P. Sneltzworther had said his announcer was just the funniest man, and Tim could not have agreed with him more. The things the announcer thought funny were just the things Tim thought funny, and finding the same things funny is a shortcut to being friends. The announcer, whose name was Brent, liked funny things to happen as well as to be said. He roared with laughter when the seat fell out of the chair somebody was going to sit on or a toy snake jumped out of the piano as the player opened it, and Tim laughed even louder. After the very first broadcast, they were conspirators, planning wilder and better jokes for Hiram's next Hour.

Oddly enough, as well as being perfect about jokes, Brent loved music. Tim had found this out at his first rehearsal; he played several pieces of music and found that discussing music with Brent was like discussing it with Mr. Brown. It was looking at Mr. Brown's letter with Jeremy Caulder's list that made Brent ask about the piano. Tim had, of course, told Mr. Brown all about his hoping to rent one, and Mr. Brown had written, "Hope that piano comes soon."

"What's this about a piano?" Brent asked.

Tim explained everything. And Brent said, what were they

191

waiting for? They would go out and choose the one to rent right away.

John drove Tim back from his rehearsal and was the first to hear the good news that the piano was on its way. He was not pleased.

"Coming next week! But, Tim, your aunt won't let it inside the house."

Tim patted John's knee. "Don't worry, Dad. Bella said that when the Lord sent my piano, He'd fix it with Aunt Cora where it was to be set down."

Tim rushed to tell Bella about his piano. And the next morning, when she brought Aunt Cora her breakfast tray, Bella stood by the bed, her wrinkled face looking serious. She explained that the piano was coming and was not put off by squeaks and moans of horror from Aunt Cora.

"It's no use fussing and fretting. That piano's coming into this house, and all there is for you to say is where it's to sit."

Though she would never have admitted it, Aunt Cora was scared of displeasing Bella for fear she would leave. Also, though this, of course, she did not tell Bella, at her Thanksgiving party a number of the guests had said it was a pity there was no piano in the house so that they could hear Tim play. So though her voice whined more than usual and she kept her eyes shut while she spoke, Aunt Cora said, "Clear that chiffonier out of the living room; the piano can stand in its place. Now go away and leave me."

Bella hurried downstairs to Tim so fast that she arrived at the bottom breathless. She clasped her hands.

"I have said time and again the Lord would fix it, and He sure has."

As soon as the piano arrived and had been set down in the living room, Tim rushed off to tell his news to the Antonios. Although the Antonios would stop getting money in their

192

money box when Tim stopped playing in their drugstore, they were as pleased at Tim's news as if he had brought them a present.

The great trouble about Christmas in America was that everybody gave everybody else presents, and more than one present; it seemed to be almost a competition of giving.

"It's frightful," Bee said to John. "What on earth are we to do if all the people we know send us something? You know how generous Americans are, and we can't live up to it; we haven't the money."

John found a way out. It was not a very grand way, but it was the best they could do. He wrote a story of the Winter family coming to America in the nineteenth century and traveling by wagon down the Santa Fe Trail to Santa Monica as they might have done a hundred years ago. John found a printer and had copies of his story made as a Christmas-card present.

The children could not do anything like that, but they, too, did not want to be the only ones not giving in such an orgy of giving, and they all had people to whom they wanted to give presents. From an English point of view they had a lot of money to spend. Ever since Jane had been working and Bee had been getting a salary to look after her, they all had been receiving regular pocket money.

To add to the excitement, cards began to arrive from England. Rachel had dozens from the academy, and John and Bee had so many they did not know where to put them down. Jane was the luckiest of all. Dr. Smith had not sent her a card; instead he had taken Chewing-gum to one of those places where sheets of little photos are made. Chewing-gum photographed beautifully; there were two sheets, and each photograph, except one where he had moved slightly, was perfect. Jane was so pleased with them that she could not get her words out properly; she gasped. "It's him! It's him! It's as if he were here."

She was so thrilled that she could not part with the photographs; she even took them with her to the studio so she could look at them between shots.

"Show them to Shirley and everybody," Bee suggested. "They'll like to see them."

But Jane would not. She could not explain, but she did not want people fingering the photographs and talking about them; it would make Chewing-gum seem less real.

"I'll let David see them when I can get him alone, but nobody else. Chewing-gum's mine."

Just before Christmas there was a little *Secret Garden* party. Jane's-Mr. Browne made a speech wishing everybody a happy Christmas, and then presents were exchanged. Jane had bought a book for Shirley and a set of tiny animals for David, but nothing for anybody else. She did not know that one day Her-Mr. Browne had told everybody how he had met her through his dog, Hyde Park, and about the food parcel he had sent to Chewing-gum when she got the part. A few of the cast had asked her about Chewing-gum, and she had told them how his parcel had arrived very grandly by air.

"And Dr. Smith laid all the cans out in a row and let Chewing-gum choose for himself which he would eat first, and do you know what he chose? Something called Finest Liver, Inc., which was very clever of him, for he never had liver in his whole life unless it was when he was a tiny puppy and belonged to an American soldier."

It was a startled Jane who, when the exchanging of presents started, found herself holding a sheaf of envelopes. Except for David and Jane's-Mr. Browne, there was one from everybody working on the picture. There was even one from Maurice.

"Open them," said Bee. "They're cards, I think. You must go thank everybody."

But they were not only cards. Inside each card was a slip of paper on which was written, "Food parcel sent to Chewing-gum," and the name of the firm and the date the parcel had been sent.

Jane sat surrounded by envelopes, the cards in her lap, the slips about the parcels in her hands.

Bee was overcome by everybody's kindess.

"How wonderful, darling! Just think, there must be enough food to keep Chewing-gum in luxury for years and years! Run and thank them all." Jane got up. Her eyes were not shining. She looked her most black-doggish. She went into her dressing room. Bee followed her. "Jane, what is the matter? You're behaving abominably. Scowling like that when everybody's been so good to you!"

"May I have your sewing scissors?" Jane asked.

"What for?"

Jane was bent over the photos of Chewing-gum. "Ssh, I'm counting." Then, after a minute: "There are just enough to give one to everybody. Maurice can have the one where Chewing-gum moved."

Nobody expresses thanks for presents in a more pleased way than Americans. Even Maurice, who could not see Chewing-gum clearly in his photo, caught something of the American manner. He managed to sound as if a photograph of Chewing-gum were one of his best Christmas presents and added that he seemed a handsome dog.

"And he couldn't have said anything else," Jane told Bee, "because it's true."

Bee thought Jane had behaved very well, and to tell the truth, it had surprised her. "It was nice of you to give the photos; everybody's very pleased," she told Jane.

Jane looked her worst. "So. they ought to be. They are the loveliest photographs any of them ever saw."

Christmas Day was quite perfect. The children had stockings just bulging with presents. After church there was a glorious Christmas dinner in the middle of the day, with everything that should be there and lots extra. In the afternoon John took the family out in the car to deliver special presents. The first was Tim's for the Antonios. He had bought them scented candles to burn in front of their best picture. The Antonios were terribly pleased. They kissed Tim on both cheeks and gave him an enormous box of chocolates.

The family did not drive up to the Fossils' front door since Bee said they must not be asked in or they would be late and annoy Aunt Cora, so Tim was sent with Rachel's parcel. In it was a needlebook she had made for Nana, a calendar for Aunt Sylvia, and for Posy a little pair of silver ballet shoes on a brooch.

To Jane's great disappointment there was nobody at home at the Does'. She had hoped to see David. It had worried her that only he and Her-Mr. Browne had not given her presents. It was not that she wanted a present from David, but he said so little, and it's difficult to know if a person likes you when he doesn't talk to you. If David had given her a present, it would have been a sign that he liked her, and that might mean, before the picture was finished, that he would like her enough to teach her his magic. Jane left her present for David on the empty porch; as she got back into the car, it seemed as if some of the shimmer of happiness that covered the day had gone.

At Aunt Cora's the house was full of people. There was a huge Christmas tree in the living room blazing with lights, and around it were more parcels than it seemed possible could be meant for one house. All the family had gorgeous things, but each of the children had one present which was so perfect it made all the others seem unimportant. Rachel had a huge box from Posy. In it were the special black tunic and tights Manoff liked his pupils to wear, one pair of new ballet shoes, and one pair of worn ones. On the worn ones was written, "I wore these the first time I danced the Sugarplum Fairy. Hope they bring you luck. Love, Posy." As she undid her other parcels, Rachel's heart felt as if it were singing.

"Posy's shoes! A pair she's actually danced in! Oh, lucky, lucky me!"

Tim had a huge box from Brent. Goodness knows where Brent had found it, but what was in that box might have been invented especially for him and Tim. There was not a practical joke missing. Pools of India-rubber ink to lay beside an overturned inkpot. Things that lifted plates. Things that squeaked and grunted and jumped. They were all there. Tim was spellbound by such a multiplicity of jokes.

"Look, Mom! I can do something new every day the rest of the time I'm here."

Even on Christmas Day Bee could remember that jokes of that sort every day might not be a riot with Aunt Cora.

"Wonderful, darling. Do you think that tomorrow you and I might look at each one separately and decide what to do when?"

Jane thought her most beautiful present was the first she opened. It was a lovely little wristwatch. On the card with it was written, "From Hyde Park and me with best wishes. Your Mr. Browne." But presently she opened a parcel which made her forget there were any other presents in the world. It was a plain cardboard box with none of the grand American fixings of massed bows and flowers. Inside was something done up in brown paper. And inside that were exact duplicates of David's reed pipes. On a piece of paper David had written, "Merry Christmas. I'll teach you to play these. David."

The evening finished with carols. Tim played, and everybody stood around the piano. On the top of the piano, where Tim could keep his eye on it, was Brent's trick box. Rachel was hugging Posy's old shoes close to her. Jane, wearing her wristwatch, held the box with her pipes. As Tim crashed out the opening chords of ''Oh, Come All Ye Faithful,'' everybody's eyes, even Aunt Cora's, were bright, but nobody's eyes shone quite so much as Jane's.

23

Ella

There is often a grumpy nothing-nice-will-ever-happen-again feeling after Christmas. The Winters usually had severe attacks of this, but this year so much was going on they missed even a touch of it. Even Rachel remained gay long after Christmas. Her dancing lessons stopped for a while around Christmas, but there were Manoff's Saturdays. To Rachel, Manoff's dancing mornings were so exciting that all the rest of Saturday after them she went around in sort of daze. She tried to tell her family what it was like.

"Of course, most of it's much too difficult for me, but just being there is simply superb. Manoff shows us steps, three or four at a time, some of them terribly difficult. When he does fast ones, it's like fireworks just going off, and when he does slow ones, they all slide together like water coming out of a tap."

"Splendid, dear," said Peaseblossom. "Wonderful chance for you; up the Winters!"

For Tim there was no question of Christmas grumpiness. There was that absorbing box of tricks, and there was *Hiram's Hour,* with Brent and more tricks. In spite of John's, Bee's, and Peaseblossom's efforts, Tim managed to work three tricks on Aunt Cora: the ink one on her desk, a cat's meow from under the cushion of her chair when she sat down, and a snake in her bath. The last was so realistic that Aunt Cora had hysterics and had to go to bed for the rest of the day with not only a nervous but a dizzy spell. The hysterics caused such confusion that even Bella was cross, and Tim could see he had gone too far. He knew for certain he had gone too far when John told him that he was a pestiferous little horror and that if he played one more trick on Aunt Cora, the whole box of jokes would be burned. Tim said, "Don't fuss, Dad. I won't do any more to her. As a matter of fact, I won't even do one in a room where she could go. But I wish I didn't have an aunt who's like that."

Fortunately all the jokes were a riot on *Hiram's Hour*. The audience adored them, and the men who sang about Mr. Hiram P. Sneltzworther's secondhand cars adored them. Driving home after the broadcasts, Tim would describe in detail the cast's and staff's reactions to every trick played on them. John would say, "Fine, old man, but what did you play?"

"Chopin's *Fantaisie-Impromptu* and then Mendelssohn's *Rondo Capriccioso,* and oh, Dad, I forgot to tell you about the spider that came down in front of the lady who was singing. . . ." And off Tim would go again, describing other tricks played and not-very-well-told versions of Brent's jokes.

Peaseblossom found Tim's calm acceptance of all that was happening to him annoying. She had never thought him sufficiently impressed by the goodness of Jeremy Caulder in offering to give him lessons. She had been really shocked at the offhand way he had treated Mr. Caulder's suggested list of music for the radio program. She thought it sad that after she had sat in, as she usually did, to listen to Tim on *Hiram's Hour* and been impressed and moved by his playing, all he talked about when he came home was water spouting out of trombones or a trick played on the gentlemen who sang the singing advertisements. Bella, who always listened to *Hiram's Hour* and rocked to and fro, did not mind a bit that all he talked about was tricks and jokes. Though she had heard the

200

program, she enjoyed it all over again with Tim, laughing until she ached. But not Peaseblossom; she felt all the hilarity showed disrespect on Tim's part for a gift for piano playing. She tried in a hinting way to make him see her point of view.

"It's a wonderful opportunity for giving pleasure that few boys of your age have the chance to give."

These discussions always went on during Tim's supper. He would eat stolidly while Peaseblossom talked, and she always hoped he was being improved by what she said; but she was always disappointed. Tim enjoyed *Hiram's Hour*s so much he found it impossible to be serious after them. While Peaseblossom talked earnestly about how much Debussy, Mendelssohn, Bach, or whatever music she was discussing could mean in people's lives and how perfectly splendid it was for a Winter to have a chance to be that influence, Tim was thinking of better and brighter tricks. When Peaseblossom finished talking, he would say something like "I wonder if Brent could put some stuff on the microphone which would make everybody hiccup. Hiccups would be gorgeous, especially if you had to sing."

Peaseblossom tried not to let herself be discouraged, but after one *Hiram's Hour* she lost her temper. It had been a particularly riotous program, so riotous that Tim came home in what John, describing it to Bee, called a "thoroughly-above-himself mood," and it was a long time before Peaseblossom could get in her talk. At the end of it Tim said, "Brent's got the hiccup stuff. He's going to use it on a lady singing 'Cherry Ripe.' "

Peaseblossom gave a snort.

"Disgusting! A lovely song like that ruined by horseplay! Your Mr. Brent should be ashamed; after all, there are listeners who love music. Do you know that the first bars you played tonight were ruined because people had not stopped

201

laughing at Mr. Brent's 'crack,' as you call it? And those notes lost in all that laughing are lost for good.''

Tim had finished his supper.

''Not really. I forgot to tell Dad I'm going to make gramophone records. There's a gentleman coming to see him about it.''

Peaseblossom's hands, holding the tray, shook.

''Really, Tim! Make gramophone records! A wonderful compliment, and you forget to mention it!'' She put down the tray. ''I simply don't understand you. If you can't take pride in yourself, you might at least be proud for the family. Records! Our side's doing splendidly, but you lack the team spirit.''

Tim flung his arms around her.

''Do you think you could make me a little tiny bag with a sponge in it full of red ink? I thought I could squeeze it just as Brent announced I'm going to play and he'd think my nose was bleeding.''

Peaseblossom picked up the tray. ''I shall do nothing of the sort. Good night.''

Immediately after Christmas David started to teach Jane to play her pipes. Hearing the little soft-calling music David's pipes made, Jane thought that after a few lessons she could make the same sounds, but not a bit of it. To play pipes requires patience and a certain natural ability. Jane had neither. If it had not been David who was teaching her, Jane would have lost her temper at her very first lesson. She was clumsy with the pipes, and instead of David's magic tune, dreary squawks came out of them. It was the most difficult thing Jane had ever done to go on trying hard and to look fairly pleasant at the same time. But somehow she managed it, for she feared that otherwise David would not think her worth teaching. As usual, when anything was going wrong, she kept it to herself. She said to Rachel, ''You just can't imag-

202

ine how easy it is. Of course, I can only practice between shots when Mickey isn't there, but if he was, he'd fly straight to me."

Rachel spoke to Bee about this.

"I do think, Mom, you ought to ask David to teach Jane go-away as well as come-to-me tunes on that pipe. Just think what Saxon Crescent is going to be like if she plays her pipes there. Full of cats, dogs, pigeons, sparrows, and, I expect, sea gulls."

Bee was surprised. "I will, darling, if I get a chance, but I'm amazed that she's supposed to be learning fast, for she makes the most ghastly noises; I spend my time apologizing about it."

One day, when David and Jane had done all their lessons in the morning, and had an almost free afternoon, David said, in the middle of a pipe lesson, "Reckon that's better."

Jane was overwhelmed at what, from David, was terrific praise.

"Do you really reckon it was? Oh, I am glad."

David turned his pipes around and around. When he spoke again, his slow words seemed more pushed out of him than usual.

"Tomorrow they'll be shooting almost all my creatures."

"In the garden?"

David had a worried look. "Yes."

Jane's eyes shone. "How gorgeous! I've done that scene with Miss Steiman, and I thought only Mickey was there."

David was not listening to Jane but following his own thoughts. "Bob'll be all right, but the rest aren't ready to meet folks; I'm 'feared they'll be scared."

"You mean they won't work even with you?"

"Alone they would, but I can't be everyplace."

Jane gazed at David, hardly believing what she had heard.

203

"You mean you want me to help you with them? You'd let me help?"

David nodded. "So they won't be scared."

As always, when David was using his creatures in the picture, he had them on the set well before the shooting began. In this scene Colin had already been helped down the steps and was sitting on the grass and Mary was gardening. As Jane's-Mr. Browne had planned the picture, Dickon brought a baby lamb to show Colin and was to give it to him to hold while he sat under a tree and piped. Presently a little fox, four rabbits, Bob, the squirrel, Mickey, and a crow and a cock pheasant would be sitting around or on him. Nobody interfered with David or his arrangements for his creatures, for he alone knew what was best for them. When, therefore, he told Mr. Phelps he wanted Jane to be on the set early, Mr. Phelps, though surprised, passed on the message to Bee.

To Jane the time spent in the garden with David and his creatures before the shooting began was something she was to remember all her life. David had in his arms an almost new lamb, which he stroked all the while he was talking. He spoke even more slowly and softly than usual. He said the lamb was called Ella and was terribly scared, so he would give her to Jane in a minute to get her accustomed to strange people holding her. Presently he did just that. First he told Jane to pick up a feeding-bottle of milk which was under a painted rose bush and then to sit down. Jane hardly breathed as Ella's soft little helpless body was laid on her lap. Would Ella stay? Would she? For a moment it looked as though she would not. She gave a terrified start.

"Stroke her," David said. "Stroke her; then give her the bottle." Jane stroked and whispered loving words; then very gently she lifted the bottle and put the nipple into Ella's mouth. For a second nothing happened; then Ella gave a wriggle to make herself more cozy and began to suck. Jane dared not speak; but she looked at David, and her eyes would have told him Ella had settled down even if he had not been able to see for himself she had.

David began to talk again. He said that somewhere about were old friends of Jane's that she had met before: Andy, the cock pheasant; four of the rabbits, Joe, Arthur, Mary, and Ann; Pedro, the fox; Jack, the crow; and, of course, Mickey and Bob. Then he began to pipe, and what happened was real magic. Mickey, of course, came first. Then two little eyes twinkled from behind a clump of tulips, and Bob hopped out. David stopped piping for a moment and threw a handful of food toward Jane. Then he piped again, and one by one the four rabbits were out nibbling; then, very shyly, the baby fox crept out from behind a peach tree and crawled up to David. Then, with an I'm-not-afraid-of-anybody caw, Jack, the crow, flew from a lilac bush onto David's shoulder, and last of all, Andy, the pheasant, hopped onto the path and stood still, gazing at David with his head on one side. Jane went on stroking Ella and hoping and hoping that just one of the creatures would come near her.

"If they do," she thought, "I'll be helping David, and I'll be starting to be part of taming them," and in her mind she added Chewing-gum to the group. Not the Chewing-gum she knew, who was not obedient and inclined to chase any bird he saw, but a new Chewing-gum, who sat down beside her and looked at Ella with worshiping eyes.

Presently Bob had eaten all the nuts near him, and he skipped toward Jane. He looked at her thoughtfully: Was this the girl he knew? Yes, of course it was. As if she were not there, he picked up a nut that was almost touching her knee. Two of the rabbits, Joe and Ann, seeing how little disturbed Bob was, had a word with each other. Jane could imagine what they were saying. "That's the girl David's brought along to see us. That's a good-looking lettuce beside her. Let's have a nibble.''

Jane's-Mr. Browne's voice came from somewhere behind David.

''Can you get rid of them without frightening them? Then we'll get cracking.''

David got rid of his creatures by getting up and taking Ella from Jane and wandering off with her down the garden. As he went, the animals scuttled and the birds flew after him.

Jane's-Mr. Browne took Jane and Maurice through their scenes. The sequence was that Dickon, having wheeled Colin into the garden, had gone to fetch his creatures. Mary, with her rake, was weeding, and as she weeded, she talked to Colin, who was sitting on the grass beside her. They were discussing the magic in the garden, which was not only bringing the garden to life but also making Colin's legs strong so that he could walk. That scene finished as Dickon's pipes were heard and was the beginning of the scenes with the creatures in them.

Maurice, as usual, did his scenes with Jane faultlessly, and Jane was better than usual. She was so eager to get to the scenes with David that she could almost be nice to Maurice without thinking of him as a chipmunk. All the same, the time it took to take the first shots bored her dreadfully, and she needed nobody to tell her to look up with a face shining with pleasure when at last she heard David's pipes.

Maurice was told not to move. Jane was to take a few steps toward David. In the first scene with the creatures only Ella was to be used. While Jane's-Mr. Browne was explaining to Maurice what he wanted him to do and what he wanted him to feel, David whispered to Jane that it should be all right. Full of the milk Jane had given her, Ella had gone to sleep and most likely would not know that she had been in

Maurice's arms. Jane looked at Ella. "Lucky Maurice," she thought. "It would be Maurice who has to hold her."

It was decided not to disturb Ella by rehearsing her. David pretended to give her to Maurice, and Maurice pretended to take her; but the real giving and taking waited till the cameras were rolling.

Jane had nothing to do in that scene except look interested; that was no trouble at all because she was. Her eyes on Ella, she watched David cross to Maurice and very softly put the lamb in his arms. Ella was either a very light sleeper or not as fast asleep as David thought, for the second Maurice touched her she opened her eyes and on seeing him leaped out of his arms and out of the picture. Jane's-Mr. Browne said quietly, "Cut"; they would start the scene again. They started it four times, but it was no use: Ella just would not be touched by Maurice. It was a new experience for Jane to see a scene being shot over and over again because somebody else was doing it wrong.

"I bet Maurice blames Ella," she thought. "But I know just how Ella feels, and I don't blame her at all."

Presently the lights were switched off, and Jane's-Mr. Browne and David had a long talk. At the end Mr. Phelps came up to Jane.

"David thinks the lamb'll come to you. Mr. Browne'll try it that way."

Another rehearsal took place. As Jane heard David's pipes, she was to drop her rake and go sit on the grass beside Colin while he said his line: "It's Dickon. Oh, I hope the creatures will like me."

That scene went badly. Maurice was furious that Jane was to hold Ella.

"Come on, Maurice," Jane's-Mr. Browne said. "You said those lines all right at the first take. Now all the life's gone out of them."

Maurice made an effort, and after a few tries, because he really was a good actor, he got the lines fairly right, but never as well as he had the first time. The moment the lights were switched off he ran to his mother, his face scarlet with temper.

"Talk to Mr. Browne, Mommy. I'm the star of this picture. People will like to see me holding a lamb. It will make a lovely still. I won't have that Jane holding her. It's my scene. Mine. Mine. Mine."

Mrs. Tuesday went to Jane's-Mr. Browne.

"Little Maurice is upset. He was so looking forward to cuddling the lamb; besides, it would have made a sweetly pretty still. I do hope you won't disappoint him; he is such a highly strung little boy and so easily upset."

Jane's-Mr. Browne was used to Mrs. Tuesday. In every picture there was some place where she thought Maurice did not have enough to do and so might be upset. When he could, Mr. Browne gave in to her but not, of course, if it spoiled his picture. This time he couldn't give in because nobody could make Ella do what she didn't want to do. He explained this to Mrs. Tuesday, but Mrs. Tuesday was not satisfied.

"I shall have a talk with Mr. Bettelheimer. My boy's the most wonderful little boy Bee Bee studios have ever had under contract, and I won't have him slighted."

Jane's-Mr. Browne told Mr. Phelps to call Jane and Maurice onto the set.

"I guess Mrs. Tuesday needn't worry any," he said. "My bet is Ella won't go to Jane either. In that case we won't have the lamb in the picture."

Jane had said nothing since she had been told she was to hold Ella. The hairdresser fussed with her hair, and the makeup woman mopped her face with a tissue; but she never opened her mouth. She stood with her eyes shut, clasping her pipes. When Bee asked if anything was wrong, she only shook her head, and Bee supposed she was playing some game. But it was not a game. Jane was using her will. Over and over again she was repeating to herself, "If Ella comes to me, I've begun to learn magic. She's got to come to me. She's got to. She's *got* to."

There were no words in the first scene with Ella. As David came slowly toward her, Jane could hear her own heart beating. Ella was not asleep, and David was stroking her. David came nearer and nearer. The cameras were rolling, the lights blazing down on the garden. Then David was beside her. He knelt and gave her Ella. For a second it was uncertain whether Ella would stay. Then Jane, stroking her gently, whispered a line that was not in the script. "Stay with me, darling. Stay with me."

Jane's-Mr. Browne said, "Cut," and mopped his forehead. Mr. Phelps grinned.

"If you make pictures for the next fifty years, you'll never get anything more natural than that." He broke off. "What's happening?"

What was happening was that Maurice was having a screaming fit. As the cameras stopped rolling, he threw himself on the ground and kicked and howled.

Because of Maurice's hysterics, the other scenes with Ella and the creatures had to wait until the next day. Bee took Jane home in a taxi. Jane was so quiet Bee asked if anything was wrong. Jane looked at her, her eyes shining.

"Nothing. It's been the most beautiful day of my whole life. I had all that time with David's creatures, and none of them minded me. Ella lay in my arms, but I never thought I'd hold her in the picture."

Bee had felt very awkward while Maurice had hysterics. She had kept out of Mrs. Tuesday's way, but Mrs. Norstrum had shaken her head and said it was unlucky, that Mrs. Tuesday might go on being upset for days.

"I'm rather sorry about that, darling. It's nearly the end of the picture, and we don't want Mrs. Tuesday or Maurice getting upset."

Jane gave a pleased wriggle.

"I do. His screaming was the most beautiful part of the most beautiful day."

24

What Happened in February

Peaseblossom had to hover about Rachel's and Jane's door to stop them from talking at night; but they often whispered all the same, and in the mornings there was unending chatter from the time they woke until breakfast. It was something new for the sisters to have so much to say to each other. Of course, doing quite different things all day made a difference, but it was not only that. Jane had been rather like a frostbitten rosebud, all tightly stuck together, and now, little by little, her petals were uncurling. There never seemed to be enough time to say everything. Rachel heard every detail of the crisis when Jane held Ella and Maurice had hysterics. She heard all about the grown-ups' discouraged talk about Maurice's hysterics, and John's saying to Jane, "Don't gloat, you little horror. If all I hear is true, Maurice had plenty to gloat over in the first two or three weeks they were making the picture."

Rachel, though, was entirely on Jane's side.

"Oh, I wish I'd been there! I'd love to have seen how Maurice looked."

One Saturday night Jane heard something from Rachel that no one else knew. Rachel had a new ambition. At Manoff's Saturday class the pupils had been shown steps from a new ballet Manoff was going to use in his repertoire. It was a ballet about birds. The corps de ballet had an entrance as birds; they did little pecking steps like rather scared birds hopping across a street. Somehow the class could not get what Manoff wanted, but Rachel, in the back row, got it exactly, for at Manoff's Saturdays she felt herself rather like a scared bird hopping across a street.

"I was just holding the attitude at the end when, imagine, Monsieur Manoff said, 'Little friend of Posy's at the back, come here.' "

Jane despised humility. "Doesn't he know your name yet?"

"Goodness, no, of course not. I couldn't be lower than I am. Most of the pupils belong to his ballet, but the grandest people come as well. Dancers from all the film companies and even some people who have come especially from places like New York and Chicago for refresher courses. Apart from being a marvelous dancer himself, he's the best teacher in the world."

"I bet you're better than lots of them. What did he say when he called you?"

Rachel hung out of bed, leaning toward Jane and speaking in an awed whisper.

"He said, 'This little girl is better than any of you. Show them, my child.' I had forgotten to curtsy when I came to him, but I remembered then and did a big one, saying, 'Maître,' the way we do; then I did the steps."

"Well? What happened after that?" Jane wanted to know.

"That was all."

"Didn't anyone clap or anything?"

Rachel was shocked. "At a Manoff's Saturday? Of course not! It's not like that at all. Only it made me think of something. When Posy Fossil was younger than I am, she danced for Monsieur Manoff and he told her she was to come to his school at Szolva and he would make her into a beautiful artiste. Oh, Jane, suppose, just suppose, he was to say to

212

me, 'You will stay with me and I will make you into a beautiful artiste!' "

Jane sat up. "Stay here? All alone when we go home?"

"It would be awful, but I would if he asked me. Imagine being like Posy someday. You can't think what it's like when she dances. Even all those grand pupils stop talking if she dances alone. She's got all the things: precision, elevation, and something extra. When she holds an attitude or moves from one step to another, it's like butter melting in a saucepan; it's all soft. I can't explain."

Jane lay down again. Though she would not have said so, she thought Rachel marvelous. On the few occasions when she had seen her dance, she had been very proud of her. Naturally Rachel did not know this, for Jane's way of showing she felt proud of her was to be rude about her dancing.

"I don't think butter looks nice melting. Would Dad let you stay?"

"I think so. You know how he feels about our working at our own things."

"If the Bee Bee studios wanted to put me under contract, Dad wouldn't let them. He told me that when I got the part of Mary."

"That's because it's not your thing. Besides, you couldn't stay here alone. If Monsieur Manoff let me join his company, I think I could live in the same places as Posy. Either Nana or Aunt Sylvia travels with her. Imagine the glory of living with Posy!"

Peaseblossom opened the door. Both Rachel and Jane shut their eyes. Pleaseblossom stopped for a moment, then shut the door and went away. Rachel and Jane raised their heads from their pillows and listened until they heard her go downstairs.

"What I was going to say," Rachel whispered, "is that you

213

wouldn't want to go on in films even if they wanted you, would you?''

Jane could not let that pass. She did not want to act in pictures for the rest of her life, but she did very much want the company to want her to. So she said, ''I wouldn't mind if David and all the animals and birds were in the picture.''

''Even then you wouldn't. You'd be bored. You'd want Chewing-gum. It's different for me. My dancing isn't something that's happened in California; it's been always.''

Jane did not answer that because she was asleep.

It was a few days after this talk that John had his bit of good news. He had been working hard on a book ever since the first day he arrived at Aunt Cora's, but he had taken time off to write a short story. He sent it to the *Saturday Evening Post,* and when the news came that the magazine had bought it, he was like somebody who finds the first primrose after a hard winter.

''This deserves something special,'' John announced. ''What about going away for a weekend of sight-seeing? We could combine it with your birthday, Tim.''

Tim bounced with excitement. ''Death Valley. You did promise Death Valley.''

Rachel turned pink.

''I can't. I can't go away. I can't miss a Manoff's Saturday.''

John looked less cheerful. ''Not even for once? Just as a celebration? I know old Jane can't come, but I had hoped to have you.''

Rachel hated to seem mean about it, but there was so little time left. If Monsieur Manoff was to take her as a pupil, she must not miss a moment of his classes. She came to John and rubbed her cheek on his arm.

''I'm sorry, Dad, but I can't.''

John raised her chin.

''All right, puss. If you can't, you can't. It'll be just

214

Peaseblossom, Tim, and myself. Unless you'd like to come, Cora.''

Aunt Cora turned quite pale at the thought.

"Death Valley! No, thank you. Besides, even if there weren't Tim's party to fix, I'd be so nervous something was going wrong I'd be as fidgety as a coot the whole trip.''

John had not expected or, to be quite honest, wanted Aunt Cora to say she would go, and his mind had skipped ahead of her answer.

"I wish you could come, Bee. It'll be no fun going without you.''

Peaseblossom, trying not to look like a martyr, said, ''You shall go, Bee. I'll take charge of Jane at the studio. I shall enjoy it.''

Though nobody had ever guessed it, Aunt Cora was longing for a day at the studio. Already several of her friends had asked if she had been up to see her niece working at the studio. So now she said, trying to make it sound as though she were being noble, ''There's no need for anybody to miss the trip. I'll take Jane to the studio.''

At first it was planned that Bee should take Aunt Cora with her to the studio on the day before she left for Death Valley, but then John had a better idea. He said they all had been saying they wanted to see Jane at work; what about Bee's getting permission for the whole family to go up on Friday afternoon?

The family and Aunt Cora arrived early for the afternoon's shooting. Jane's-Mr. Browne was there. He told Mr. Phelps to take Rachel and Tim around and show them the lights, sound apparatus, and cameras while he himself escorted Aunt Cora and John around the painted garden.

It was now April in the garden. In a Technicolor film there are always brighter skies and more flowers than there would be in real life. John stood at the top of the steps and let out a low whistle.

"My word! 'Oh, to be in England, now that April's there,' in glorious Technicolor."

Aunt Cora was not good at quotations and had come to look not at gardens but at film stars. She smiled politely at the garden.

"Very pretty. I shall go and find Bee. She wants to introduce me to everybody."

Left alone, John and Jane's-Mr. Browne walked down the steps into the garden. John said, "Had a bad time with Jane, didn't you?"

"Terrible. I guess those days when I had to get her to look pleasant were about the worst I'll ever live through."

"Well, it's nearly over."

"You'll be surprised when you see her on the screen. They've been working hard at it in the cutting room because if we need a retake, it'll have to be done before you leave next month. I'm glad you're taking Jane home. I'll bet that when the big shots see the finished version of this, they'll want Jane under contract. What a fate! She'd play bad-tempered girls for the next four or five years, and some poor devil would have to direct her. But not me. No, sir, not twice!"

John grinned.

"You needn't lose any sleep over her. She'll be on the *Mauretania* next month. Mind you, if I thought she would like it, and she had an offer, I'd arrange somehow to let her stay. But she'd hate it, bless her. So would I. We've had a glorious time here, but I'm not planning to leave one of my children behind as a souvenir of our visit."

Rachel and Tim had a very interesting afternoon. Everybody made a fuss over them. Rachel was extraordinarily pretty, and Tim nice-looking, and both had very good manners.

One of the electricians said, "I'll bet those two little birds came out of a different hatching from the one that gave us Jane."

And that, in different words, was what everybody was saying. Luckily it was a day when Mickey was in the picture, so Jane was in a very good mood and never noticed that people were talking about Rachel and Tim. Also, she was having a sniff of the grandeur she had always wanted. Rachel, Aunt Cora, and Peaseblossom were very impressed by her dressing room and by the way the hairdresser and makeup woman attended to her.

"Isn't Jane important?" Rachel whispered to Bee.

Bee was by now used to the studio.

"Not really. It looks grand, but it happens to them all."

During the afternoon a camera man took several stills of them all, some with Jane and some alone.

"May as well have some good pictures of all the family," Jane's Mr. Browne said to John.

Very early the next morning the family in great excitement set off for Death Valley, though it was miserable leaving Rachel and Jane behind. John had decided with Bee not to tell Jane where they were spending the night because it would be just what she would most enjoy. They were planning to spend Saturday and Sunday nights in Yosemite National Park; that would give them all Sunday to see the park, particularly the bears that lived there.

"Poor Jane," Tim said. "She would have taken her pipes and played them to the bears."

Bee laughed. "That's the first thing which has consoled me for leaving Jane behind. If the noise I've heard coming out of her pipes is what she would play to bears, I should think they'd eat the lot of us."

Jane had behaved very well. She came down to the front door with Rachel in her dressing gown to wave good-bye to

217

the family, and though she hated seeing them go off without her, she did not look a bit black-doggish.

"Splendid of Jane," Peaseblossom said to John. "She's more disciplined than one would think."

"Whatever else may be held against old Jane," John answered, "I never knew her to go back on anything. We warned her that if she played Mary, she would miss seeing all the lovely things Rachel and Tim would see, and she has. This is the first long trip; but there's hardly been a day when I haven't taken the other two and shown them some new beauty, and all she's seen is a film studio."

It was a lovely trip. Death Valley was desert, glittering sand, barren rocks, and dismal beyond all belief. Yosemite was just the opposite. It was beautiful and had everything in it that anyone could want: Indian caves, an enormous tree supposed to be nearly four thousand years old, and a fallen-down tree which was so big that a row of cars had been photographed on top of it; there were waterfalls and, a long way off, the bears. It was real winter in Yosemite, as it had been most of the drive up the mountains to get there, and everything was covered with snow. This, from Tim's point of view, was one of the best things about it. When they left to return to Santa Monica early on Monday morning, Peaseblossom said, "What an experience! What scenery! You'll never forget it, will you, Tim?"

"Never. When I tell Mr. Brown I met bears walking loose in the snow just as if they were dogs, he'll never believe me."

Aunt Cora found her two days at the studio thrilling, and she did something Bee had never done: She made friends with Mrs. Tuesday. Aunt Cora liked celebrities, and because Maurice was well known in pictures, she thought he must be

218

interesting and sweet, and she did not care how much Mrs. Tuesday talked about him.

The Saturday shooting passed off easily for Jane. It was a day when David and Mickey were in the scenes, and she was always happy on those days. Monday, however, was a different story. It began by Jane's being rubbed the wrong way. She had thought they were going to shoot some scenes with Ben Weatherstaff, but the actor playing him had a cold, so instead Jane's-Mr. Browne decided to take the last of the interiors. Jane hated interiors because they were always with Maurice and never with David, and she looked as disobliging as she felt. After lunch David walked into the studio. He had been feeding his creatures and had looked in to give Jane a lesson on the pipes. At once all Jane's bad temper vanished. She forgot she had ever been cross. Then a hand was laid on her shoulder. There was the teacher from Miss Barnabas's school.

"Come, Jane. We can make a start on that arithmetic you missed this morning."

Arithmetic! It had never been Jane's favorite subject, but arithmetic instead of playing the pipes with David! It was too much. She forgot David was listening. There was no Bee to say the soothing thing, only Aunt Cora talking hard to Mrs. Tuesday. All the very worst rose up in Jane. She stamped.

"I won't do arithmetic. Go away and leave me alone."

The teacher looked sad, for she had thought Jane was improving, yet here she was, even worse than when she had first come to work in the studio.

"Jane!" the teacher reproved her. "That's not at all a nice way to talk. Come at once."

Jane's eyebrows almost met, she was scowling so. She spoke in what was nearly a shout. "I won't! I won't! I won't!"

Aunt Cora jumped. "My! Jane! Whatever did I hear you say! We need some ice water to wash out that mouth."

Mrs. Tuesday was glad to see Jane behaving badly because although she had stood up for Maurice on the day he screamed and said he was highly strung, she had really been a bit ashamed for him. Now she made a remark not likely to soothe. "Now why choose today to act this way? Upsetting your poor aunt."

Poor aunt! That was more than Jane could bear.

"She's not a poor aunt; she's a rich aunt. She's got everything, and all she does is just lie in bed while people who are staying with her clean her house."

Jane's raised voice caught Mr. Phelps's ear. He hurried over in time to hear the last remark.

"What's the trouble?"

Jane was shaking with temper. "I won't do arithmetic."

Mr. Phelps turned to the teacher. "I'll bring her right over." Then he looked at Jane; his voice was frighteningly severe. "Come over here." He drew her out of earshot of Mrs. Tuesday and Aunt Cora. "Did I say that I wouldn't know you for the child who started in this picture? Did I say that maybe folks were wrong in thinking there wasn't a pin to put between you and Maurice when it came to conceit and contrariness?"

Jane was furious with herself. Why had she lost her temper? She had been exactly like Maurice. She scratched the floor with one toe.

"She talked about arithmetic just as David and I were going to play the pipes."

"And why shouldn't she? She's doing what she has to do, and you know it. It's no pleasure to her to teach a puffed-up child arithmetic or anything else."

"I'll go now."

Mr. Phelps looked less severe. "And don't go looking like that. You've a face that would sour an apple. Smile at the teacher, and tell her how ashamed you are."

Jane was turning to go. Then she stopped and looked pleadingly at Mr. Phelps. She lowered her voice to a whisper, for what she had to say was very private. "Would you ask David if he could wait for half an hour?"

"Will you apologize nicely?"

Jane nodded.

"Get along then."

Mr. Phelps did ask David to wait. As soon as Jane had done her lessons and was dressed for the next shot, she went off to look for him, terrified as to what he was thinking of her. She was half afraid that he would have refused to stay. She tried to think of something that would explain her bad behavior, but she couldn't because there was no explanation. She need not have bothered. David said in his slow voice, just as if there had been no interruption, "Play those four notes which call Mickey."

The family was home by the time Jane and Aunt Cora got back from the studio. Aunt Cora had enjoyed her day so enormously that she had forgotten for the moment Jane's badness. She was, for her, quite animated and talked so much it was difficult for the rest to get in their stories of Yosemite and Death Valley. In the end everybody was talking at once, until Bee put her hands over her ears.

"Be quiet a minute, please. Jane and Tim must go to bed."

Tim was sitting at his piano. "But I wanted to play to Rachel and Jane what a bear's growl sounds like."

Bee knew Tim had not heard a bear growl, but she did not give him away. "Not tonight, darling. It's your bedtime, and you want a particularly long night if you're to be ready for your party tomorrow."

Jane gave Tim a pitying smile. "You'd better make the best of the first part of your party, my boy, for you'll hate it after six o'clock. Do you know what Aunt Cora's done? She's invited Mrs. Tuesday and Maurice.''

25

Tim's Birthday

Tim's party was a success. What Aunt Cora had called "darling children" turned out, to Tim's surprise, to be nice children. There was a very good treasure hunt, and various games with prizes, and a magnificent tea with a great pink-and-white cake with Tim's name on the top and nine pink candles.

At six o'clock the mothers and fathers of the children, as well as lots of other grown-up people, arrived. To begin with, that part of the party was all right. Posy came; that pleased Rachel. Then suddenly Mrs. Tuesday and Maurice arrived, and the Winters were forgotten.

Tim and Rachel stood in a corner, watching Maurice being introduced to people by Aunt Cora. Rachel was filled with unwilling admiration. She said, "Of course, he's an awful show-off, but I must say he does it well."

Tim sighed. "I do wish Aunt Cora weren't here. I'd do one of my best jokes on him."

Rachel glanced at him anxiously. "You do remember you absolutely promised."

"I know I did, but it's not breaking my promise to wish Aunt Cora weren't here. It isn't often I agree with Jane about anything, but I do about him."

Bee, with Jane, had been driven back from the studio in Maurice's car. She came up to them and kissed Tim. "Had a good party, darling?"

"It was, but it isn't improved since that Maurice came."

Bee looked around anxiously to make sure that Mrs. Tuesday wasn't about. "Don't you start that, Tim. We've enough trouble with Jane. He's all right, really."

Tim looked reproachfully after Bee. "It's sad what things even the best mother can say."

Jane joined them. She had a very Jane-ish expression. "I hope you're enjoying having him here. Isn't he awful? I had to drive home in his car, sitting by him. Luckily Mrs. Tuesday kept on talking, talking, talking, so I didn't have to say anything. It was a good thing, for if I had, I would only have said, 'What a pity you couldn't hold Ella, Maurice.' "

A group of people were gathered around Mrs. Tuesday. Sentences flowed across to the children.

"Such a wonderful actor . . . My, you must be proud. . . . He's so cute. . . ."

When Mrs. Tuesday spoke about her son, her voice was awed and reverent. "He is rather special, though, of course, a terrible responsibility. I don't look upon him as my son but as a child who belongs to the world and has been trusted to me to bring up."

The Winters turned away their heads and made faces to show what they thought. Tim made a sound like somebody who was going to be sick.

John, whose face had expressed nothing but politeness while Mrs. Tuesday was talking, took advantage of everybody's looking at Maurice to move away. He came over to the children.

"What are you bunched together here for? Hop it and get some plates, and hand them around. And you'd better go and wash, Tim; your fingers must be sticky, and I expect any minute now your aunt will want you to play."

Jane put a hand in John's and tugged at his arm to make

224

him lean down to her. "Isn't he even worse than I told you?"

John laughed. "I'll grant you he's unlucky in his mother. The poor kid hasn't a chance."

When everybody seemed to have gone, Aunt Cora asked if the family would tidy the living room a bit as she hated to see it all mussed up. And if Tim would excuse her from his birthday supper, she would go right up to bed.

As soon as Aunt Cora was safely upstairs, Rachel burst out: "Stop tidying. Posy hasn't gone; she's in the kitchen talking to Bella. She danced Mrs. Tuesday for me in the hall, and I said she must dance her for you."

Only Rachel had seen Posy's dancing imitations. Posy danced Mrs. Tuesday so that nobody could miss whom she was imitating. They all laughed so much they ached. Tim and Jane had to lie on the floor, and the others had to stuff things in their mouths so Aunt Cora wouldn't hear. Once Posy had started her dancing imitations, it was difficult to stop her. She danced Maurice. She danced Bella. Finally she danced Aunt Cora. That was the best of all. John whooped and hiccuped with laughter, and the tears streamed down his cheeks. Bee had to hold her hands as well as her handkerchief over her mouth to hold back the sound of her laughing from Aunt Cora, and the children rolled on the floor. Only Peaseblossom did not enjoy it. She thought it very bad taste and said, disapprovingly, "Very clever, I know, but we mustn't forget how good Aunt Cora's been to us; that's not our way, is it?"

Rachel could see from the look in Posy's eye that in another minute she would dance Peaseblossom, but luckily the door opened and Bella's beaming face looked in.

"Your supper's on the table, and seeing Miss Cora don't feel so good, I fixed her place for you, Miss Posy."

*　　*　　*

After Tim's birthday it was frightening how fast the time passed. One minute their leaving seemed weeks away, and the next, boxes were being packed, and on John's writing table were piles of labels with "Mauretania" on them, or "W" or "Cabin Class."

The photographs taken at the studio arrived. They all were good, but there was one of Rachel that rather startled the family. Rachel had worn one of the prettier of Posy's frocks and had brushed her hair loose and tied a ribbon around it, but otherwise she was just her usual self. The photograph was really what is called a speaking likeness, only somehow Rachel looked not just pretty but downright lovely.

"Goodness!" Tim said. "You look like a movie star."

Peaseblossom made disapproving, clicking noises. "Tch! Tch! Very nice just for once, but I prefer you with two sensible braids."

Jane thought Rachel looked marvelous. She had seen lots of stills of herself, and she never looked like that. But she was not jealous. After all, there was the still of her holding Ella, which she would not have exchanged to look like Rachel or anyone else. All the same, her tongue could not twist itself around nice words. The best she could say was "It reminds me of pictures of Maurice."

Bee was delighted with the photograph. In her mind she had already framed it and put it on a table in the drawing room in Saxon Crescent.

"They say we can have some more," she said. "We must get some for friends at home, and the grannies must each have one."

John said, "And Mrs. Bones. And you should send one to Madame Fidolia, Rachel. She'll like it for her office."

26

Good-bye to the Studio

It was a pity, but Jane drove to her last day at the studio in a bad temper. First of all, her plans had been upset. Her idea had been to drive to the lot just before school finished, say good-bye to everybody, and then have lunch at the same table in the commissary with David. After lunch David was to take her to say good-bye to his creatures, and then all the family and Aunt Cora were coming to see the film. Bee and Miss Barnabas upset these arrangements. Miss Barnabas had told Bee not to take Jane away from her school one day before she need. That with all the good-byes Bee would have to say and last things to do, it would maybe help to have one of the children out of the house. It had been a help, and it had suited from another point of view. Aunt Cora liked going to the studio and liked lunching in the commissary, so on the last days, after shooting had stopped, Aunt Cora fetched Jane from school, and they lunched on the lot before they drove home. It meant that Aunt Cora as well as Jane was out of the house.

John drove Jane to school that last morning and saw she was angry. "What's the trouble?"

Jane was shocked that she could have a father so blind to what was fair that he had to ask a question like that.

"Would you like to be pushed off to lessons on a day when Tim's been allowed to spend the morning saying good-bye to the Antonios and Rachel's gone with Aunt Cora to buy food for the farewell party?''

''I see your point, but let's be fair: Nobody knew you didn't want to go. We thought you'd like a chance to say good-bye to them all, especially David.''

''Of course I want to. But I meant just to come in when lessons were over. And another thing: When a person is giving good-bye presents, that person should choose who is to have them.''

John did not pretend that he did not know what Jane was talking about. Bee had come to him several weeks before about Jane's presents. ''We can leave the studio people,'' she had said, ''to Jane, but we must see that she gives something really nice to Miss Barnabas and Miss Steiman; they've been terribly kind, and I'm sure Jane hasn't always been easy.'' John had agreed with Bee, and a beautifully bound book of poetry and a dozen lovely handkerchiefs had been bought.

Now he said, ''So that person should if that person could be trusted to say 'thank you' properly to people who have been good to her.''

Jane stuck her chin in the air. ''I've written in the book, and I'll say polite things to Miss Steiman.'' She lowered her voice. ''But inside I'll be thinking, 'I hope she gets an awful cold and needs these handkerchiefs soon.' ''

''You're a little horror. I can't imagine how I came to have such a daughter. For goodness' sake, don't spoil our last day, and do try to leave a good impression behind. We don't want everybody in the Bee Bee studios in the future saying, 'As cross-looking as that English child Jane Winter.' ''

Jane was carrying Miss Steiman's parcel as if it smelled. She had learned what she was to say by heart, but the way she said it was not a credit to Miss Steiman's training in inflections, for there were no inflections at all and no pauses either.

"I've come to say good-bye and to thank you for taking so much trouble with me and to give you these to remember me by." Then, in quite a different voice because what she was thinking got the better of her: "Mom chose them and paid for them. I didn't."

Miss Steiman needed very little to make her feel good. Jane being polite, Jane bringing her a present were quite enough to make her sure that her belief that all children were sweet really was right. She kissed her.

"Now isn't that kind. Oh, Jane, what perfectly beautiful handkerchiefs! Every time I use one I'll surely think of you."

Jane gave Miss Barnabas her book before school. She had written, under Bee's instruction, "To Miss Barnabas to say thank you. Jane Winter." Miss Barnabas said thank you and kissed Jane, but she broke off lessons a few minutes early to say a proper thank-you and good-bye. She made a little speech. She showed the school her book and said she was going to treasure it.

After Miss Barnabas had finished speaking, all the pupils came to say good-bye. Jane for once was embarrassed; they were all so nice that Jane by herself thought of the right way to say "thank you." She asked them to put their names and addresses on a piece of paper, and she promised to send each of them postcards of London when she got home. Even as she made the offer, she could see that she was not going to like carrying it out. She saw herself at the table in the dining room at Saxon Crescent writing postcard after postcard until her hand ached.

Jane said a proper good-bye to Mrs. Norstrum and Shirley. She had brought Shirley a new plastic bubble-blowing kit because she had used up so much of Shirley's. Shirley had for Jane a lovely book full of pictures of Los Angeles. The two girls had seen each other every day while *The Secret Garden* was being made, and they had said all the things they had to say and knew each other well. Saying an official good-bye seemed silly. So they just smiled at each other. Mrs. Norstrum was the one who said things. She gave Jane a parcel for Bee. She said she had always thought English people were stiff, and knowing Bee had shown her that lots of them were just as unaffected as Americans. She did not say she was sorry to say good-bye to Jane, because she was a straightforward person who did not say things just for pretense, but she did say they would always remember Jane, as was true.

Jane had not meant to say a special good-bye to Maurice, but she had to because Aunt Cora was talking to Mrs. Tuesday when Jane, her arms full of presents, came out of the schoolroom. It was a short good-bye. Jane said, "Do you want a postcard sent you from London?"

"No," Maurice answered.

Jane nodded. "I thought you wouldn't. Good-bye."

Jane was glad when lunch was over and she and David, with Mr. Doe and Aunt Cora far behind, were on their way to the place where the creatures lived.

David opened the gate into his little zoo. "I brought them all over to say good-bye."

"Ella, too?" Jane asked.

"Sure, I've brought Ella."

It was like making the scenes with David in the picture, only better, because there were no cameras or lights to scare the creatures.

What seemed a pause in time was broken by Aunt Cora. Her whining voice rang through the zoo.

"Jane, Jane, you really must hurry. They're showing the picture in just a quarter of an hour."

At Aunt Cora's voice, all the creatures disappeared back into their cages and pens. Jane's eyes blazed.

"She's frightened them. She frightened them away. I could kill her."

David had not moved. "They'll come back."

"Because of your piping, you mean? Oh, David, before I go, will you tell me something? Is my pipe playing good enough for me to be a tamer yet? Is it?"

As usual, David took a long time answering.

"Taming wild creatures isn't just piping; it's how you feel. They know that."

"But they like me. Ella sat in my arms when she wouldn't look at Maurice, and Bob likes me, and Mickey and all of them."

David nodded. "They like you."

"So I can start taming creatures myself when I get home, can't I? Especially Chewing-gum? I want to start with him doing tricks."

"I don't know about tricks, but I wouldn't trouble a grown dog; he'd think it kind of mean."

"But I've been learning my pipes specially for him. Don't you think I could train him? Don't you?"

"Maybe. Don't rush at it. Start with a little bird. I figure little birds like piping."

Aunt Cora's voice whined again. "Jane, Jane, will you come? You can't keep everybody waiting."

Jane got up. "I'm sending you a book on bird watching from England. Dad says you'll like that. Good-bye."

David felt in his pocket. He brought out a small parcel. His words seemed more difficult and pushed out than usual.

"Good-bye. It's fine having known you."

Jane stumped ahead of Aunt Cora. She felt miserable, and she was not going to let Aunt Cora know it. She hated saying good-bye to David and his creatures. She wished he had been more certain about her being a trainer. It was a come-down to follow David's suggestion and start with one small

231

bird. All the same, inside, she knew he was right, and she knew that was what she would try to do. Bee and Peaseblossom did not know it, but she had hidden her pipes and meant to practice all the way to England. She stopped being miserable. She could see herself sitting on the wall of Saxon Crescent playing her pipes, and as she piped, a bird would come. Then another bird. Then another. Then the whole crescent would be full of birds and people would say . . .

"Jane," said Aunt Cora, "come and walk with me. It's downright rude, rushing ahead that way. What's that you're holding?"

Jane looked at her hand. David's present. It had no ribbon or grand paper, just a bit of newspaper and an rubber band around it. She took off the rubber band and the paper. Aunt Cora peered at what Jane was holding.

"What's that?"

"A chipmunk. I wouldn't be surprised if David carved it himself. It's a no-good, stuck-up chipmunk. I shall keep it always."

Although the children had known from the first time they went to a theater that they must not say one word at a public entertainment, both Rachel and Tim let out faint squeaks when they first saw Jane on the screen.

Of course, the film affected them all differently. Tim clapped when the wicked doctor left Misselthwaite Manor forever. John was interested in the way the story was told. Peaseblossom, Bee, and Aunt Cora cried off and on all the time. Rachel, forgetting all about Jane, was caring for nothing but Colin. Although she knew the book, she kept saying in her head, "Let him walk. Let him walk. Make his father come back quickly before that awful man kills him." To Jane it was the garden. Though she knew it was a painted garden, though she had said the lines over and over until she yawned, she sat entranced, watching the garden come alive. She

232

forgot Dickon was David; he was only Dickon to her, the boy who could bring a garden to life, could teach Mary how to make creatures obey him.

When it was over and the lights went on in the grandly fitted private cinema of Bee Bee Films Incorporated, Jane's-Mr. Browne said, "Well? What do you think of her?"

Bee mopped her eyes. "That poor Mrs. Craven, only meeting her boy when she was a ghost."

Peaseblossom blew her nose. "Very affecting. What a wonderful improvement nature made in the characters of those two children."

Tim knelt on his seat. "I'm glad that awful doctor got sent away. I hope he starved."

Rachel got up. "Colin could walk. He could walk as well as anybody at the end."

Aunt Cora powdered her nose, which was shiny from crying. "That Maurice Tuesday is certainly a wonderful little actor."

That brought all the family back from the story. They turned to Jane.

"You were good, darling," said Bee. "I forgot it was you."

Rachel looked puzzled. "Do you know, so did I."

Tim sighed. "So did I, and I liked Jane better when she was Mary."

John laughed. "You did marvels with her, Browne. Come along, kids. We mustn't keep Jane's-Mr. Browne and Mr. Phelps hanging about; they're busy men."

Mr. Phelps gave Jane a kiss and an envelope.

"There's a four-leaf clover on a brooch in there to bring you luck. I won't forget you." He pointed to his neck. "You see, I'm wearing the tie you gave me. Good-bye, you've been a lot of trouble, but I wouldn't have missed it for the world."

233

Jane's-Mr. Browne took her hand. They walked together through the lot. "Sorry it's over?" he asked.

Jane looked around at the now familiar streets, studios, and offices.

"Sort of." She looked up at Her-Mr. Browne. "You see, I'm nobody at home."

"But you wouldn't like this life."

"I might if I acted always with David and the creatures."

"That wouldn't happen. You'd go from picture to picture, maybe without playing with him again."

"All the same, I'd like to have been asked to stay. I'd like just once to have been really important."

"In what way?"

"Any way, so Rachel and Tim could see I was important. I'm not sure how. I suppose people bowing and flowers . . ." She was not certain what she did want so she broke off. "I've got a present for you."

Jane's-Mr. Browne knew just what to do when he got a present. He didn't wait until he got home to unwrap it. He unwrapped it right there in the middle of the lot. It was a good present. A drinking bowl for Hyde Park. Jane had had it specially painted for him. One one side was written, "Hyde Park," and on the other, "No bad fish." Jane's-Mr. Browne seemed pleased. He lifted her chin and looked at her.

"Thank you. Hyde Park will surely value that. Good-bye, little friend. Watch out for the mailman. Neither Hyde Park nor I are going to forget you."

27

California, Here We Go!

Time seemed to be running through a sieve. The Winters were no sooner back from the Bee Bee studios than they were rushing upstairs to change for Aunt Cora's good-bye party.

Rachel had her frock over her head when suddenly there were shouts from downstairs. Jane opened the door.

"What is it?" she called.

"Is Rachel there? Come down, Rachel, I want you."

Rachel, scrabbling at the buttons on her frock, rushed down the stairs. John was holding a cable. Jane hung over the landing rail to hear what the fuss was about. Had Monsieur Manoff asked Rachel to stay after all?

Rachel read the cable out loud.

PLEASE CABLE DATE ARRIVE LONDON STOP GLINKEN SAW RACHEL'S PHOTOGRAPH HEARD MANOFF'S VIEWS HER WORK WISHES SEE HER IMMEDIATELY VIEW ENGAGING HER GOOD DANCING ROLE NEW PRODUCTION. FIDOLIA.

Rachel's hands shook so much with excitement she could hardly hold the telegram. "Oh, Dad! Oh, Dad!"

John took the cable from her. "Don't shake it to pieces. I've got to answer it." He put an arm around her. "I told you I refused to despair of your career."

"But you said you felt in your bones it would happen here, and it never has."

235

"Hasn't it? Where are we now? Isn't that the Pacific Ocean outside? Aren't those mountains in California?"

Rachel had to hug herself with both arms. "I'm so happy I hurt."

John gave her a kiss. "That's good. It was your turn for a break. Good dancing role! Imagine how proud we're all going to be on your first night."

Jane went back into her bedroom. John and Rachel had not looked up. They did not know she had heard. "How proud we're all going to be." She scowled at the labeled luggage. "I suppose they'll forget I was once nearly a film star. Well, fairly nearly one. They'll talk, talk, talk about Rachel's dancing and Tim's piano, and Peaseblossom will say, 'We may not all be equally talented, but we can all be equally nice people.' " Then Jane remembered her pipes. She opened a drawer. Yes, right at the back under the lining paper was a lump. Let them wait. She would show them. She might start with only one small bird, but in the end she would have . . .

Peaseblossom opened the door.

"Not dressed yet, Jane? Let me do you up; the guests will be arriving soon. What were you dreaming about? Chewing-gum?"

Jane was still half in her daydream. "Partly him, but mostly lions, tigers, and elephants and giraffes. Did you ever see an absolutely tame giraffe in a circus, Peaseblossom?"

"No, dear, I can't say I ever did."

Jane spoke with superb confidence. "You will."

Aunt Cora's good-bye party was the biggest success of all her parties. Tim, after a time, gave up handing cups and plates around and went to the piano. He was feeling very happy. He was sorry to leave California, but he longed to travel on *The Chief* and *Mauretania* again. He felt much too happy to play ordinary music, so instead he played things people could sing. Presently all the guests were standing around the piano, roaring at the top of their voices. Tim finished in grand style with "The Battle Hymn of the Republic." John and Bee thought it polite of him to have finished with that, and the guests' voices rose louder than ever as they sang "Glory, glory, hallelujah." But Tim had not played for politeness or for anybody in the living room; he was playing very loud so that it would reach the kitchen, where Bella would be singing, for that was her favorite hymn.

When everybody had gone, there was present giving. After much thought the whole family had combined on a lovely punch bowl and glasses to go with it for Aunt Cora, for after all, giving parties was her favorite hobby. Aunt Cora was so pleased with her present, and so exhausted by her long day and the emotion of saying good-bye, that she had the beginnings of a nervous spell and had to go up to bed quickly so that she would be fit to drive them the next day in the borrowed station wagon to their train.

After Aunt Cora had gone to bed, the family went to the kitchen and gave Bella her presents: a vase from Rachel; a china dog from Jane; a record from Tim; and the family group in a silver frame from the grown-ups. Although, of course, they would see Bella again in the morning, it was the proper good-bye and everybody felt miserable. Tears trickled down Bella's wrinkled black cheeks.

"I sure hate to see you go. I couldn't hate it more if you were my own family."

Bee took her hands. "And we hate to leave you, Bella. You've been part of the family for six whole months."

As they would have plenty of time to sleep on the train, the children were allowed to take a last evening walk. John looked up at the stars.

"I shall remember the nights in California, more even than I shall remember the sun."

"It's the smell," said Jane. "It smells California-ish."

Rachel sniffed, then shook her head. "It isn't. It's the being warm that's so California-ish, as if the sun were still out, only not showing."

Tim was scornful. "You aren't listening. It's the tree frogs; they're the most California-ish thing of all. I shall hear ker-up, ker-up forever and ever."

Suddenly they were playing follow-the-leader up the street just as they had done at Thanksgiving. They sang their final and silliest version of "California, Here I Come."

It was the same railroad station. The same train. Even the same coach, with dear Joe, his black face spread into a wide, recognizing grin, but it was so different from their arrival. Nothing was strange now, and instead of just Aunt Cora, there was a crowd of people to see them off. Posy had rushed down to say that she had heard from Madame and wished Rachel the best of luck about the job. The Antonios were there to see the last of Tim. They had brought everything they could think of that he would like from their drugstore and seemed to mind terribly that he was going away. Mrs. Antonio was crying.

"You take good care. I burn the candle. I burn ten candles."

Mr. Antonio tried to smile, but he seemed to mind too much to do it very well. "I hate the train. I hate good-byes."

There were heaps of friends to say good-bye to Pease-blossom, Bee, and John, and they brought lovely good-bye presents. Aunt Cora would have enjoyed the fuss except that she did not care about mixing socially with the Antonios; also, she had a feeling Posy noticed this and thought it very odd, as was true. With little steps Posy was dancing for Rachel her interpretation of Aunt Cora not liking the Antonios.

They were told to get on the train. Joe pulled up the steps.

The family leaned forward, waving and shouting. The train started moving. They were off.

Jane had been squeezed to the back of the family. There had been nobody to see her off. She had not expected anybody, but it did seem mean that she was the only one without a special friend. Of course, David wasn't a railway station sort of person, but it would have been grand if he had marched down the platform, with Mickey on one shoulder and Bob on the other and perhaps Pedro walking behind.

"Now," said Peaseblossom, "we must settle ourselves. You three children . . ."

Suddenly Joe was standing by them, an enormous box tied with wide satin bows in his arms. "Miss Jane Winter?" he inquired.

Jane was so surprised she could hardly untie the bows. She took the lid off the box. Inside, on top of sheets of green paper, was a card: "Best wishes and Bon Voyage from the Directors of Bee Bee Films Incorporated." She pulled back the layers of paper. For a moment there was complete silence. Then Rachel said, "Orchids! Real film star flowers!"

Tim gaped into the box. "Hundreds of them!"

They all looked with respect at Jane. Rachel said, "This is the grandest thing that's ever happened to us."

Tim nodded. "Most likely the grandest thing that will ever happen to a Winter."

DANCING

If dancing holds a special magic for you, don't miss these charming stories. Set in England before you were born, they follow the amusing adventures of some *very* talented children.

____BALLET SHOES
41508-X-54 ....$3.25
____DANCING SHOES
42289-2-57......................$2.95
____MOVIE SHOES
45815-3-46 ....$3.25
____SKATING SHOES
47731-X-35 ....$2.75
____THEATRE SHOES
48791-9-06.......................$2.95

by Noel Streatfeild

At your local bookstore or use this handy coupon for ordering: